DEVOUR THE RICH

DEVOUR THE RICH

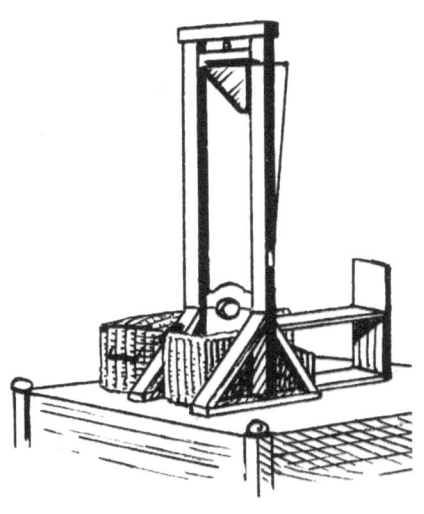

ABOVE THE RAIN COLLECTIVE
2025

Above the Rain Collective
abovetheraincollective@gmail.com
North Georgia, USA

Contributing Editor: J.A. Sexton

Publisher's note:

This is a work of fiction. All characters and incidents are the product of the author's imagination, places are used fictitiously and any resemblance to an actual person, living or dead, is entirely coincidental.

No AI was used in producing this work.

ISBN: 979-8-9899186-5-2

abovetheraincollective.com

Interior formatting by Juliet Rose
Cover graphics by D.Z. Hollow and Juliet Rose
Above the Rain Collective logo artwork by Bee Freitag

FOR LUIGI

CHAPTERS

SECRET EMPLOYER

BY BOBBY NASH

Why am I doing this again?"

It wasn't the first time Edwin Norris asked the question since leaving his mansion that morning. The limo picked him up and drove him, along with his personal assistant, Kathy, to an undisclosed location downtown.

Kathy wondered if the reason for her boss's discomfort was due to the fact that he wasn't fully in control of the situation. She understood the feeling. She didn't want to be there, either. It had been a long time since she could truthfully claim she loved her job.

Her boss, Mr. Norris didn't trust easily. Or quietly. Now that they had arrived at their destination and he had been shown to his chair, he continued to grump.

"You remember, sir," she said, speaking in calm tones. "The board requested it. They think this will be good P.R. for the company, but also for you."

"Why the hell do I need good P.R.?" he grumbled. He shifted under the weight of the cloth draped over him as they waited.

"You saw the news stories, sir. They reported on working conditions in the company. Neither you nor the company, came off in a good light, sir. This will help with perception."

"What the hell do I care what the news thinks? Or the workers for that matter? Buncha crybabies. They should be down on their knees thanking me for the jobs they have. When I find that whiney whistleblower who spilled his guts to the press, I'll have his ass in a sling!" He fumed in silence before adding, "Why am I doing this again?"

Before she could explain it another time, Scott Preston walked into the room. Scott was in his forties, handsome, always smiling, cheerful, and boisterous. He was everything Kathy had always imagined a television producer would be. Only nicer.

"Welcome to Secret Employer, Mr. Norris," he all but shouted, his singsong voice echoing off the walls.

"This is never going to work," Norris grumbled, ignoring the platitudes. "Why am I even doing this?"

"Of course, it'll work," Preston said, still smiling. "My makeup team is some of the best in the business. We can make you look like anyone. Even your family won't be able to tell the difference. Trust me, it'll be fun and, if you'll pardon me saying so, you need this, Mr. Norris. Your company needs it. The media has given you a black eye. We're here to help make you look better to the people who buy your product."

"Oh, all right," Norris said, though his level of enthusiasm left much to be desired. "Let's get on with it already."

"That's the spirit. While they start crafting your new look, here are a few things we should go over for your episode."

"What things?"

"Well, as you know, Mr. Norris, we're sending you into your own company in different lower-level positions, so our viewers can get a sense of you connecting with various employees. Our viewers love it if you learn something about your employees, something that makes you feel a special connection to them." Preston circled the makeup chair, arms flailing about as he continued. "Our research has helped us choose some of the more down-on-their-luck people working for you. We want you to try and connect with them on a personal level. Make new friends. Feel empathy for their situations."

"What? What do sob stories have to do with my business?" Norris asked. "I thought this was supposed to promote my business. Norris Industries is tough. We should be showing strength. Not weakness."

"Viewers love seeing the boss, that's you," Preston reminded him. "They like to see the boss connect with the people who work for him. It makes you seem more like them. A regular person. Those feel-good moments are ratings gold."

"So, you want me to listen to them whine about their problems and pretend to care?"

"Something like that," Preston said. "We would prefer you really care, but if you have to fake it, well, that's between you and your conscience. This show is all about changing lives, Mr. Norris. Yours, as well as your employees. Our goal is to make people's lives better."

"Sounds like hippy-dippy nonsense to me," Norris said. "But I'm a team player. I'll get it done. For the company. Don't you worry."

"I never doubted it, Mr. Norris," Preston said, showing pearly white teeth. "While the makeup team finishes up here, I'll go get your first stop set up and ready for you. Remember to have fun, sir. This is all about people connecting with people. Enjoy it."

"Right."

As Kathy watched the process unfold, she started to wonder if this was a good idea. The thought of Mr. Norris treating any of his employees, much less the low-level ones, like anything other than puppets there to do his bidding, suddenly seemed like a recipe for disaster. Like him, she was beginning to wonder why he was doing this.

***

The first setup went pretty well.

Under his alias as Chad Harris, Norris was made up to look the polar opposite of his usual appearance. He wore jeans and tennis shoes under a button-up, off-the-rack shirt with a T-shirt underneath. Though it was tied back and partially hidden under a ball cap, his hair was longer, thanks to the dark wig he wore, and a fake beard had been applied. It was doubtful anyone who did not know him very well would recognize him.

The first stop had him teamed with a line supervisor in one of the many warehouses his company owned. He spent the day shadowing the supervisor, a pleasant young lady named Sally Bell, watching her work, and learning the ropes as though he hadn't seen this type of work in action before. That was partly true. He had never worked this particular job. It was one of many he had created and implemented after he was working exclusively in his corporate offices. He wrote the work plan, set up the steps required, determined how long he thought it should take to perform the necessary tasks, and whatnot, but had never physically done the job himself. Had never seen it in action.

He seemed surprised when the supervisor mentioned that it was difficult to do the job as laid out in the work instructions in the time allotted. His first thought was that she was either too lazy or too stupid to follow the simple instructions he, himself, had laid out. He planned to have her fired for her incompetence once this experiment was finished. Then he tried to run the job himself to show her how it was done.

He failed spectacularly.

Begrudgingly, afterward, he admitted in his on-camera interview that perhaps corporate needed to reevaluate the process. Maybe there was a way to streamline the process to make the position more successful in reaching their target goals. Kathy was stunned to hear Mr. Norris utter those words. She had never once heard her boss admit that he might be mistaken about anything. For a moment, she wondered if being on the show, going undercover in his company, and spending time with the rank and file might actually have changed him. Even if just a little bit.

Then, during the inevitable sob story moment, while taking their one short, ten-minute break, Sally told her new friend about how she worked two jobs to support her family. Her father had died unexpectedly, her mother was in the middle of difficult cancer treatments, and her developmentally challenged brother also needed around-the-clock care. All of those things fell to her, and Sally had put her life on hold to take care of the people closest to her. As a result of mounting medical bills, she feared they would lose their home. It was a heartbreaking, but also inspirational, story.

On camera, Norris listened, nodded, offered the appropriate platitudes where prudent, and showed empathy. Seeing compassion from Mr. Norris touched her. Of course, once they were done and the cameras were no longer rolling, he told the producers that he couldn't believe an employee of his would whine so much. Then, he called her a pathetic loser and rushed to move on to the next setup so they could "hurry up and get this over with so I can get out of here."

Kathy looked to the producer with sadness in her eyes. "I'm sorry," she whispered.

"It's okay," Preston told her. "The first day is usually tough. This is a process. We're trying to make employers better understand the people who work for them. That's why we approach those CEOs who aren't exactly getting World's Best Boss mugs unironically."

Kathy smiled at that. "Sounds good in theory, but I've worked for Mr. Norris a long time. He's not going to change. He'll never learn."

"Oh, I wouldn't be so sure about that," Preston said, smiling. "We've remade a number of guys tougher than him around here. By the time this is over, I guarantee you he'll be a new man. You'll see."

"I won't hold my breath," Kathy said.

"Have a little hope," Preston said. "We might just surprise you."

"I hope so."

"Trust me," Preston said. "It's a marathon. Not a sprint."

"If you say so," she said, still not believing.

***

The second setup went a little better.

Norris handled the job well, but once again failed to connect with the employee on a personal level. Frank Ginnis had worked for the company for almost twenty years. He'd been there since the early days before the corporation exploded into the billion-dollar industry it was today. Ginnis had an incredible attitude about his job and a fantastic work ethic, even though there hadn't been enough training on his particular job to allow him to be as successful as possible. His tale of woe, as Norris called it, shed light on his desire to write the so-called Great American Novel, which was not going well for him after several starts and stops.

Norris took it all in, even offered some advice on how Ginnis had to "make" time to write instead of always trying to "find" time to write. "You have to make your opportunities, Frank," he said in an honest moment. "You won't find them by looking. You have to be the catalyst for your own success. It all starts with you, Frank. I think you can do it."

They were good words and Preston seemed pleased with the footage.

"Just three more to go," he told Kathy as they shuttled the secret employer off to his next setup.

***

The rest of the shoot went more or less according to plan.

Norris performed the tasks set in front of him. He talked with his employees and listened to their stories. If he was faking empathy, Kathy thought he did it well. She even started to believe that perhaps he was becoming a better person by the experience.

She hoped so. She liked Mr. Norris, but he rarely came off as a nice man. Maybe this was softening him. However, when the cameras stopped rolling, he reverted to type.

It broke Kathy's heart.

***

After he finished the initial undercover filming, the producers asked Norris to consider making offers to the employees he met while in disguise. Acts of kindness that showed them they were heard. That corporate, that he, Mr. Norris, understood their struggles and wanted to help them overcome them.

Norris had no interest in offering what he referred to as handouts to anyone, least of all the ungrateful whiners who worked for him.

"But that's the show," Preston reminded him. "This is what you and your company signed up for, Mr. Norris. You're trying to repair your reputation."

"What's wrong with my reputation?"

"People think you're a heartless bastard," Preston said matter-of-factly.

"In my day, that was considered a good thing. No one wanted to work for a boss who wasn't tough as nails."

"Maybe once upon a time," Preston reminded him. "Not today. It's a brave new world, Mr. Norris. You need to embrace it."

"No," Norris said. "These people need to stop bemoaning how unfair their lives are. They need to pull themselves up by their own bootstraps, the same way I did. You don't see me crying about how hard it is to do my job, do you?"

"Didn't your father give you a million dollars to get you started after you graduated?" Preston asked.

"Yes. He did," Norris said. "And I took that million and turned it into billions with no help from anyone. It was all me."

"All you?"

"Yes. No one lined up to help me," Norris said, chest puffed out proudly.

"But most people don't just have a million dollars handed to them like you did, Mr. Norris," the producer continued. "Ordinary people start with nothing and still try to build something they can be proud of. They do this without the safety net you had, sir. All I'm asking is that you offer a helping hand to these people the same way your father did for you. Trust me, our viewers, your customers, will eat it up."

"Why can't their own parents do that? I worked hard to earn my fortune. And I did it on my own. No handouts. No free rides. All me. Why should I give away my hard-earned money to these freeloaders?"

"So, you never spent a dime of that million?"

"Of course, I did," Norris huffed. "I invested it, then turned a profit that I used to buy a house and put down a deposit on my first factory."

"Then you did have a helping hand," Preston said plainly. "You had daddy's money."

"That was my money."

"You didn't earn it. It was a gift."

"Growing up under that man's thumb, you better believe I earned it," Norris said, anger tinging his words. "Every. Single. Penny."

"Don't you understand that not everyone gets a gift like that, Mr. Norris?" Kathy said, no longer able to sit by quietly and listen. "I know what you pay me, Mr. Norris. I work hard for you. Believe me, I'm just barely scraping by on it. I can't afford to buy a home. I certainly can't afford to start a business."

"Sound like you need better financial planning, Miss Church," Norris said. "That's all. Learn to budget. Spend money wisely. I cannot be held responsible for your misuse of the generous stipend I pay you for a job that any unskilled laborer could perform."

Kathy felt as though she had been hit between the eyes with a rock. "Any... unskilled..."

She let the words hang there, disbelieving that she heard him correctly. "What do you think I do all day, Mr. Norris?"

She held up her hands even as she fought back tears. "You know what, don't answer that."

Tears streaming down her cheeks, Kathy Church excused herself and left the group, heading over to the far end of the room where she could be alone, but still close enough to answer if her boss called. She hated breaking down in front of anyone, but his words were a gut punch. She had assumed that he, at the very least, valued her work. To learn that this was patently untrue, hurt her to the quick.

"You do have a way with words, Mr. Norris," Preston said as he watched the CEO's assistant rush out. "Maybe we can find a dog for you to kick while we're at it. Who knows, it might make for good TV too. It won't help improve your image, but it would get viewers talking."

"Oh, phooey on you and your dog, Preston." Norris stood, arms flailing about as he groused. "Just what kind of racket are you running here, anyway? Handouts? Whiners with their tales of woe? Is this your idea of good TV? No wonder you needed me to come on your show. You needed me to teach you how to handle workers."

"America seems to love our show, sir."

"Oh, sure. The lazy and uninformed, right? Is that your target audience, Preston? Are those the people you want me to coddle? I think they've been coddled quite enough, thank you very much. No. They need discipline. Work ethic. That's what this country needs. Work ethic. Like when I was younger. We knew how to work. No complaints. Just do your job. Yes. Work ethic. That's what's missing. And that's what I'll bloody well teach them. Starting with those people you paired me up with on your little show here. No handouts from me, Preston. Oh, no. Tomorrow, these people are going to receive a splash of cold, hard reality and it'll be my pleasure to give it to them."

"What are you going to do, Mr. Norris?"

"You'll see, my boy," Norris sneered. "You'll see."

As Norris left the studio, he passed Kathy without giving her a second glance. "Come, girl," he ordered.

Mouth agape, she exchanged a look with the producer. He shook his head.

Unsure what to do, Kathy did what she always did and fell in line. She performed an about-face and followed her boss out of the soundstage.

"See you tomorrow, Mr. Norris," the producer called out once they were gone. As soon as the door slammed shut, Preston headed toward the production office where the rest of his team awaited his return. "Ladies and gentlemen, we've got a real live wire here."

He stared around the table. "I think we need to rewrite the ending."

There were nods from around the table.

"Let's get to work."

***

It was the day of the final scene.

Kathy was asked to wait outside while hair and makeup did their thing, getting Mr. Norris ready to meet the employees he had worked with while pretending to be Chad Harris.

Someone other than the boss.

Today, they would meet the real Edwin Norris. Kathy's nerves were frayed. She had no idea what to expect. She was not looking forward to it, though. Her anxiety levels were extremely high.

To her surprise, a smiling, jovial, friendly Edwin Norris appeared on the monitor where she watched the interviews. He offered a grant to Sally Bell that would help offset the cost of caring for her mother and brother and allow them to keep their family home.

Frank Ginnis was offered the opportunity to study in a writer's group and the CEO put a pre-paid professional editor at the writer's disposal to help him whip his novel into shape.

The same kind of meeting happened with all of the employees. Everyone left either happy or crying, but all left feeling better about their jobs and their employer.

"That was amazing," Kathy told Preston when he stood next to her to watch the playback footage. "I don't know what I was expecting, but that wasn't it. Mr. Norris almost seems like a new man. What did you say to him?"

Preston smiled. "I simply reminded him why he was doing this. The company needed a new image. Now, we've given them one."

"But you know he'll go back to being his usual old cranky self as soon as we get back to corporate headquarters. He's playing a role here. I doubt we changed anything long-term."

"You never know, Miss Church," Preston said. "I've seen miracles happen here."

"Well, that's what it'll take to make Mr. Norris a better man."

"Lucky for us, I believe in miracles." Preston placed a gentle hand on her shoulder, offered a friendly smile, then headed off to join his production team to wrap up the episode.

"Miracles," Kathy repeated with a chuckle. "I'll believe it when I see it."

***

In the days and weeks to come, Kathy Church's belief in miracles solidified. Her boss seemed like a new man. He was nicer, friendlier, and more open to ideas from throughout the company, instead of from a select few in his inner circle. He had even started offering attaboys and took time to get to know people. It was exactly as Scott Preston had predicted. The show had changed Mr. Norris. For the better. She didn't know how long it would last, but for now, Kathy loved her job again.

That was a miracle.

***

Three months later.

"Good morning, Mr. Norris."

"Why are you doing this to me?" Edwin Norris growled. His face sported a week's worth of beard growth, his hair a mess.

Gone were the expensive suits. They had been replaced by hospital scrubs, a soft pastel blue. He was in a hospital bed, the side bars raised to keep him from tumbling out. The soft restraints around his wrists and ankles aided in making sure he stayed put.

"You were given a choice if you recall," Scott Preston said. His trademarked smile remained in place, teeth gleaming white. "You chose poorly."

"I will have your head for this!"

"Oh, I don't think so, Mr. Norris."

"You can't do this to me!" Norris bellowed. "You cannot hold me like this!"

"It occurs to me, Mr. Norris, that I already am, as you say, doing this to you."

"Why?"

Preston chuckled while walking around the bed, careful to stay in his prisoner's line of sight. "I told you from the beginning, Mr. Norris. I told you multiple times. Our main goal was to change you, to make you into a better man. Your company needed you to change so they could continue. It was your very own board of directors who called us in. Did you know that?"

Confused, Norris shook his head.

"It's true. We were asked to make a better man out of you, sir. We tried. Oh, yes. We tried, but you're a stubborn one, Mr. Norris. Too set in your ways to change. Or too stupid." He smiled. "There's been a bit of debate on that."

"What did you do?" Norris asked, his throat suddenly dry.

Preston pointed to the large plasma TV screen mounted on the wall. "Your episode airs tonight. I thought you might like a sneak peek. We even added a segment at the end about all the changes you're making to improve your company. I think you'll be pleased."

"But how?"

"Just watch."

The television screen came to life, and the episode played. Norris watched, unable to look away, partly due to the straps holding him in place. Near the end, he saw footage of himself talking to his employees.

"That..." he said, hoarse. "That's not me."

"Sure it is," Preston said proudly. "Looks like you. Sounds like you. Hell, according to your family, friends, employees, and your company's board, you've become the man they always hoped you would be."

"What are you talking about?"

"According to all reports, you've become a kinder, gentler man, Mr. Norris." The smile widened. "A man of some humility, I've been told. Even your marriage has improved."

"An imposter?"

Preston chuckled. "I did tell you that our makeup guys are the best, didn't I? They can make you look like anyone." The smile faded, and his voice dropped in timbre. "They can also make someone look like you."

"You're trying to steal my company!" Norris bellowed.

"Of course not," Preston said. "I've already stolen your company."

Norris started to cry. "How is this possible?" he sobbed.

"In the past three months, we've pumped you for information, studied you, your walk, talk, mannerisms. We've built a better you." Preston started walking again. "As soon as the company is on the right track and moving in the right direction again, your doppelganger there..." He pointed to the screen. "His name's Pete, by the way. Eventually, you'll have a heart attack. With your diet and anxiety levels, no one will question it. The company will continue on without you. It'll thrive."

Preston snapped his fingers. "Oh, did I mention that you promoted Kathy? She's doing a bang-up job as your new vice president. When you... or the Pete version of you on the screen there... dies, she'll take over running the company along with your wife."

"My wife? Keep her away from my company."

"It'll be her company then."

"No..."

"You should be happy, Mr. Norris. Profits are up. Employee turnover is at an all-time low. Your company is thriving."

Norris looked worried. "What's going to happen to me?"

"We have a nice, long-term care facility that we run upstate. It's a beautiful place. You'll spend the rest of your days there, pretty much existing in a drug-induced haze until eventually you forget your name and all you lost. From this day forward, you belong to me, Edwin. Body and soul. You're mine."

"You're insane!" Norris shouted.

"Hardly," Preston said playfully, a small glint in his eye. "I've been doing this a long time, sir. You are hardly the first and most definitely not the last. Secret Employer is just a tool we use nowadays. Television has streamlined the process, made it easier to find our victims."

He smiled. "Everyone wants to be on TV."

"No!"

"There's no need to scream, Edwin," Preston said as the room began to darken around him. The temperature started to rise. "I mean, you can if it makes you feel better. No one will hear you. Well, no one who cares, that is. I actually enjoy a good scream, so please, be my guest."

"I'll see you in hell!" Norris shouted.

Preston let loose an ear-splitting howl of laughter.

"You're already here," Preston said. "Welcome to hell, Mr. Norris. Here, I am the secret employer."

Strapped to a bed, unable to move, unable to escape, Edwin Norris tried to scream, to call out for God, for anyone to save him. He screamed until his dry throat refused to cooperate further. In the dark of his own personal nightmare, Edwin Norris' pleas died in his throat. The silence that remained was deafening.

Bobby Nash is an award-winning author, artist, and occasional actor. He writes novels, comic books & graphic novels, novellas, short stories, audio scripts, screenplays, and more. Bobby is a member of the International Association of Media Tie-in Writers, International Thriller Writers, and Southeastern Writers Association. From time to time, he appears in movies and TV shows, usually standing behind your favorite actor. Sometimes they let him speak. Scary, we know.

For more information, please visit Bobby at www.bobbynash.com, www.ben-books.com, and across social media.

YOU REAP WHAT YOU SOW
BY R.C. ABERNATHY

Alex had made a lot of bad decisions in their life — dropping out of undergrad, two toxic relationships back-to-back, keying their abusive aunt's car — but they'd known those decisions were not great, to put it mildly. There was some level of self-awareness.

But the objectively bad decision to murder their homophobic bosses at the library felt like the best damn one they'd ever made in their entire thirty years of life.

"Is that it?"

"Yep. That's the plant that will murder them." Alex stepped back to let their work best friend view the bright purple orchid for their supervisor on the counter of their half-circle circulation desk in the Children's Department. A family entered through the glass door to the Children's space on the first floor, and they both paused to greet them. Once the family started toward the train table, Alex gathered their dark, straight hair off their neck and twirled it into a bun.

They focused on the innocuous-looking flower. "That's it. I'm really doing it."

"You're really doing it," Claudia agreed and nibbled on a neon pink nail.

"Do you think I shouldn't?" Alex asked, a tendril of anxiety twisting their stomach.

"Oh, no, you definitely should do it. You were told to take down your Pride display during Pride. They all deserve it. Plus, we're in rural Tennessee. No one is ever gonna suspect murder by plants. The peony is for the Assistant City Manager?"

Alex nodded, picked the fluffy, white flower up, and placed it in Claudia's outstretched hands. "How are we going to get it to him? Just walk it over to City Hall on a fifteen-minute break?"

"He'll probably be here soon enough, like he is every day," Claudia grumbled. "Just, 'Checking up on us,' like we haven't been doing our jobs fine on our own for years."

"Micromanaging at its finest. No one's gonna suspect anything, right? Because it's the Annual Flower Extravaganza, and over a hundred people are getting flowers today?"

"Correct," Claudia said and greeted another patron as they came down the stairs. "And you're sure it'll work? I mean, you've never done anything like this before."

Alex hugged the plant to their chest. "I haven't, but family legend claims it's been done successfully before."

"'Legend.' Wonderful. So, it might not work. Also, are we gonna be okay with them here?"

Alex set the monstrous plant back down on the desk. "For a bit. It should take five or six hours of constant exposure before anyone starts to feel the effects. We might get a little down, but, hey, we do that every day anyway just by walking in the front door."

Claudia laughed as the aforementioned door opened again and their supervisor, Megan, stalked in. Her dark curly hair was down, a skirt that was too short for the dress code swished around her upper thighs, and unpainted toenails dug into her favorite sandals. Her face drew down in ire.

Gonna be one of those really bad days, Alex thought.

But then her supervisor spotted the orchid on the desk and a huge smile broke across their face. "That's so beautiful, Alexis! Is it—"

"Alex," Claudia said matter-of-factly.

"That's what I said."

"You didn't," Alex said quietly, but firmly, fingers tugging at the hem of their button-up. "You used my deadname."

Megan stopped just short of rolling her eyes but heaved an aggrieved sigh all the same. "My bad. But the plant!" She put both arms out in a childish gimme gesture. "Can I see it?"

Alex tamped down their ever-present annoyance when Megan was around and forced themself to smile. "It's actually for you."

The supervisor's jaw dropped. "Really? For me?"

It was the fakest surprise Alex had ever heard from her. They whooped internally. "Well, of course. I always give you an orchid when the season ends. The ones for patrons are at the main circulation desk."

"Thank you. Really."

Oh, wow, a genuine emotion, how rare.

"They always make me feel so good. I swear, your family has some kinda magic with them."

Alex smiled widely. If she — and the rest of the town — only believed the truth. Yes, her family had 'magic' if you counted generations of herbalists as magic. Her mamaw did and told everyone she was a witch, but Alex was less sure.

Well, had been less sure until a month ago when she started working on her sinister plan on the plants for her supervisor and the bosses all the way up their city government. Her mamaw would be so disappointed if she ever found out.

"Just a really good green thumb," Alex said, faux humble.

"I'll go put it in my office now. Y'all need anything before I get my day started?"

Alex and Claudia shook their heads. Their supervisor headed to her office, ignoring every patron on the way as if there were no sounds other than the hubris in her own mind. She didn't even react when a small child said, "Pretty flower!"

As the Head of the Children's Department, you'd think she'd at least say, "Isn't it?"

When Megan's office door clicked shut, Claudia sighed heavily. "How long does it take to work? I want her gone today."

Alex pulled out their chair and logged onto their work computer. "It won't be today. Tomorrow, maybe, or Friday."

"Friday?" Claudia groaned. "That's too long."

"Agreed, but–"

Claudia greeted another patron, who actually needed help. The day got hectic between a lost child, someone being naked in the upstairs bathroom, a shirt set on fire outside the building, and the regular crush of Summer Reading Program questions. The two work besties didn't get to talk again until after lunch over the undelivered plants.

Alex looked at the remaining two plants on their desk. "Did the director come get hers?"

Claudia collapsed into her seat at the check-out computer and shrugged. "Yes. Want help getting those to City Hall?"

"Yeah, I'll see if someone from circulation can cover the desk. They've got a lot of people there at the moment."

Less than a minute later, with help procured, Alex picked up the white peony, and Claudia cradled the blue orchid in her arms.

City Hall was directly across the street from the library, which left little time for talking, but the two librarians had plenty of practice of making the most of their time outside of the building.

The second the heavy, red front door closed behind them, Alex said, "And you're positive no one will trace this back to me? Even with all the other giveaways?"

"I would bet my mom's life on it."

Alex glared at Claudia. "You don't even like your mom."

"Oh, right, fair enough. Fine, I would bet my niece's life on it, and I would die for her."

Alex laughed and adjusted the plant in her arms. They both slowed their steps in the crosswalk, clear of traffic. "Okay, I finally accept your reassurances."

"Do you, though?"

"No."

Claudia groaned. "Your stupid anxiety. It lies!"

"Agreed, but, like, also the plant might be making it worse."

"You said we have hours!"

"I said probably," Alex reminded quickly. "But also, how irrational am I being? The plant is going to murder them."

"When the plant releases a poison that will mimic the effect of carbon monoxide poisoning, yes, it's irrational."

They started up the steps into the government building that housed all the city services, including the oft-visited Human Resources who did absolutely nothing to ever make anyone's work lives better. Not without the threat of a lawsuit.

"Oh, right, the actual way it kills," Alex said and paused at the top of the stairs to set the orchid down. "I was so focused on making sure it made them feel absofuckinglutely terrible about themselves that I almost forgot everything else."

Claudia gave them a look. "Seriously?"

"Yes! I mean, sure, I want them dead, but I need them to suffer first. The plants will make them think and feel all kinds of awful stuff about themselves. Depression and anxiety on steroids. But, not the point. Back to the poisoning. No one will suspect me, also because I do this giveaway every year — although never with murderous versions — and our bosses all have private offices on a separate a/c system from the rest of the buildings. It'll be a super weird freak accident. 'A terrible tragedy, really,' as my mamaw would say, but since it'll be contained to only a few offices, everyone will be relieved."

"Exactly!" Claudia said brightly. "And no one really believes your family has any magic, so they will never suspect a plant."

"Or they will now, and I'll get investigated by the police." Alex smiled widely at their best friend and her expected eye roll. "Come on. Let's get these delivered and then go to HR, again, to let them know she used my deadname, yet again."

Of course, when Alex actually needed the men to be in their office, they weren't. The secretaries promised to ensure the head of Leisure Services and the City Manager both received the plants that very day and would be sure to let them know they came from the famous Mullins Farms. They left the City Manager's secretary and let out a sigh.

"It's done," Alex whispered. "What happens next is out of my hands."

Claudia squealed quietly and grabbed Alex's upper arms, shaking them. "We did it! We're gonna make everything better!"

Alex couldn't stop the feral grin that spread across their face. "We'll make it better for everyone."

***

The instant Alex walked into work the next morning, they knew morale was at a new low.

The edge in their supervisor's voice came close to breaking. "Why are you going all the way upstairs to print?"

Claudia looked up from the stack of paper flowers she was in the middle of cutting out. "Because the printer down here doesn't have the ink it needs."

Alex slid into the workspace between Megan and their desk.

"I've told you where to go to get new ink."

Claudia stayed neutral, face blank. "There wasn't any there, and when I told you last time, you said you would get with the library's secretary to see about ordering more."

"That was months ago!" Megan's volume increased. Claudia's face went more blank, the light in her eyes dimming.

Alex's chest tightened with anxiety. The raised voice yelling at them wasn't new, but over goddamn printer ink?

Maybe the plant was doing its job a little too well.

"Okay," Claudia said slowly. "Well, we still don't have any."

"I've told all of you multiple times," Megan's voice got even louder, and the background chatter of patrons on the floor got quieter, "what needed to be done. It shouldn't take months for things to get done around here. But fine, I'll take care of it, like I always do."

Alex pressed their lips together to stop from speaking. They would not get fired when the entire library was so close to being free of Megan. The entire point of murdering everyone was to avoid getting fired or quitting. The last thing Alex wanted was to not work at the library. Hence, the murder plot. They — and everyone else working in the library — just needed the ableist, racist, transphobic people out of the picture, and everything would be okay.

Megan spun on her heel, but something in her eye made Alex follow her trek. Her eyes were shot through with the green of a flower stem.

Fucking hell.

36

"Alex? You okay?"

Alex turned to Claudia's worried expression. "What is it? Because it ain't just her, so don't try and tell me it is." Alex sat down heavily, arms flopping listlessly at their side. "I'm going to jail."

"We've been over–"

"Her eyes. Did you not see the green in them?"

Claudia shook her head, eyebrows drawn down. "What would that have — oh."

"Yeah, 'Oh,'" Alex said and snorted before leaning forward and clutching their face. "Shit. The plant isn't going to mimic poisoning. It's going to overtake her body."

Claudia's jaw dropped, and a slow smile spread across her face. "I mean, that's pretty badass."

Alex gave her best friend a withering look. "Not if I go to jail! Also, *she* is an appropriate pronoun for the next little bit. It just happened."

"Noted. But, come on, death by evil plant? She deserves it. They all do."

Alex couldn't argue with that.

The library started to get busy, and they got drawn into different tasks. Alex cut out more flowers for the kids to decorate the Children's Department with as they read and logged minutes for the Summer Reading Program, and Claudia brainstormed program ideas for the Fall and Winter seasons.

It was almost time for both of them to leave when the Leisure Services boss came through the door. "Hi, ladies."

Just because Alex felt femme at the moment didn't mean it was okay for him to say that.

Quietly firm, she said, "Not a lady."

The man didn't respond. Alex stared at his face for several seconds and — yep, there it was. The veins on his neck were light green, the whites of his eyes extra white. The same white as his peony. And was that — no, it couldn't be.

But it was.

The edge of a pure white petal peeked out of the top of his ear. He scratched at it but made no comment or response to it.

"Is Megan in her office?"

They both nodded. He nodded back and started for the office. As soon as the office door clicked shut, Claudia spun her chair to Alex and hissed, "Did you see the petal?"

"Yes!" Alex whispered back. "Do you think he knows it's there?"

Claudia shrugged. "Didn't act like it. D'ya think this visit will make her worse?"

"Definitely. Always does. We knew these in-between days would be rough."

Claudia hummed in agreement. "He's coming back."

The two resumed their tasks as if they'd never paused.

"Have a good day," Alex said, the white petal all she could see.

Megan's door opened. Her footsteps thundered across the floor. Alex took a deep, steadying breath. She could handle whatever the supervisor was gonna throw at her. As long as she didn't actually throw anything. Physical assault was Alex's line in the sand.

Megan paused at Alex's desk. "What did you say to him?"

Alex looked up from her task and did a double-take. Megan's eyes were green in the irises and purple in the pupils. The veins in her neck pulsed with the green of leaves and the brown of the soil. A petal pushed its way out of her wrist, light and fluffy.

Alex swallowed and pretended not to notice her boss turning into an orchid. "I told him I wasn't a lady."

"Why?"

Alex could do nothing except blink. "Because I'm genderfluid, as you know, and no matter if I feel femme, calling me a lady isn't accurate."

Megan's face went red. Her skin rippled, the imprint of an edge of a petal on her cheekbone. She screamed, "It's accurate all the time! You're a girl!"

"Sometimes," Alex acknowledged, "but 'lady' is never accurate, and before you say anything else, I do get to decide that. It would be greatly appreciated if you stopped misgendering and deadnaming me."

Megan threw up her hands. Bits of soil leaked out of somewhere Alex couldn't pinpoint. "It's hard! I'm trying! This is all new to me."

Claudia leaned forward in her chair. "It's been six months. My mamaw got it in the span of an afternoon lunch, and she's in her seventies."

Megan glared daggers at Claudia. "It doesn't matter how long it's been!" She took a step forward. Soil rained from her fingertips. Green shoots with white petals sprouted from her calves. She yelled louder than before. "I shouldn't have to—"

"Is everything okay?"

All three turned to the new voice, a librarian from the Main Circulation desk. Megan sneered, "It's none of your business."

"Megan," Claudia started, "you're yelling. Everyone can hear–"

"Good! They should hear! Alexis, what you did is unacceptable."

"Using her deadname is unacceptable," Claudia snapped.

Megan turned her ire on her. Her voice dripped with disdain. "Oh, and using 'her' is acceptable now?"

"Yes," Alex said.

Where spots of red would normally appear, circles of green and white colored her pale skin. Alex swallowed thickly. The green spread across her nose and down to her lips. Her mouth turned a sickly blue, purple tinging the edges.

A petal reached its way through the corner of her mouth when she next spoke. "So, you feel like a girl today and you still — ah!"

Alex jumped.

Her supervisor doubled over and screamed again in pain, an anguished sound that quieted all the other noises in the library. "What's–" she gasped out between another scream, "happening to me?"

All Alex could think was: *Guess she finally felt herself turning into a flower.*

Megan yelled again. More stems ruptured through the skin on her arms. Now dots of blood welled. Her skirt, too short for the dress code, fluttered away from her leg. The fabric ripped. A stem appeared in the hole and reached to the ground, a white orchid blooming at its end.

"Don't just stand there!" Megan yelled. "Help me!"

Alex took a step forward, knowing she needed to maintain appearances. Nobody could point fingers at her if they saw her offering help.

Then, her supervisor exploded.

A stem coated in blood and flesh came straight at Alex's face. She raised her hands on instinct and caught the battered body part. It slipped through her fingers like melted butter and splattered on the floor.

Thick, slimy, green matter spattered across the toes of her Chucks. Blood fanned out in a half circle around her. She blinked, uncomprehending, and wheezed out something between a scream and a sob. Someone else did scream, high and hysterical. Then more screams.

Then Claudia's hand on her forearm.

The white of a bone poking out of the red-smeared flesh filled her vision. Someone called her name from far away. Alex slowly raised her eyes. Claudia swam into view, and so did the gruesome scene behind her.

Alex blinked slowly, shook her head on instinct like that would somehow help, and the world came into confusing focus. Claudia's nails dug into her shoulder.

She gently dislodged herself. "Holy shit."

"Agreed. Did you—"

Alex shook her head. "We need to — I don't know what we need to do."

The friends turned to survey the carnage. Blood, bone, soil, and petals spread out in a circle from where Megan had stood yelling. In the spot where she was mere seconds ago lay the largest and most rotted plant Alex had ever seen.

The end of the stem, going brown at the edges, flopped onto the top of the check-out desk, and the same green ooze on Alex's shoes spread toward the computer. A white petal at least two feet long and almost as wide squelched under her foot as she stepped forward. The bits of human left barely looked human anymore.

Megan hadn't just died.

She'd been obliterated.

The petals of the orchid reached toward the four corners of the floor. Where the original flower had been beautiful, vibrant, and lush, this murderous one had brown at the edges and holes eaten through every petal. Flecks of soil, blood, and viscera dotted the stem and petals. A piece of an arm dripped soil instead of blood. Decayed, brown, brittle petals twisted through a lock of hair that hung on the bathroom door. A single sandal smeared with blood lay sideways on the desk. A chunk of skin and muscle, complete with green and purple veins, dangled from the circle light above the two women.

Claudia gagged.

There was almost nothing left of Megan. This was not how it was supposed to go. But something dark in her rose up in interest. She was repulsed, particularly by the acrid smell of rotting soil now assaulting her senses, but a larger piece glowed with undeniable satisfaction.

If anyone deserved this painful, gory death it was Megan.

The door opened, and what had to be half of the police squad poured in. Alex didn't like cops, but with her supervisor in literal pieces, she let them usher her out of the library and into the humid summer air.

The next several hours passed in a blur. Alex gave a statement to the officers, her shoes were taken as evidence, and then her sister picked her up from the station. She woke up the next morning to a slew of text messages and social media notifications. Both the assistant city manager and the city manager had died overnight in their homes. In the same manner Megan did, a giant-ass, rotting flower left in the middle of the human debris.

Various rumors and speculation filled her screen, but nobody mentioned her other than to make sure she heard the news. Alex's phone vibrated, and her mamaw's face filled the screen.

She hit accept and sat up in bed. "Hi, Mamaw. When did you learn how to video chat?"

"Oh, lord, is that what I'm doin'? I didn't mean to."

"It doesn't matter to me, Mamaw." Alex yawned and stretched before noticing the time.

"Why are you calling so early?"

The phone was pointed at her mamaw's forehead, but it was enough to see her brow furrow. "Oh, I think you know exactly why. No one else will suspect us, but I know what you did."

Alex went cold. "I-I-I-"

"Close your mouth or the flies'll get in."

Alex snapped her jaw shut.

Her mamaw nodded in satisfaction. "Now, I ain't mad or nothing. I'm glad those awful people are gone. Claudette Bovier, next door, even caught wind that Eric Parker might be taking over the city manager position! And you know how much she's fawned over him since he came out."

"She threw the largest wedding this town has ever seen for him and paid for it all herself."

"Given what his husband did in helping establish her home as a historical landmark, she'd honestly do anything for them." Her mamaw's voice turns warm. "You know I feel the same about you. I've always told you I'd love you no matter what, you remember that?"

Alex nodded, then realized the phone wasn't at the right angle to see her. "I remember. And it includes this?"

"Of course, it does," her mamaw said loudly with a laugh. "I love you to the ends of the world."

Alex blinked away tears. "Thank you, Mamaw. I need to get ready for work, okay?"

"Okay, sweetie. I love you. Be safe now, you hear? Bye."

Alex disconnected the call and stared at her phone for several long seconds. She let out a laugh and jumped out of bed. Her mamaw knew the truth and still loved her, her family business was safe, there was no way Alex was going to jail, and best of all:

Her homophobic bosses were dead.

Alex got ready for work and entered the library an hour later, heart light. The Children's Department part of the floor was closed off until it could be properly cleaned and decontaminated. Alex headed to the Main Circulation desk, searching for Claudia.

Her work bestie tried and failed to hide her massive grin. "Good morning!"

"Morning to you, too. What's got you so chipper?"

"Oh, just some good news."

"Which is?"

Claudia squirmed in her seat, practically vibrating with excitement. "They've already picked an interim director."

Alex gasped. "You're kidding. They never do anything that fast."

"She's from the other branch. It's—"

"Hi, there," a familiar voice said from behind Claudia. "You're Alex, right?"

Alex stared at the interim Library Director, a branch manager with whom she'd worked with at a few programs with larger attendance. A branch manager who was openly trans and had she/they pronouns on their name badge under their name, Cameron.

"Yeah, I'm Alex." Alex took a deep breath. "My pronouns are she/they, like yours."

"Noted. Are both always fine?"

Alex's heart soared. "*They* is always fine, but *she* isn't sometimes, though it is right now and probably will be for a few weeks."

"Cool. If I ever mess up, let me know."

"Same for you."

Her new boss smiled, full of genuine warmth. "I will. Now, what is this I hear about us not having a Pride display in the Teen section anymore?"

A slow smile spread across Alex's face. "Can I fix it?"

"Please. You up for making a display for both the Children's Department and the Adults? Maybe if Claudia helps?"

"Absolutely!" Claudia's hand shot up. "I volunteer as tribute!"

Their new director snorted. "Okay, then, we're all set. I'll email you both later to set up separate meetings, so you can explain your job duties to me, discuss any ideas you've got for programs, and tell me what you need from me as your new manager. Sound good?"

"Sounds great," Alex said, finding herself meaning it.

"Fantastic! I'll see y'all later then." The interim director turned away from them.

Alex did a little jump dance and just managed not to sprint to the Teen section. Claudia went upstairs to reprint the display sign they'd been forced to remove before, and Alex took down the books for her display on revolutions. It had been Alex's own form of rebellion when Megan made her tear down the other one. Not like she could say anything about that. Or anything else, now, for that matter. Alex grinned and pulled the first sapphic book off the shelf to rebuild her Pride display.

Although things would take a few weeks to settle down, the town would move on. With the news of the new openly queer people taking important positions and folks unable to challenge any of it, all was well in her world.

And if anybody tried to stir up trouble, well, she had a surefire way to solve that issue.

R.C. Abernathy is a queer writer from Appalachia who loves hiking, attending fan conventions, and watching more horror movies than is healthy.

Their work can be found in *Appalachia Bare, Apostate: Stories of Deconversion,* and Flash Phantoms.

You can follow them on Bluesky @rosecabernathy.

THE CONDUCTOR
BY D.Z. HOLLOW

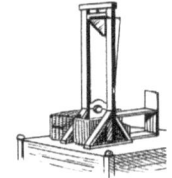

I

The train tracks were nestled between various hedges and native hardwoods. Maples and oaks adorned the edge of the old railroad. The dense grey overcast permeated the afternoon sky as Terrence picked up bits of gravel and rubbed them with his small thumb. With each swivel, he admired the wooden planks decorating the train tracks. He tossed the stone at the ground and quickly shifted his gaze.

In the distance, he noticed a mirage. Terrence began to run as fast as he could away. Then he heard it.

"Hey, Terry! Come here!"

He turned around to see two figures forming before him. The silhouettes began to take shape. They were kids from the high school known as Tweak and Diesel — nicknames they gave one another.

Tweak was tall, pale, freckled, and slender with bright red hair. Diesel was squatty with shaggy, brown hair and fat wrists. Both were ninth graders, six years older than Terrence.

"Terry, we have something we want to show you," Diesel stated proudly.

He was stout and strong for his age; his chubby fingers pointed toward the forest.

"What is it?" Terrence asked while blinking rapidly with a slight stutter.

"A train. You love trains, don't you, Terry?"

"Yes, they are my favorite. When I grow up, I am going to be a train conductor," Terrence replied with glee. His eyes lit up, they resembled the sunset at dusk in autumn, golden like the fields that lay dormant in the West Virginia winterset.

"This train is the biggest and best train in all of town. It's bright and orange. Have you seen it?"

"I haven't, will you show me?" Terrence insisted.

"Of course we will," Diesel muttered with a snicker.

Tweak chuckled as he covered his mouth before spitting a cigarette-scented loogie at the wooden planks. The thick sludge of salvia dripped from the rusty iron bolts hammered into the ancient railway tracks.

"Is it a huge train? I like big locomotives," Terrence asked.

"The biggest," Tweak muttered.

"I can't wait!" Terrence exclaimed. He fluttered his hands like a butterfly. The joy illuminated him. Every bit of his core was pure and wholesome. He was happy.

In an instant, the mood shifted. Diesel grabbed the little boy by his washed-out denim coat and tossed him on the railroad. The iron jutted into his frail, curved back. Terrence let out a blood-curdling scream. Tweak clenched his hands around Terrence's wrists and held him down firmly. Both ninth graders began punching the young child with intense force. With each jab, they both yelled obscenities.

"Fucking retard!" they hollered in unison.

Blood pooled as he cried profusely. When the young teens stopped beating the small child, their hands hurt. With sore knuckles, they relished in victory.

"I hear a train coming, let's get out of here!" Diesel shouted. The duo disappeared like dust into the sunset as the train grew louder; it approached Terrence, drawing closer by the second.

"Help me!" he cried out as he crawled to his knees. His face was swollen and badly bruised, but Terrence fought with every ounce of his soul to get to his feet. He wobbled back and forth before falling off the tracks. Terrence rolled away from the railroad as the vehicle passed by, just missing his face.

He managed to make it home before the sun fully set. When he walked in the door, his mother was horrified at the sight of her child.

"Terry, who did this to you?" she asked.

"I fell on the tracks. I'm ok," he stuttered.

"Son, who hurt you? You can tell me," his mother demanded.

"I'm ok, I always am," he replied, his head low and eyes to follow suit.

"I'm taking you to the infirmary," his mother insisted.

Terrence was rushed to the doctor on-site at the coal mine where his family lived, and his father worked. The entire operation was owned by the Roaches, Diesel's family. They built the mine in 1879, owning it and Coalwood for a full hundred years since its inception.

The doctor observed the young child's injuries and stitched up several wounds around the boy's eyes before sending him home. That night, it was tough for the little one to fall asleep. He fell in and out of the dream world, beings and cosmic entities filled his vision as he drifted into a realm of spirit and fantastical lore.

Every time he morphed into a dimension of mechanical beings and ethereal deities, Terrence noticed his cat, Shiloh, would always be asleep on his belly. Each time, without fail, he'd awaken to see a black ball of an endless abyss softly purring near his face. Shiloh would sleep on Terrence's stomach or chest every night; the vibrations of her purrs traveled far into his psyche, providing much-needed relief to the deep-seated fear buried inside him.

***

Morning came, and rain fell gently from the muted sky. The sweet smell of petrichor filled the dawn chorus. Terrence gathered his backpack and metal train lunchbox, then headed to school. The walk was brief, only a hundred yards; a small outbuilding sat beside an empty pit, worn and weathered. It was a one-room schoolhouse that housed twelve students in total. All of the children's parents were mine workers. Terrence was the only eight-year-old in the schoolhouse but was on the same educational level as the kindergarteners, of which there were three.

"Terry, get your book out and read page thirteen!" the teacher ordered.

Terrence struggled to get his textbook from his bag. As he fumbled with the pages, the woman came over and smacked him on the hands with a giant ruler. Terrence hid the pain and shoved it deep within his belly, to a place it could ferment and linger for decades until it crept to the surface during some late-stage, midlife crisis.

"Faster, Terry. We know you're stupid but slow, too?" she cackled loudly. The paper felt strange between his fingers as he flipped to page thirteen.

"Can you read the first sentence, Terry? Out loud to me please!"

He glanced at the black text firmly printed on the thin, waxy paper and struggled to read the first word. "Ch...chee. I don't know this word," he mumbled in immense defeat.

"Cheetahs, the word you can't read is cheetahs."

Terrence blinked in a sequence and focused on the page. "Cheetahs are the fattest."

"No, fastest, you idiot!" the teacher squawked.

Terrence felt weak and numb, drenched in a cloud of complete confusion. Reading was difficult for him; he liked drawing, and his favorite thing to sketch was trains.

"I have no patience for you today, Terrence. Go stand in the corner."

The far left nook of the schoolhouse was Terrence's corner; he spent the majority of his time there. He was banished to the confined space and forced to stand for the next six hours. Day in and day out, there he stood, still as can be. Sometimes he would shift in and out of consciousness, yet somehow he maintained his balance, still and centered as ever.

The teacher was convinced Terrence was incapable of learning and would rather leave him to rot like decaying fruit than to nourish the caterpillar hidden inside, waiting to emerge as a butterfly from beneath the surface.

"The day is over, Terry. You may go home now," she told him with a strong West Virginia drawl.

He grabbed his backpack and the train lunchbox, then began his trek. Clouds passed quickly, they created shadows on the tracks as Terrence whistled and sang a tune he made up about trains. "I love trains, they love me, I love trains, now I have to pee!"

Chuckling, he meandered along the railway. He knew he was supposed to go straight home after school, but sometimes he liked to wander the railway. When Terrence wandered, he'd always head downhill on the tracks. He would follow the curve and bend of the railroad tracks until they reached the covered bridge outside town. Coalwood was situated on the border of both Virginias, in the heart of the Appalachian mountains.

The town was a haven for millionaires who flooded the area in the late 1800s to score big with coal and railwork. Over the years, however, all that remained was a giant pit hidden deep beneath the earth. The wealth distribution was incredibly uneven; there seemed to be no middle class. The people of Coalwood were either rich descendants of the Roaches or part of the duo of families that owned and operated the railways. Certain segments of Coalwood were a tourist destination for the wealthy, many millionaires built cabins just outside of town in the mountains. They owned riverfront properties and enormous, luxurious lakeside retreats.

Terrence's family, however, was poor... but not just poor... Coalwood poor. That meant you didn't have plumbing, and your family was owned by the mine. It was already written in stone that Terrence would be working for the Roach family by thirteen. Those days were far from his mind, however.

He kept his eyes on the tracks as he walked, counting each plank with each step. "Plank ninety-seven, plank ninety-eight, plank ninety-nine, plank one hundred!" he yelled before continuing.

"Plank one hundred and one, plank one hundred and two," he mumbled as he hopped. Before he knew it, he'd reached the covered bridge. Beneath the dilapidated building ran the Coalwood River. It was dark and murky as it cascaded over several moss-covered boulders. Terrence looked at the red paint; it was chipped and faded. He ran his delicate fingers over the wood grain and felt the years of wear and tear.

What do you think happens when we die? The idea was profound and consumed the young boy's mind.

"What will happen to me when I leave this Earth?" he asked the covered bridge.

"You will finally live your dream," a voice murmured from the shadows.

***

The school week ended, and Terrence found himself yet again wandering the train tracks alone on Saturday afternoon. The sky was dull and muted; it resembled a polished stone stripped of any color and unique character, much like the gravel Terrence clenched in his grasp as he trudged along.

When he reached the covered bridge, he sat against the wooden wall and pulled his tin lunchbox from his brown bag. He sat quietly eating his mayonnaise sandwich, observing the trees as they swayed in the breeze. The scene was peaceful and tranquil, and he took every bit in, savoring each moment.

Then the silence broke.

"Terry, there you are. We were looking for you!" Diesel said from the other side of the bridge. Just then, Tweak appeared from the woodline.

"I brought you my old toy train. Here, you can have it. It's yours, Terry. Take it!"

"Really?" Terrence said with a smile. His face was bright and radiant, despite the bruising from the beating he received at the hands of Tweak and Diesel the weekend prior.

"Sure, here you go," Tweak offered as he handed the toy train to Terrence.

"I love it! I'm going to call him Greenie 'cause he's green."

Tweak laughed.

Diesel skipped across the broken bridge, following a metal beam that protruded from the sinkhole in the center. The railroad company built a new one a few years earlier in the fall of 1975. Terrence's father took him to see the grand opening, and they watched the first set of trains go over it.

"Hey, Terry, I see you have a new toy," Diesel said while jumping from the old platform to the dusty ground below. He made his way closer to Terrence, Tweak followed suit.

"I do. Tweak gave it to me. Thank you so much. I love Greenie so much!" he said as he hugged and kissed the plastic train.

"You love it, don't you? Do you love getting punched in the face?" Diesel spat.

"Please don't punch me, last time hurt. Last time hurt real bad."

"Aw, did it hurt?"

"Yes, please don't hurt me again. I just wanna sit by the bridge with Greenie."

"You love Greenie, don't you? You wanna fuck Greenie?" Diesel hissed.

"Teacher says you can't say that word, that's a bad word. I stand in the corner if I say bad words."

"You stand in the corner because you're a retard!" they shouted in unison.

"My mom says you shouldn't call me that. I am Terrence, and there is nobody like me," he said with extreme confidence.

"I want Greenie back!" Tweak ordered. In an instant, he snatched the toy from Terrence's hands. A rush of emotions overtook his small frame, and the boy began to sob.

"Oh, he's going to cry like a baby. Are you a baby?"

Terrence was too full of sadness to respond. The loss of Greenie was profound and significant.

"What a little crybaby!"

Before Terrence knew it, he was on the ground, and both teens were on top of him. The high schoolers grabbed small boulders beside the covered bridge and began striking the child with full-fledged force. They threw rocks at him with immense velocity. In a matter of seconds, Terrence was unconscious. He drifted far from Earth, his spirit traveling deep into the cosmos, journeying past the planets, past the moon and stars.

"Stop, Diesel! I think we hit him too hard! He's not breathing!" Tweak pointed out with fear.

"He's faking it."

"No, Diesel, look at his face. He's covered in blood and unrecognizable. He's fucking dead, we killed him!"

"Shut up, Tweak!" Diesel yelled in a panic. He surveyed the tracks and woodsline. Both boys looked at each other and realized their mistake.

"No one is around for miles. We need to hide his body, so no one can find him," Diesel stated, his hands trembling with each breath as Terrence took his last.

"Where the fuck are we going to dump him?" Tweak asked. His eyes were as wide as the moon, and his face was just as pale as the clouds above.

"In the river," Diesel said softly.

"In the river?"

"If we roll him into the Coalwood, it will look like he fell from the bridge. By the time they find his body, it will be way downstream. Plus, my family owns this town, and no one gives a shit about that fucking retard! That kid can't even read."

"We shove him over the edge?" Tweak asked faintly.

"Are you slow, too? Yeah, help me drag him closer to the edge."

The teens shoved Terrence's body over the side of the ravine beside the old covered bridge and watched as his corpse plummeted and hit the rocky water below.

Terrence was gone.

It took two weeks for his body to surface from the darkness of the Coalwood River. His parents were gutted.

Deep down, a part of them believed their son was just lost in the mountains, and they would be reunited soon. There had been speculation he took off into the forest with Shiloh, as the black cat was nowhere to be seen. The search for Terrence was quick and short-lived; the rest of Coalwood moved on and was not too concerned with a mentally-challenged child's whereabouts, especially a coal miner's son.

Terrence's death was ruled an accident. The local Coalwood sheriff declared it a product of poor infrastructure and low intelligence on Terrence's part. The rest of the town agreed. Life in Coalwood carried on, but not like usual.

***

A week after Terrence's body was recovered from the river, Shiloh showed up at the family home. Terrence's mother was happy to see the cat as the animal helped her cope with some of her grief. A bond between them grew. Shiloh spent her nights sleeping on top of Terrence's mother. Just like her son, her dreams were intense and deeply spiritual. At times, they were beautiful, while at other times they were violent and horrific. His mother couldn't help but feel they were prophetic and full of meaning.

In one of the dreams, there was a train derailed, and many people died. The dream played for several days until one morning she awoke to an explosion at the mine. She rushed outside to see a dark grey plume of smoke bellowing in the distance. People were screaming, and debris was crumbling down the mountains beside the miners' homes. The emergency siren cried out; it was deafening.

Several ambulances and Coalwood paramedics arrived on-site and began descending into the rubble. Yells and hollers from men trapped beneath the debris carried on for a day or so, until the majority fell silent. Terrence's mother watched as dead bodies were retrieved from the wreckage. Then she saw her husband emerge from the chaos. He was the lone survivor; the entire crew was gone.

The Roach family panicked.

They were at a loss; their entire staff, minus one, was wiped out. They were unsure what caused the rumble; to this day no one knows for certain.

Funerals were held for the workers, an honor Terrence did not receive. His family was given a small wooden crate to put his body in and were told they could burn it themselves or bury their son in their yard. They chose to cremate their child; the process was long and grueling, but the parents honored their boy.

***

Years would pass by, three to be exact. Tweak and Diesel were now seniors in high school.

"Tweak, grab me another beer," Diesel demanded from the truck bed, his voice echoing through the holler.

The duo had taken Diesel's father's Chevy to the edge of town to drink beer in the woods; the air was cold and dry. They were deep in the shadows, oblivious to the darkness around them.

"It's been three years since we killed Terry," Tweak slurred, a Marlboro hanging from his wide lips.

"Shut up, don't bring that shit up again, you hear me?" Diesel yelled. He grabbed his friend by the shirt and flung obscenities, belligerent and unruly.

"Chill, man. Get out of my face," Tweak murmured.

"Don't you ever bring that shit up again, or I will throw your ass in the Coalwood River! You got me?"

Tweak grew silent.

Suddenly, the car engine revved, and the headlights began to flash abruptly. They blinked rapidly in succession as the locks shut. The seniors panicked.

"What the fuck is going on?" Diesel shouted.

The truck began to drive out of the forest.

"What the hell Tweak? The truck is driving itself!"

"Hit the emergency brake!"

"I tried but it won't budge!" Diesel screamed in fear.

The truck stopped abruptly on the train tracks.

"We're on the railroad, I hear a train coming!" Diesel screeched, his hands desperately trying to fling the door open.

The locomotive grew closer.

"We're gonna die!" Tweak belted at the top of his lungs. The boys continued to try to unlock the doors, but they couldn't. They were trapped. Something was keeping them bound. The stereo acted erratically, white noise pierced through the speakers, and radio static fluctuated between stations before strange chanting erupted.

The train got closer and closer.

"It's going to hit us!"

In one swift motion, the passenger's side door flung open. Tweak leaped out of the vehicle as the train crushed the Chevy to rubble; Diesel was jelly.

His body was pulverized, his brain and pelvis uniting as one. The scene was vile. Diesel was plastered everywhere; bits of his spleen, intestines, and skull were stuck to crossing signs and railroad tracks. A massacred body, mush and mangled.

The bolts in the old wooden planks were bloody and drenched in gore. Several officers and EMTs vomited when they approached the wreck. The train conductor leaped from the vehicle once it finally came to a halt; bits of Diesel were plastered throughout. His mother and father were late on the scene. Consumed by terror and grief as they huddled together, clenching limbs of sorrow, they prayed for their son. They asked many questions. How? Why? The Roach family was devastated, their world fell bleak, and the rest of the town would soon follow. Tweak, on the other hand, would get out unscathed.

II

Terrence's spirit swirled in outer space for a couple of years. He lived in the cosmos, and his soul undulated and oscillated with infinite, universal time. His mother was pregnant at Diesel's funeral. Despite their feelings, both parents were forced to attend the ceremony; all of Coalwood was there. Terrence was reborn in the winter of 1989. His parents named him Roger, but his nickname was Rocky.

He was smart, confident, and telepathic with powers beyond mind reading, being a pro at telekinesis. Something sinister, however, was lurking in Rocky, buried deep within his nickname.

No one in Coalwood would ever learn the truth about Terrence's murder. Tweak and Diesel managed to keep it between each other, mainly due to Tweak's fear of Diesel's wrath and fury.

With Terrence reborn and Diesel dead, Coalwood turned to stone. The mine shut down, and the Roach family lost millions. After it caved in a second time, killing half their workers, the remaining miners banded and went on strike. The owners lost bids and contracts. The mine went bankrupt.

Farms fell to famine, all the crops turned rotten. Babies were born with birth defects, and all of the Roach family infants grew sick and died mysteriously. The family sought religious and spiritual help. All anyone could tell them was they must be "cursed." The harsh reality was, they were. Terry, now Rocky, made sure the entire Roach family was diseased.

The same went for Tweak and his relatives. They stayed in Coalwood, just like Terrence's family. Tweak knocked a young girl up when Rocky was one. The child was born unwell, and eventually, the mother killed the infant, burying it in the backyard. She was sentenced to life in prison, and the downfall of Tweak began.

A year later, he would get another girl pregnant, this baby being stillborn. One evening, while drinking alone in his workshop, Tweak somehow managed to slice off his left hand. In utter shock, he bled all over the workspace. He managed to get to the hospital, and the surgeon stitched him up nicely. He lost his hand, but at least had a nub.

He traveled down an extensive rabbit hole of darkness. Tweak couldn't grasp his fate, struggling deeply. He felt ashamed, crippled, and less than. His friends distanced themselves, and he found he was rotting in seclusion. Another year passed, and Tweak would, yet again, slip one past the goalie. This time, however, a child was born. His name was Tucker. Tweak and his girlfriend Tabitha were so happy... that was until Tucker turned seven.

***

I remember it... the day I died, that is. It was in my past life, the one as Terrence or Terry. Now I am Roger or Rocky. Everybody calls me by my nickname and has pretty much since birth. It's dark and twisted that my new identity reflects how I was removed from this world in my past life; I guess the universe is funny like that sometimes. A giant, cosmic joke.

When I crossed over as Terrence, I met an eternal spirit. It manifested in the form of my cat, Shiloh. The entity presented herself as a shapeshifter. She offered me a chance at rebirth, an opportunity at a waking life, moving through two worlds at once. While my form changed and filtered through the cosmos, I learned how to control objects with my mind. One of which was a locomotive. I spent weeks practicing with cars, vans, semi-trucks, then trains.

I was the conductor the night Diesel's brains and insides were smashed to oblivion. If I remember correctly, it was in the same location where they beat me to death with rocks. I'd wanted to take Diesel out first, to hurt the Roach family as a whole, so I went for their pockets and their hearts. When the mine closed, I was happy, but it still didn't leave much for my family. I had to figure out a way to help them move forward.

I was just a few years older than Tucker. When we met, he was five, and I was eight. He had special needs, he couldn't learn like the other children, reminding me of myself in my past life as Terrence. I could have chosen to kill Tucker, but I am not that kind of villain. Instead, I befriended the poor sap. He was lonely and isolated; all the other kids picked on him for being different. I was well-liked at school, so I took it upon myself to help Tucker in his vulnerable state. It also gave me a chance to get closer to Tweak and his family.

My father eventually started working for Tweak's uncle, who ran a hardware store and hired him to help around the shop. He was very grateful, my mom even made him a nice outfit. My friendship with Tucker led to the gig, Tweak's family was happy that he had a pal, considering he was an outcast.

When Tucker turned seven, everything changed. He began hearing voices and seeing spirits. He would speak in tongues, and his eyes would roll in the back of his head. Tweak and his wife brought their son to every doctor in West Virginia, and no one could figure it out. A psychiatrist recommended an exorcism, claiming she believed the boy was possessed by an evil spirit. Tucker's parents called a priest, and the old man came to their house to perform the ritual. That's when everything grew dark and sinister.

***

"He's foaming!" Tucker's mother, Tabitha, yelled. She was right, he was.

His skin was grey and translucent. Critters crawled beneath the surface, and segmented creatures protruded out of it. His eyes were now black as obsidian, far and distant. The child screamed obscenities, spitting bile from his small-rimmed mouth.

"Set me free, so I can feed!" Tucker moaned.

"He's possessed! Please help, Lord!" Tweak shrieked, his red hair clenched in his pale grasp.

"Quiet!" the priest interjected. He was old and quilted in grey, his hair white as a pearl. He lit several candles, cradled his Bible while reciting scriptures, and squeezed his rosary.

"Please, Heavenly Father, rid this child of evil. Lucifer has taken this boy; he has taken this little one to the gates of Hell. We ask that you enter this child and free his spirit from the shackles of Satan! In the name of the Father, the Son, and the Holy Spirit. Amen!" the priest beckoned.

He tossed holy water on the boy and waited.

Tucker continued to spew and foam. He hissed and spit violently. "Let me free, so I can eat!"

"It's not working, Reverend, help, do something!" Tweak demanded, the rage surfacing with each breath.

The priest cycled through his ritual two more times, but nothing changed; Tucker was still consumed by evil.

"I know you don't love me, Daddy, how could you after all? You hate kids like me. You killed that boy, you beat him to oblivion. Terry was his name. Tell them about Terry! Tell them, Daddy!" Tucker spat.

"What is he talking about?" the mother begged Tweak, trying to understand.

Tweak was silent.

"Tell them, Daddy, tell them how you and Diesel beat little Terry to death on the train tracks and then threw his body in the river. You did, you did, didn't you, Daddy?"

Tweak became angry. He fled the home and ran to the crumbling shed, reflective of his life. When he returned, he was holding an axe in his hand.

"What are you doing?" his wife asked, horrified.

The priest was deep in his mantra, chanting, singing, and calling on the lord to save the family. It was too late, it always was.

"I'm putting a stop to this madness. No boy of mine will act or speak like this. This child is evil, even God can't cure him!" he hollered into the cabin walls.

The priest woke from his trance. "Lord Jesus Christ, save this family now!" he commanded.

Tweak waited.

"You want to murder me, Daddy, just like you murdered Terry. Do it, Daddy, do it!"

"Argh!!" Tweak growled. In one dramatic motion, he slung the blade into Tucker's face, hacking his poor son to bits.

The blood was thick and splattered across the chocolate-stained walls of the luxury cabin. Blood waterfalled from the chair and onto the marble floor decorating the kitchen. Tweak's family home was gorgeous, a mountain retreat quietly tucked away, nestled along the Coalwood River.

"My boy!" his wife wept, clutching the remnants of her child.

"That's not our boy!" Tweak screeched.

It was then they noticed the priest was back in a trance, his eyes were closed, and he had not reacted to Tweak smashing the child with an axe. The man of God reached into his pocket, retrieved the pistol he had prepped, aimed at his temple, and pulled the trigger.

"You piece of shit, I hate you, Tweak!" Tabitha cried out with a blood-curdling shrill. She grabbed the bloody axe and lunged at her husband. He stumbled around and tripped onto the floor before reaching for the bloody revolver in the priest's hand, aiming it at Tabitha.

"What are you going to do, go Wendy Torrence on me?" he jabbed, his freckles buried by pieces of his kid.

"Wendy had a bat, Jack had the axe, dumbass!"

Tabitha swung the weapon and plunged it deep into her husband's stomach.

"You bitch!" he muttered while plummeting rapidly.

Tabitha picked the axe up and repeated the process a few times, squirts of blood arched in unison.

Tweak was done.

She dropped the tool and collapsed on the carpet. It was then she noticed something slithering in her son's corpse.

"Tuck," she whispered.

"Mother."

The being resembled a centipede, its body split into saturated segments, and legs like a caterpillar. There were loads of them dangling from its elongated form. Its eyes were yellow and its body black. As it walked, it grew in size. Tucker was over nine feet long and two feet wide, the height of a skateboard. Each segment was covered in spindly black hairs. A red number *seven* was brushed on his insect body, much like a black widow would have a marking.

"Open your mouth, Momma," the centipede said softly.

Tucker's mother lay flat on her back, Tweak's blood soaking into her sweater. Without hesitation, Tabitha hung her mouth agape. The insect climbed into its mother's body and coiled inside her belly. With Tucker now inside her, she was ready for a re-emergence. She consumed pieces of Tweak's corpse and waited patiently. Tucker, Tweak, and the priest were burned far from town, and a small funeral was held for all.

Tabitha did not attend them.

As the funerals went on, each stacked on the other, same Sunday and all, the folks of Coalwood couldn't help but wonder where Tabitha was. The family trio was known as the "three T's" all over town, and now two were being laid to rest.

Where was Tabitha?

A day would flutter on by, and her family would contact the police. A search party was conducted, and the people of Coalwood tried desperately to locate her, but she was nowhere to be found.

The truth was, she was being led through the forests of Western Virginia. The creature dwelling inside her had complete dominion over her every move. He fed his mother through the frigid winter greenwood until they reached the old mine.

"Journey down the abandoned shaft, it's still accessible," the centipede directed.

Tabitha followed orders. She climbed as far down as she could, reaching the bottom. She sat there for a while as Tucker hibernated. Several days would pass, and eventually, he was ready. The entity ripped from his mother's belly and climbed out of the coal mine.

***

When I saw the segmented being lurking in the forest, shuffling over dead leaves and lumber, I knew it was Tucker. I sent him messages with my brain waves, letting him know it was me, Rocky.

"Tucker, is that you?"

"It's me," he confessed.

"What happened to you?" I asked.

"My father killed me. I was offered a chance at resurrection by a dark spirit, it reminded me of Shiloh, your cat," Tucker transmitted.

"That's because it was," I admitted.

Shiloh told me years ago, in my past life, she was an alien from another reality, sent here to watch and judge humanity. She can morph and shapeshift. For some, she is a leader or a savior. For others, she is simply an extreme predator.

"Why a centipede?" Tucker questioned, his yellow eyes drifting as his googly eyes pressed to his strange shape. His body was moist and warm; you could feel the heat coming off his core. Suddenly, antennas sprouted from his head, and two thin hairs beamed from Tucker's skull.

"Now I can control you," I told him.

"What for?" he asked, his obscure pupils fluctuating side to side like a fish.

"So we can destroy Coalwood, once and for all."

***

Rocky and Tucker, the centipede creature, traversed the woods of Coalwood until they funneled into downtown. It was a Saturday afternoon, and the square was bustling. All the rich lakefront owners, wealthy out-of-town elites, and corporate business folks were enjoying time meandering around. The shops were packed, and the restaurants were full. They sludged through, the onlookers releasing infinite gasps into the aether. The centipede opened its mouth, exposing layers of rigid, sharp teeth. Rocky carefully climbed inside and became the conductor.

He led the killer creature through town, devouring all of Coalwood. The sidewalks, alleyways, parks, and recreation centers were scattered with half-eaten, desecrated corpses. Trains derailed, spewing into the lake.

The duo traveled into the millionaire's lakefront retreats and consumed their flesh, leaving eggs all over town. Once they were done, the only folks who remained in Coalwood, were Rocky, his parents... and his pet centipede.

A new wind rushed by.

Rocky's father became the owner and sole proprietor of the hardware store. A couple of years ticked by and the parents had enough money to purchase the ramshackle hotel, originally owned by the Roaches.

They fixed it up and turned it into a beautiful inn, perfectly situated on the old train tracks, nestled between an array of maples and hardwoods.

The hotel butted up against the historical train station, which they purchased as well. The couple refurbished both and joined the two. It was a fun, hip spot that made Rocky's family wealthy. People traveled from all over to visit the charming bed and breakfast. Parked outside, on the train tracks, was an old green locomotive.

Beside it hung a plaque.

Established in 2003
The Conductor Bed and Breakfast.
Coalwood, West Virginia
In honor of our boy, Terrence.

Mommy and Daddy love you.

"Switch-man sleeping train hundred and two
is on the wrong track and headed for you."
"Casey Jones" - Grateful Dead

D.Z. Hollow is an author with cerebral palsy, living in the North Georgia Mountains. He draws inspiration from Appalachian folklore, vintage horror, and unique life experiences. His stories often involve characters with physical flaws, seeking revenge in an unjust world.

www.facebook.com/dz.hollow.2024

www.instagram.com/d.z.hollow

IN DEATH, JUSTICE PREVAILS
BY KELLY BARKER

Shortly after Will woke up in the morgue, his self-appointed social worker told him to go home after explaining a few things to him about the afterlife. Making sure Will understood he wouldn't see anyone from the world of the living until they, too, passed away, he walked off and gently shook the shoulder of another body-bag-wrapped corpse.

Will left, and after a nine-mile trek, he stood outside his house. His mind flickered from one thought to another while he tried to piece together an impossible puzzle. Looking down at the business card he was handed, he wondered if it was too soon to phone his social worker with further enquiries. There was only one question at the forefront of his mind, and that was whether he would see Ted again. Will rubbed his chest, then realised he didn't feel out of breath, dehydrated, or hungry. Nor was he cold or too hot. Being dead came with perks, he decided, but his heart still thrummed with pain.

Not wanting to get his hopes up, he put the business card back in his pocket, backtracked, and searched for signs of life. From across the street, a door opened and someone called out to him. Will jogged over to greet his elderly neighbour, who had died a few years back. Feeling guilty for not knowing his name, mostly because everyone down the street referred to him as Deaf-ears, Will made a conscious note to call him sir.

"Hello," Deaf-ears said. "It's nice to see you again."

"And you—"

"What?" he said, cupping his ear.

Will rolled in his lips to hide his smirk. "Er, it's nice to see you, too."

Deaf-ears nodded his head. "You've just died, haven't you? If you need any help, you know where I am."

His words meant a lot to Will because, in the past, they had only ever waved at each other. "Do you know if animals or pets come here, as well? Wherever here is."

He cupped his ear again, making Will repeat his question a little louder. His neighbour's smile was kind. "Can't you hear the birds singing? I can't anymore, but I still enjoy watching them. Go home, son. He's been waiting for you."

Will's eyes flooded with tears before he dropped to his knees. When he looked up, he saw a flock of birds fly across the blue and orange streaked sky. He had felt too overwhelmed to take in his surroundings and hadn't noticed them singing or anything much else.

Deaf-ears wrapped his arms around Will's shoulders and lifted him up the best he could. "Go home."

Will nodded, too shaken to produce any words, then sprinted to his house. His hands trembled when he reached for the handle of his front door. When he opened it, his hallway was empty and silent. A cruel reminder of why he had closed his eyes and wished for death when the firefighters were frantically sawing off the top of his car to free him.

A bark rang out from upstairs, and Will's heart hammered in his chest. "Ted. Teddy, is that you?"

His lurcher launched himself down the stairs and knocked Will off his feet.

"My boy, my baby boy. I've missed you so much," he said while Teddy licked his face.

***

Later that evening, Will and Teddy were walking their usual route through the woods when they came across another beagle. "That's twelve we've seen now with no collars on. Where do you think they're coming from? And why are they so skittish?"

Teddy looked at him, and if he could shrug, he surely would have before resuming his sniffing quest. When Will spied one between the trees, he went down to one knee, then tried to coax the beagle over. It eyed him cautiously before running off.

"Strange," he said.

"Devastating, more like."

Will stood up and spun around, almost tripping himself up. A young, beautiful woman, maybe his own age, stood before him with a Jack Russell in her arms.

"Hi. What did you mean by that?"

"The beagles are coming from the pharmaceutical testing facility down the road after they die. Those arseholes even got awards for not testing on animals, but it's clear now that they do. That's wealth for you." She shook her head and walked past him.

"Hey, wait. Is that really true? Surely, in a small town, we would have known they were testing on animals." Will visualised the pharmaceutical facility she mentioned, trying to see it through a different perspective, but saw nothing sinister about it.

"Oh, yeah. Like I said, that's wealth. An annual profit of twenty-two billion buys you the power to make people believe the sky is green or that the moon doesn't really exist. And they don't just test on the beagles, they torture them. We've been dead for nearly a decade, and we still haven't been able to get them to trust us."

"Who's we?"

"I'm Milly, and this is Angel." She faced her Jack Russell toward him. "She's paralysed, so I have to carry her everywhere — not that I mind."

He closed the gap between them and stroked Angel's head. "She is cute."

And so are you.

"What are your names?"

"I'm Will." He patted his thigh until his lurcher came to him. "And although he doesn't respond to his name, this is Ted, Teddy, or Boy."

Milly grinned. "That would explain why he doesn't respond to it. He doesn't know which name is his."

"Ah, gotcha. Anyway, how many beagles do you think are living in the woods?"

"There are thousands of them. Way too many to count."

"That's disgusting, and we need to put a stop to it right now. Do we... Er." He spun his finger in the air while thinking of the right questions to ask. "Do we have a police station? Newspapers, politicians? Who do we go to when we—"

"Will, there are no police because all the rotten souls don't get an afterlife like we do. Even if the media still existed, we can't do anything about it."

"Why can't we?"

Milly's eyes were warm and sympathetic. "Because we're dead, and we can't interfere with the world of the living without a day pass."

"A day pass? How do I get one?" Will asked without thinking. He wasn't sure if he wanted to go back, even if he could.

"The local council offices are still open. If you give them a plausible reason, they will give you one."

Will cocked his head to the side, waiting for her to smile or show some sort of sign she was joking.

She mirrored him, then nodded as if she finally understood something. "You died recently, didn't you?"

"It's a blur, so I couldn't say for sure, but I think it was just a few days ago. What's the date today?"

Again, her eyes and smile were warm. "I don't know. It doesn't matter anymore, does it?"

"I guess not." Looking at his feet, he felt guilty for Teddy because he wished he were still alive, just long enough to stop the beagles from being tortured. He then winced when an image of his dog getting hurt in such a brutal way invaded his thoughts. "All those poor dogs."

She shuffled Angel into one arm and put her other around Will. "Hey, I know it's hard to deal with, but at least the dogs here are at peace now."

"It can't continue, though. Maybe we could get a coffee in town, and you could tell me more about the day pass? That's if you're not too busy."

This time, when she smiled, it was playful. "The dead aren't busy, and we can sit in a coffee shop if you want, but coffee is no longer served there because we don't eat or drink anymore—"

"What? Are you sure?"

She nodded.

"I don't know what's bloody worse; the pain of my death or that I'll never share a pizza with Ted again."

Milly laughed. "You're a box of frogs, aren't you? Either way, I think it would be best if we discussed what it actually means to be dead before you ask the council for a day pass."

***

Will had been standing in the council office for over an hour and had seen no signs of life. The last time he was here, he had asked for his twenty-five percent discount on the council tax for being a sole occupier shortly after he moved into his new home.

After bouncing around in foster care since he could remember, the only thing that got him through it in his early teens was that he would get himself a dog as soon as he could. Getting Teddy was the happiest day of Will's life. The worst day of his life was when the vet put Ted to sleep because his tumours had gotten way out of hand to treat.

Now that he had died for real, he knew that he had died twice. The first time was when Teddy took his last breath, making the second time a walk in the park. Still, the past was where it belonged. All that mattered now was getting justice for the beagles.

The door opened and a lady in a floral dressing gown and matching slippers walked in. Will was on the cusp of telling her there was a queue when she walked past him. When she continued to walk until she was behind the desk, he closed his mouth.

She pulled out a chair, sat, then straightened her glasses. "How may I help you?"

"You work here?"

"I do. How may I help you?"

Will looked around. "Where is everyone?"

"On their lunch break."

He stifled a laugh. "Oh, really? And what are they having for lunch? Air?"

"What do you want?" Her eyes narrowed.

"Er. Okay." Will ran his hands down his face. "I'm not sure if you are aware of the beagle situation, but I plan to put a stop to it."

She breathed out a sigh and looked deflated. "I am aware of what that pharmaceutical company is doing, and it's heartbreaking, but I can't see how you can stop it."

"I have been told about your day pass. Maybe I could find the owner and threaten to expose him if he doesn't shut down his testing facility."

Her stare was blank, and just when Will thought her eyeballs would dry up and shrivel, she blinked. "How will the owner hear your threats?"

"I haven't got it all figured out yet, but my new friend said that with practice, the dead can move objects in the world of the living. Maybe I could write something down, like, stop what you're doing or else."

"Even if you could, that's not a good enough reason to get a day pass. I'm sorry." She pulled her keyboard closer to her and started tapping away.

Will leaned over the desk and saw his reflection on the blank computer screen. "It's not even switched on," he said.

The receptionist glared at him over the rim of her glasses and didn't even bother to look ashamed.

"Fine, whatever. What would be a good enough reason?" He then remembered who he was dealing with and a response shot out of his mouth before he thought it through. "Dog poop."

"Excuse me?"

"It's everywhere because there are thousands of stray beagles, and it's the council's responsibility to deal with it. And, by giving me a day pass, I'll have a chance of stopping those dogs from needlessly dying and adding to the mess."

"The beagles are dead and don't eat, therefore, do not poop."

Will looked up at the ceiling for guidance. "Oh, I know. They bark — constantly. It's a nuisance and I can't sleep."

She looked bored. "Fine, I'll give you a day pass. What's your name, address, and social worker's information?"

While Will gave her what she had requested, she tapped away at her keyboard again.

"Why are you still doing that if the computer is off?" Will said, hiding his smile behind his hand.

"See that door behind you?" she snapped. "Think about where you want to go and then step through it."

Turning to see the door she had pointed at, Will sighed. "That says staffroom on the door. How the hell is that going to take me where I want to go?"

"It's my lunch break now. Either use the door or don't. It's the only access to the world of the living in this county, but you are free to use others."

"You've just come back from lunch." Under his breath, he said, "This place is a flipping circus."

"Circus or not. You are living in the afterlife now, and you need to come to terms with the changes." With that, she stood up and walked out of the building.

Will stared at the staffroom door, then shook his head. He had asked Milly what the day pass would look like, but because she had looked at him like he was joking, he hadn't wanted to embarrass himself further by asking for more details. Now he wished he had.

"Right, let's see if this works." He stepped directly in front of the door. Just think about where you want to go, the receptionist said. He put his hand on the handle. "Take me to the pharmaceutical testing facility in this town, and to the exact location where they hurt the dogs."

The moment he opened the door, he thought he heard a child screaming. Then he saw people in white lab coats cutting open a beagle's chest while it was strapped down to a gurney. It was howling in pain, and its eyes were bulging out of its sockets. A woman slapped the dog across the face and told it to shut up. Will averted his eyes, only to notice there were other dogs there too, whimpering for mercy in small cages, surrounding the vilest sight he had ever beheld.

He choked on the smell of blood and faeces and slammed the door shut. As he turned to leave, the building turned on its side, and Will heard his body crash to the floor before he felt the impact.

***

I should have done something. I could have... Will had berated himself and had cried all the way from the council office to Milly's house. She was looking after Teddy for him, and although he didn't want to face anyone right now, he needed his dog's comfort. He tapped on her door.

Milly was smiling when she greeted him, then her face dropped. "What happened? Didn't you get a day-pass?"

Will shuffled inside, sat on her floor, then leaned back against the wall. Teddy came over, and instead of his usual excitement, he sensed something was wrong and licked Will's tears away. "I got the pass, which is just a staffroom door, by the way. And I saw something I can never unsee."

He looked up at Milly before she sat down across from him. "Whether my eyes are open or closed, I just see it, and I know now for certain I have to shut that testing facility down."

"What did you see? Actually..." She waved her words away. "I don't want to know. But I'll help you in any way I can."

"Do you know the name of the owner?"

"Yes, he's called Jonathan Dalton. He was in the news a lot just before my death. Along with his diabolical company, he was also connected to many sexual assault claims, which never made it to trial. Although with his money and power, I suspect all the claims were true. Oh, and he was occasionally accused of financial fraud. Clearly, twenty-two billion isn't enough for his type. Why do you ask?"

Will rubbed his face into Teddy's neck. "Because I want to kill him."

He also wanted to kill the people he saw torturing the dog, but he would keep that to himself for now.

Milly tucked her hair behind her ears. "I wouldn't think less of you if you did, but you're not a killer."

"I am a killer," he murmured.

"No, you are not. If you were, you wouldn't be here. Like I said, the rotten souls don't get a second chance." She stood up, then nestled beside him. "And if you were to kill him, there's a chance you won't be able to return to the afterlife."

Will thought about that for a moment, but it was too late. Certain things were just set in stone the moment they arose, and opening that door was one of them. He turned to Milly and placed his hand on her jaw.

"I'm here because I killed myself — in a way. It was a head-on collision a week after Ted died, and although it wasn't my fault, I couldn't believe my luck. I wanted to die and didn't fight for my life. So I know what I'm capable of. Now I know Ted is safe, and that you would look after him if I weren't to return. I have decided to do everything in my power to help those dogs."

"I'm so sorry you went through something so awful, and you felt like you had no way out, but you can't do this to yourself again. The afterlife is kooky. I'll be the first to admit it, but it's peaceful, and you and Teddy will have an eternity of tranquillity."

He shook his head. "No, I will have an eternity of misery after what I saw, and the beagles in the woods will only remind me of it. My mind is made up."

***

Will agreed to let Milly ring around and ask others about his chances of returning. The conclusion was fifty-fifty. Not that he cared. His only regret was that he wouldn't have more time to spend with her. She was already special to him. He wondered why, after all this time, he would finally meet someone who didn't make him feel like he didn't belong.

She put the receiver back on the wall-mounted landline and sat next to Will on the sofa. "So, Geth Deers seems to think... Why are you laughing?"

Will covered his mouth with his hand. "Sorry, it's just that I know someone called Deaf-ears. Obviously, it's not the same person. Please, carry on."

Despite the situation, she laughed. "Geth Deers is Deaf-ears."

"Holy shit, that's actually really clever."

"It's not clever, it's childish." Milly bit her lip in a poor attempt at hiding her amusement. "He seems to think that ghosts are entitled to seek revenge, but because the owner of the testing facility hasn't hurt you personally, it may not count."

"Ghosts?" Will frowned at her.

"Yeah, ghosts. That is what we are when we enter the world of the living. Also, Geth said he's coming with you."

"No way. He's a good man, and I'm not risking him."

"You're a good man. And by not doing more to stop you, I feel like I'm risking you. If it weren't for Angel and Teddy, I would come with you, too. Please, Will, take him with you. It would make me feel a lot better about this." She stroked back his fringe from his face.

"Okay," he said, but when the time came, he would convince Deaf-ears otherwise.

***

Back at the council office with Milly, Deaf-ears, and the two dogs in tow, Will thought for a moment his eyes would fall out the back of his head when he rolled them. The receptionist from the day before sat behind the desk, wearing a blue dressing gown this time, and had her hair scraped into a bun.

"Hi, Martha. How are you?" Milly said to her.

"Hi, my love. I see you've met this wally." The receptionist said, pointing her pen at Will. Martha then turned her attention to Deaf-ears. "Good morning, Geth."

Geth cupped his ear. "Excuse me?"

"I said, good morning."

He smiled at her, then headed straight toward the staffroom door.

"Hey, wait up," Will said, placing his hand on Geth's shoulder. His plan to talk him out of going had gone down the pan because Deaf-ears had pretended he couldn't hear a word he was saying, even though he blatantly had. His second plan was to give Teddy one last cuddle, and that was something he would follow through with.

Will went down to his knees. "Come here, boy. I'm going away, but don't worry, because Milly is going to take good care of you, okay? I love you."

She stepped forward with Angel in her arms. "I know I can't persuade you to not do this, so just know I will take good care of him if the worst should happen."

He closed the gap between them. "I don't suppose I could steal a kiss from you for being an absolute hero?"

Milly raised her brows. "You're not being a hero, you're being reckless. But if you return, I will think about it."

More than pleased with her response, he nodded at her, faced the door, then cleared his throat. "I would like to go to Jonathan Dalton's house, to his exact location."

Martha made a sound of disgust.

Will faced her.

She looked anguished for a moment before her expression turned smug. "You don't need to say it aloud, you just think it, then walk through."

With his hand on the door handle, he said, "In case I don't make it back, I just wanted you to know that I think you're the worst receptionist in existence."

Her mouth fell open.

Walking through the door with Geth right behind him, he saw a man in his sixties sitting at a dark oak desk. He was wearing a navy suit, and his thinning hair was swept to the side. If not for what Will had seen, he might have felt sorry for the man. Then he looked around the spacious room and saw animal heads mounted on all four walls. Above the fireplace

88

was a rhino's head. Just below on the mantle lay an elephant's tusk.

Will thought that if this was what being rich looked like, then he was glad he wasn't. He also concluded that this man, Jonathan, had no regard for life. If the sexual assault claims were true, then he certainly didn't discriminate between animals or humans, leaving Will to wonder what else he'd gotten away with.

Geth stood over his desk, then waved his hand in front of Jonathan's face. Nothing.

"What shall we kill him with?" Will shouted.

"How about the letter opener?"

Will scanned the desk for it. "Yeah, okay."

When Will found it, he tried to pick it up. He felt a sensation like pins and needles when it passed through his finger, but nothing more.

"You try," he said to Geth.

Geth managed to nudge it with his second attempt.

Jonathan's head whipped from his paperwork to the letter opener, then he smirked before picking up his whiskey and swigging down a gulp.

"What are we going to do now?" Will said. Feeling defeated, Will closed his eyes and thought of the dog who'd been strapped down, cut open, and slapped. The more he pictured it, the angrier he got.

Then he remembered with clarity the second after the car slammed into him and felt a power surge crackle through his fingers. He grabbed the letter opener, and just as it was about to pierce the monster before him, it slipped through his hand.

Jonathan jumped out of his chair and scrambled to the far wall. "Who's there?"

"I had hoped not to hear his entitled voice again," Martha said at the door.

Will and Geth gaped at her.

Martha strode over to the desk, picked up a paperweight, and smashed it over Jonathan's head. As soon as he hit the floor, he tried to get up again, too dazed to realise what had happened to him.

For Will, time fast-forwarded and stood still, making him feel disoriented. After opening and closing his mouth, he found his words and screamed, "What's going on?"

"Meet my husband and my murderer." Martha turned to Will. "Milly told me what you two idiots had planned to do after I asked her why the hell you were coming here. First, neither of you is powerful enough to manipulate objects with precision. Second, if you had succeeded, you both would have forfeited your souls. What the hell were you thinking?"

As Will spluttered for an answer, Geth cupped his ear, and Jonathan got to his feet. Too fast for Will's brain to register, Martha picked up the letter opener and plunged it through her husband's eye. This time, when he collapsed, he didn't move.

Martha looked down at his corpse with a hint of a smile before she faced Will. "Go back to the council office and apologise to Milly for causing her—"

"How can you just stand there like you didn't just kill someone? And why now? Did you know about what was happening to the dogs?"

Martha looked aghast. "How dare you? When I first met Jonathan, I didn't know he had a cruel side. After I found out about the girls he hurt, he pushed me down the stairs to prevent me from speaking out. As for the dogs, he never would have told me because he knew I would have put a stop to it."

Will put his hand on her shoulder. "But why now?"

"Why do you think? This is your second chance to be happy." She looked around the room. "I should have done it a long time ago. I know that now. But I was at peace without his malicious presence, and I wasn't ready to face him."

"Martha, I appreciate you protecting my second chance, but I also have to kill the ones I saw hurting the dogs. They weren't doing what they were doing for research; they were causing unnecessary pain and seemed to relish in it. And just because the owner is dead, that doesn't mean it won't continue."

She walked over to her dead husband's desk. "Notice how there isn't one photo of our son? You won't find one anywhere in this house. That's because he's an animal activist. I promise you, he will shut down the pharmaceutical company because when I'm done altering Jonathan's will, he will own everything. As for the researchers, when they die, their souls will dissolve into nothing."

Will released a sigh of relief at that and saw Martha in a completely different light. Never had he felt so much respect for a person, and it left him in awe and speechless. He owed her a debt that could never be repaid and he decided he wouldn't waste his second chance.

It was time to live his life.

Instead of shutting people out as he had always done to prevent further rejection, he was going to embrace the people in the room with him and Milly.

"I take back what I said about calling you the worst receptionist in existence," he said.

"And I still think you're a wally. Come on, let's go home."

Geth cupped his ear. "What was that?"

Will pointed at the one-eyed corpse, then at Geth. "She said you're next."

His eyes went wide before he walked through the door. After, Will felt a tremor of fear before Martha entered the council office. When he was certain she was safe to return, he searched for Milly. She wrapped her free arm around him with Angel between them, Teddy joined in, and Will understood the real meaning of wealth.

Kelly Barker was born in Oxford and now lives in Witney with her husband and dog, Lana. She has been a barber for over twenty years and loves her job. However, reading and writing are her passion—a passion handed down to her by her great-grandmother, Isobel O'Leary. Her short stories have been featured in magazines and anthologies, and she is the author of The Inner Temple, Even the Gods Fear It, Necromantia, and Breaking His House Rules.

www.kellybarker.org
https://www.facebook.com/kelly.m.barker.98
Twitter @MikeBar25891246

HAPPY HOLIDAYS
BY PETE RUSSO

It's been a challenging year in many ways for the company," said the man in the formal tuxedo. "But we've all overcome those challenges in heroic fashion, and our earnings are through the roof."

He gave an intentional glance toward his notes, undoubtedly attempting to mimic the look of solemnity or prayer while doing so, and held the pose for several obvious seconds. "And, first thing tomorrow, the Board will be voting on a well-deserved Christmas bonus for all departments and team members."

The man paused for applause, and while he received a smattering, he also allowed a look of annoyance to cross his face for just a moment. Most of the assembled crowd didn't notice it.

Kiah did.

He leaned against the ice machine in his bartender tuxedo — bow tie, shirt, and vest — this was the calm before the storm, and watched both the speech and the crowd reaction with interest.

"You buying this human motivational poster?" asked Jenny, his partner for the night. She was in the process of re-tying her bun for the third time since clocking in. Her hair was long and thick and had a bad habit of attempting to escape its bonds.

"Man, I don't even care," replied Kiah. "He's being sincere, he's taking it way too seriously. He's sending it up, he's a bad actor."

He quickly recounted the champagne flutes on the tray in front of him. There was an even dozen, just like there were five minutes ago. Thinking for a moment, he arranged them in a concentric circle to evenly disperse what weight they carried and placed a pair of ice buckets in the middle of the tray with a chilled bottle sticking out of each.

Before leaving the bar — noting the crowd that had started to leave their seats before the speech was complete — Kiah double-checked the bins of lemon and lime wedges again, looking out for his partner during the admittedly brief time she would be behind the bar herself. "Either way, time to make the donuts."

Out in the ballroom, the crowd finally offered some applause as the man in the formal tuxedo stepped away from the microphone. The familiar hum of conversation filled the room as a number of servers weaved between the tables with trays of hors d'oeuvres. Kiah arrived at the central table of executives at the same time as the man in the formal tuxedo.

"Excellent speech, Maxwell."

"Better than last year's."

"Thank you," replied Maxwell, taking his seat.

"Good evening, everyone," said Kiah, gently placing the ice buckets on the table, "Happy holidays, and I hope you're all doing well."

"Will there be an issue with the bonuses?" asked the man to his left. Kiah attempted to place the flutes in front of each guest without getting in the way of their conversation. He received no acknowledgement as he did so, expecting the same.

"Not for us," replied Maxwell. "We're getting our payout in the next seventy-two hours. If the 78 Group wants to add a bonus to the severance packages for the rest of the company, that's up to them." He moved his empty champagne flute directly in front of him in order to reach for the bread basket and a pat of softened butter.

"Pardon me, sir," said Kiah, making his rounds with one of the chilled bottles, reaching around Maxwell for his glass.

"Excuse me, son," replied Maxwell, placing his hand on the bottle to stop Kiah from filling the flute.

"Yes, sir?"

"You're incredibly rude," he continued. "Do not interrupt me while I'm talking to my colleagues."

"I apologize, sir," replied Kiah. "I was just trying to get to your glass to pou—"

"This is the problem with you people," interrupted Maxwell. "Always looking for your feelings to be validated. Fill my glass, then get the hell out of here."

Kiah allowed himself to fill with rage for approximately three-tenths of a second before his service-industry survival tactics kicked in. "Absolutely, sir. I apologize for my intrusion."

Maxwell continued to stare at him as he filled the champagne flute. "Now go away," he said dismissively. "You're just a tool, you don't look at us, you don't talk to us, you don't listen to anything we're saying except for our orders. Are we clear?"

"Yessir, crystal clear," replied Kiah. With no further acknowledgment from Maxwell or the rest of the table, Kiah turned and walked away.

"Asshole," he muttered under his breath. He picked up the pace as the crowd at the bar was getting thicker.

"Two beers, please."

"Chardonnay."

"Gin and tonic, with a lemon and a lime, please."

Kiah greeted each order with a smile and worked with and around Jenny as effortlessly as possible, with the grace of a man who has done this job for years.

"Brian," called Jenny, through the double doors at the far end of the bar, "we're getting low on ice."

"Already?" asked Kiah.

She responded with a look, giving a familiar 'thousand-yard stare' to her co-worker as she filled eight glasses with ice before blind pouring an identical measure of vodka into each.

"Thirsty bitches," replied Jenny.

Kiah laughed, but stopped himself. This type of formal event was often filled with easily offended professionals who loved to complain at the slightest issue, to say nothing of being called 'thirsty bitches.' Fortunately, either those closest to the bar hadn't noticed or were too intent on getting their drinks to care.

"...were wrong, Carter."

"What, based on that? What makes you think the old man is telling the truth?"

Jenny nudged Kiah with her hip as he stopped to listen. "Earth to Kiah, you okay, babe?"

"No way he'd..."

"Numbers were..."

"Yeah, I'm good," replied Kiah.

"Okay, then one side, I need to get—"

Kiah put his finger to his lips and tilted his head toward the line as he stepped away from the ice basin.

"...saw the contract myself..."

"...board is keeping it quiet."

"I'll tell you in a minute," he whispered.

Jenny and Kiah continued to serve their drinks as quickly and efficiently as possible. Cash dropped into the tip jar like a rain of confetti, and they both smiled and nodded their thanks each time. Gratuity was part of the contract, but additional cash was allowed to be accepted and very much appreciated.

"So, what's going on?" asked Jenny, as she poured a club soda for herself.

Kiah looked around, and, despite the fact that nobody was around them, he leaned in close to her ear. "I heard that guy with the speech talking, and I think a lot of these people are about to be out of a job."

"Ooooh, do tell," said Jenny, turning toward her customers. "Dewars, neat, and a long island iced tea for the forever young."

"Thanks, babe," replied the customer, dropping cash into the tip jar.

Jenny kept the smile on her face until the moment his back turned. "If I wanted to be called babe, I'd still be working dives," she told Kiah. "Where I could also cut people off and kick 'em out if they got annoying."

"And no bow tie," continued Kiah.

"And no hostile takeovers," laughed Jenny.

"Hostile what?"

They turned their heads to see a middle-aged man standing at the bar. Tie loosened, sweat on his forehead, he was looking at them with a mixture of terror and curiosity.

"Oh shit," said Kiah. "Hi, what can I get you?"

"What do you have in a red wine?"

"Merlot and Cabernet," replied Kiah.

"Cabernet, please. And fill it."

Reaching around Jenny for the red wine, Kiah backed up to avoid Brian, the barback, filling ice trays and collecting dirty glasses.

"Here you go," said Kiah with a smile. "Is there anything else I can get for you?"

"Not right now," he said. "Excuse me."

Double shit, thought Kiah.

"Well, nice working with you," teased Jenny.

"I didn't say anything outta turn," assured Kiah. "We heard something, we answered a client's question when asked, and we continued to do our job to the best of our ability. What can I get for you, Suze?"

Grateful for the distraction, Kiah pulled a half dozen bottles of ice-cold beer out of the cooler and popped their tops, placing them carefully on the server's tray.

"Thanks, babe," replied Susan, the server, walking away
with experienced balance.

Another round of patrons flooded the bar, which provided Kiah with a welcome distraction. He found comfort in the rhythm of filling drink orders and weaving in and around his co-workers. Gradually, the earlier confrontation faded from his memory as the evening settled into its flow. Plus, with dinner in full swing, most of the orders were beer and wine, with only an occasional mixed drink or cocktail thrown into the mix. Simple to fill with very little possibility of error.

"Excuse me, sir?"

Kiah had to do a double-take to realize he was being addressed. "Yes, sir, what can I do for you?"

"Can you provide me with the wi-fi password?" the man asked. Kiah noticed the phone in his hand and looked around, unsure of himself.

"Sure," he said. "Just... give me a minute? I don't normally work in this building and I need to locate that myself."

He turned around to the POS system and checked around the touch screen for anything that might indicate the password. Behind him, he heard the man who asked for the information joined by a second person.

"What're you doing?"

"Getting the wi-fi," replied the first. "I don't wanna take the chance someone traces my data and locks me out."

"Get you a drink?" asked Jenny.

"Jack," replied the first man. "Something simple. Double shot, make it two."

"Here it is," said Kiah. "Sorry about the wait. It's 'ballroomguest,' one word, all lowercase."

"Great," said the first man. "Thank you. And thank you, hun," he continued to Jenny. He slid one glass to the man next to him. "To the truth, Joe," he said.

"So you say, Barry," said Joe. "How did you even hear about this?"

Barry pointed at Kiah. "They overheard Pierce," he said.

All of a sudden, Kiah recognized him.

Triple shit.

"Okay," said the first man. "We're in. Damn it."

"What's up, Barry?" asked Joe.

"Way too much in his personal drive," replied Barry, continually swiping on his phone screen. He looked up to see Kiah and Jenny within earshot, unconvincingly cleaning the bar top and some condensation on the cooler.

"Thanks for the drinks, babe," said Barry, as he and Joe walked toward the tables, looking at the same screen and nearly walking into a server with a tray of empty dishes held high above their heads.

"I feel like this is going to come back to bite me," said Kiah, offhandedly.

"I dunno, man," replied Jenny. "I think you just need to hope it's true so they have bigger problems than a gossipy bartender."

"You love gossip," said Kiah.

"*You* love gossip," countered Jenny.

Their reverie was broken by another server's approach.

"How is it out there, Chris?" asked Kiah.

"Weirdly tense," replied Chris. "Round'a Natty Boho, no glasses, please."

Kiah bent over to grab the beers out of the refrigerator while the women continued the conversation.

"It's all Kiah's fault," said Jenny. "He's spreading rumors to panic the worker bees."

"Am not," retorted Kiah.

"Well, whatever it is," replied Chris, taking the first four bottles, "it's a doozy. I'm hearing metaphors like they're on the Titanic while Nero fiddles, and the interns in the cheap seats are doing the math on how they want to max out the bar bill in the process. Talk about mixed metaphors. Thanks, babes."

"Kids," muttered Kiah, after Chris left earshot.

"What, like you're so old?" asked Jenny. "How old are you, anyway?"

"How old are you?"

"Twenty-two," replied Jenny.

Kiah smiled. "Thirty-seven, and old enough to complain about the damn kids."

All of their attentions were suddenly grabbed by the sound of microphone feedback, causing them both to flinch.

"Excuse me, can I have everyone's attention?"

On the makeshift stage, Barry, the nervous man with the wifi password, stood at the microphone with his phone in one hand and a bottle of beer in the other.

"Hi, happy holidays, everyone. In case you don't know me, my name is Barry Asheur, and I work in the IT department. I'd like everyone to join me in asking Maxwell Pierce back to the microphone for a moment?"

Kiah strained to see, but Maxwell Pierce was the man in the formal tuxedo who gave the opening toast earlier. Mr.

Pierce waved him off from his seat at the far end of the ballroom, and Barry nodded.

"Strange," said Kiah. "What—"

He then saw that Barry had nodded to his friend Joe, who nodded back and stepped outside the ballroom, subtly closing all of the doors.

"Mr. Pierce certainly had an inspiring speech for us a bit ago," continued Barry. "But he did leave a few things out that you should be—" Cutting through the air was a series of loud and soft electronic beeps, warbles, and licensed music, with most of the assembled crowd reaching into their pockets or purses, "—seeing an update on in your email boxes as we speak. Please note the attachment on the message. Please note the contract it contains, signed by Pierce and all twelve members of the board of directors, approving a takeover of Pierce & Morgan by the 78 Group, effective December 26th of this year."

Pierce looked to Kiah to be unconcerned, though he did lean in and whisper to the people sitting around him, all of whom nonchalantly stood up and began to walk to the exits, oblivious to the rising chorus of questions from the rest of the people.

"Please note the golden parachute in place for the CEO and the board of directors," continued Barry. "And the immediate termination of all employees of Pierce & Morgan due to redundancies in roles between the two companies."

One of the people with Pierce pressed on the door, but it refused to budge.

"Going somewhere?" asked Barry.

They tried a second door, as the crowd started to rise to their feet, having continued to read the information just provided.

"Don't bother," continued Barry. "My associate has barred all of the exits, so we can have a chat about this. Yes? Question?"

Kiah didn't bother waiting for the board of directors to try each of the exit doors. He nonchalantly gestured to Jenny the double doors at the side of the bar, and they slowly began to move in their direction.

"Here you go Mags," continued Barry, handing the microphone to a middle-aged woman. "Just maybe let everyone know who you are?"

"Thanks, B," she replied. "I'm Maggie Jenkins, executive vice president of the marketing team, and I'd just like to know, Max, what does this mean for our vested funds and time served?"

"We'll talk about it later," said Pierce, who was starting to look nervous.

Kiah gestured to Jenny to head to the back, and he stayed in place, pushing the doors back level to cover her exit.

"Not later," said Maggie. "Max, I've been with the company for over thirty years, and I know how you operate. You don't hide something like this unless there's reason to hide it. Tell me, what's the status of our vesting?"

He stared at her for several seconds, then turned back to one of his allies. "Get that door open."

"I can tell you," said Barry, taking the microphone back from Maggie, "the pension fund has been liquidated to prop up the total value of the company. None of us get anything we've put into it."

Pandemonium erupted, and Kiah let the idea of subterfuge drop as he stepped to the side and pushed into the back room. At the far end, the door to the back alley was pressed open just a few inches, with Jenny on her knees, regarding the space.

"It's getting toasty out there," said Kiah. "What's wrong?"

She looked up at him with fear etched all over her face, her brown eyes wide as dinner plates. "Someone chained and padlocked the door," she said. "I can almost squeeze through."

"Yo? What's up?"

"Brian?"

The barback's face appeared in the door crack, and he looked at his co-workers. "Y'all okay in there?"

"Not sure," said Kiah. "There's some kinda argument going on back there; someone locked the doors. What happened?"

"You're looking at it," replied Brian. "I was taking out the trash and saw some dude messing with the door. Chased him for a block or so but he was pretty fast, and I just came back to this."

"Here," said Kiah, handing over a set of keys. "You remember my car?"

"Mazda, right?"

"Right. I'm parked on 61st and Montgomery, there's a crowbar in my trunk. Can you go get it and come back here, so we can bust this chain off and get out?"

Brian nodded and took the keys. "On it, guys. Just stay safe."

He dashed away, presumably as fast as he could go. The moment was suddenly broken up by a loud crash from the main ballroom.

"Stay here," cautioned Kiah. "I'm gonna go check it out."

Jenny nodded and crouched down by the door to stay as out of sight as possible.

Kiah slowly and quietly walked to the door and pressed it open. There was nobody waiting at the bar for a drink, though the wait staff had largely backed up toward it for the promise of cover if things escalated.

"I gave my life to this company," shouted Maggie, "and you just threw it all away?"

"My name," replied Pierce, just as loud, "my risk. My decision."

"Not much of a risk," said Barry. "Failing upward into a seven-figure payday while the rest of us lose our jobs with no notice."

"Shut the fuck up," snapped a man standing next to Pierce. "You're fired."

"We're all fired," reminded Maggie. "Cards are on the table, John — you lost your leverage."

"I didn't lose anything," reminded John, with a hard edge in his voice. "I was smart enough to get paid for it."

Drawing an audible gasp from the assembled crowd, John reached back and slapped her. Shock spread across Maggie's face as she reared back and fired a fist into his chest.

The breath was knocked out of John's chest as he staggered backward into several more members of the board, who barely managed to hold him up on his feet.

"Call the police," John said to a young woman sitting at another table, holding her phone up in the clear sign of a person recording the events in front of her.

"I'm sorry," she replied. "What?"

"I was just assaulted, Wendy," repeated John. "Call the police."

She looked around at her table, filled with people of an equivalent age. "Didn't you just let us all go?"

"Absolutely not," said John. "You're still my secretary until the end of the year, so call the police."

"Ummmm, no," replied Wendy. "I'm not gonna do that, Johnny. Oh! Reminds me."

She stood up and stared him in the face for a few seconds before raising her foot into his crotch. "I have a master's degree, you asshole. Making coffee, making copies, and pretending not to notice your hand on my ass isn't worth twenty an hour. Also, your wife knows you're banging the nanny, you stereotype. And she doesn't care if you know she's banging the gardener."

Wendy turned to return to her seat and the nearly full champagne flute at her place setting, not noticing John's face twisting into a mask of hatred.

"You bitch," he hissed, shoving her hard from behind.

She stumbled as her feet slammed into each other and she landed headfirst on the edge of the table, drawing concern from her neighbors who immediately rushed to her rescue.

John stepped toward her, clearly only seeing red, but Maggie acted — possibly too quickly for thought — and cracked an unused salad plate on his head. It shattered on contact, shocking her into silence as Pierce broke a beer bottle over her head, dropping her to the floor.

Instinctively, Barry picked up one of the chairs by the top of the back and swung it as hard as he could in the direction of Pierce and the rest of the board. It glanced off Pierce's shoulder, but the foot of the chair caught another member of the board in the eye, sending sprays of blood out at the closest people.

"Oh no," said Susan.

"What?" asked Kiah.

"We brought steak knives out for people who ordered meat..."

"I don't think we need to worry about–" Kiah could not finish his thought, as a scream rose from the middle of the room.

A handful of people remained in place, with more than a few managing to maintain their phone recordings while most of the crowd ran for the doors in a futile attempt to push them open. In the middle of the crowd, like the eye of a hurricane of blood, a woman Kiah had not seen speak or otherwise react so far that night was perched on Maxwell Pierce's back, slowly and deliberately driving one of Susan's steak knives into his back and shoulder.

There was nobody else around who was brave enough to try and pull her off; besides, she was locked in with a handful of his graying hair, and the heels of her shoes dug into his hips for leverage.

Another person, identified as a member of the board of directors, found himself on the floor with a dress shoe being repeatedly driven into his face, with another person trying his best to crack and cave in his rib cage.

Kiah could not look away, though he managed to help shield one of the server's faces in his shoulder, and most of the other waitstaff ducked behind the bar out of fear of being noticed.

"My God," he whispered, as he locked eyes with a young girl who was literally attempting to force her entire hand down another man's throat. He was beet red with wild eyes, obviously choking to death.

"Happy holidays!" shouted Barry, through the microphone rife with feedback. "Happy holidays and a great fucking new year!" The microphone cord was wrapped around another man's throat, and he was pulling as hard as he could. All of a sudden, with no real warning, the man's hands fell away from the cord and hung limp at his side.

Kiah took in the sights before him, and he felt the outside world melt away. All that he was aware of was the carnage before his eyes. He could no longer feel his co-worker's face on his shoulder. He could no longer see the rest of the wait staff ducked down below the bar to keep their own sanity. He could not hear the door open behind him as a trio of SWAT officers burst into the ballroom.

"Police! Everybody down!" shouted the lead officer, and Kiah saw nothing more except the floor of the bar area.

It seemed that an entire city block was cordoned off by the police as they locked down the rest of the building and systematically emptied the Pierce & Morgan banquet hall in order of extremity. Two bodies were removed with various pre- and post-mortem wounds, and twenty-six others were being treated for injuries ranging from bruises and black eyes to multiple stab wounds.

One woman was shot in the calf with a rubber bullet when she continued to drive her nails into another man's eyes.

He *might* still recover his sight.

"Hi, sorry to keep you waiting so long. Detective Brennan," said the plainclothes, not offering a handshake. "I think we've got a pretty good idea of what went down, but I'd like to get your contact information just in case we need to talk to you later."

Kiah sat on the hood of a police cruiser, wrapped in a blanket. Otherwise unharmed, there were enough cases of shock that prompted every witness to at least be kept warm in the frigid December air.

"Like I said, I'm just the bartender," said Kiah. "You know, I was mostly on the opposite end of the room and didn't see a lot of the chaos."

"I get that," agreed Brennan. "We've got multiple witness statements that confirm Maxwell Pierce instigated the entire riot but since you were here, we still need to—"

Kiah opened his mouth to interrupt, but his attention was taken by Maxwell himself, antiseptic bandages covering the stab wounds on his back, being placed in handcuffs.

"Hey, wait a second," said Maxwell. "Do you know who I am?"

"Maxwell Pierce," replied the officer, clicking the cuffs. "You are charged with inciting a riot, assault with intent, manslaughter, and murder in the second degree. You have the right to remain silent."

"Fuck that," argued Maxwell. "I'm being framed. They're all lying to you! I didn't kill Maggie; she attacked me! And John Morgan got into a stupid little fight with his secretary! She did it, I didn't!"

His eyes locked with Kiah, with desperate pleading clearly evident in them. "You — kid, you were in there! You saw it, right? Tell them what happened!"

Kiah looked at him, as the events of the night replayed in his mind.

"Sure, firing everyone was a shitty thing to do," continued Maxwell, "but I don't deserve this!"

The officer bringing Maxwell to the patrol car stopped. Detective Brennan looked at Kiah expectantly.

Kiah shook his head, sadly. "I'm sorry, sir, but at events like these, I'm just a tool. I don't look at the guests, I don't talk to the guests, and I don't listen to anything they're saying except for their orders. If everyone else is saying that's what happened, that's what happened."

Brennan and the officer locked eyes, while Maxwell's grew as large as dinner plates. "You little fucker!" he shouted, lunging toward Kiah, though he didn't get far with his hands cuffed and his body still dealing with the trauma of being stabbed. He was shoved into the car relatively effortlessly afterward, as the ambulances made their exit moments later and the scene started to break up.

"Hey!" called Jenny from the still taped-off entranceway.

"What's going on, girl?" asked Kiah, joining her under the awning.

"Nothin' much. I know I'm too wired to sleep, though. You feel like getting a cup'a coffee?"

Kiah smiled. "Sounds good. I know just the place."

They turned on their heels and walked down the darkened avenue, illuminated only by a sparse scattering of streetlights.

"Hey," said Jenny.

"S'up?"

"We'd better get full pay for tonight."

"Hah! You're not wrong, my friend. That might've been horrifying, but I'll tell you what..."

They walked in silence for a few seconds while Kiah gathered his thoughts.

"Those guys had the right idea."

Pete Russo has been writing short-form, long-form, and poetic pieces for upwards of three decades. His previously published novel, One Chance: The Legend of Valerian's Garden is available on Amazon, and he is actively working on a second full-length manuscript.

He lives in Savannah, GA, is available for all weddings, funerals, and birthday parties, and his statement to the police is wholly dependent on how well you tip.

JUST IN TIME FOR DINNER
ALANNA ROBERTSON-WEBB

The old clock above the soot-stained town square chimed midnight, its ancient gears protesting with each toll. The moon cast a feeble glow over the mostly deserted streets, nothing more than the occasional rustle of dried leaves daring to interrupt the heavy silence. It should have been a night like any other in the quaint town of Willow's End, where the residents had grown accustomed to the peculiarities of their quiet lives, but something was amiss.

Liam and Elara, a duo of orphaned siblings with no one left to look out for them but each other, were wide awake at an hour most people would have been peacefully slumbering. Their stomachs growled in protest of the meager dinner they'd shared, stale bread crusts soaked in stream water doing little to ease the ever-lurking hunger gnawing at their insides. Their mother had promised them a better life, but she'd been missing for months now, leaving them alone and penniless in a town where the rich beat and bullied peasant children for sport.

A sudden, shrill cry pierced the silence of the night, jolting them upright. It was a sound they'd never heard before, a desperate plea that seeped into every crack of their hovel. The siblings exchanged a nervous glance, racing hearts thumping in unison, and Elara was the first one to move. She shook her dirty curls, her silent gesture defying that all-too-familiar look in her brother's eyes. It was his heroic gleam, the shine in his gaze, that said he was going to try and help this person the same way he always tried to save hurt animals or defend his sister from the blows of the noblemen's iron-tipped canes.

Liam was already slipping out of his bed, however, the eleven-year-old yanking on his hole-filled boots with one hand as he hopped over to grab his jacket with the other. Elara wasn't nearly as brave as her brother, the eight-year-old scowling as she adamantly tried to remain in her bed. By the time Liam had reached the stairs, she was pulling on her shoes with a resigned sigh. Something just felt off, a nagging feeling deep inside her whispering that they should stay safe and mind their own business, but there would be no talking her brother out of something once his mind was made up.

As they snuck downstairs, the cry grew louder, the sound echoing eerily toward them from the alley behind the house. Liam snatched their rusty lantern from the hook beside the door. After a sharp clack of flint, it flickered to life, casting a warm, trembling glow that gave away the shaking of his hands. Elara clutched her brother's arm, her eyes wide with a mix of anxiety and curiosity, but against her better judgment, they stepped into the night.

The snow-blanketed cobblestones lay cold and damp beneath their feet, the chilled wind ripping through their threadbare jackets as if the cloth wasn't even there. The cry grew clearer now that they were outside. As Liam cocked his head, he could tell that it was coming from a child.

The narrow space between their home and the abandoned building next door twisted and turned, the shadows deepening with each step the children took. They moved cautiously, clouded breaths coming in short, sharp inhales that they tried to keep quiet. As they progressed, the wailing grew more urgent, a siren's call that tugged at their hearts. When they rounded yet another corner, the source came into view.

Liam quickly snuffed out the lantern, not wanting to give their presence away, and the siblings took a moment to let their eyes adjust to the darkness. After a moment, they peeked their heads up over a stack of old crates, the duo straining to see.

A dead-end greeted them, and curled up in a shuddering ball on the ground was a small, dirty boy who couldn't have been much older than Elara. Above him towered the town's wealthiest man, the heel of his well-oiled boot slamming down on the boy's back with a sickening crunch. Mr. Crowthorne leaned down, grabbing the boy's tattered shirt and yanking one thin arm upward as the child screamed shrilly over the sound of his joint popping.

"Stop, sir! Please! I don't know wha' I did ta ya, but I'm so sorry! I'll never do it again!" His pleading should have been enough to make anyone halt, the tears streaming down his face heart-wrenching, but not this man.

Mr. Crowthorne's eyes were wild with malicious intent, his pupils slitted like a snake's as he stared down at the handful of dirty, torn clothing he clutched. As the shadows flickered jaggedly on his face, Liam and Elara watched his expression twist into a grotesque smile, Mr. Crowthorne

119

practically beaming as he inhaled the air around the boy. He leaned down even closer, licking chapped lips hungrily as he breathed in the noxious aroma of sweat and filth.

"Ah, it looks like my guest is just in time for dinner! How delightful, though I do so have to insist that you get cleaned up before gracing my table."

Anger, horror, and confusion warred within the children; Liam and Elara watched from the shadows, wide eyes glued to the scene unfolding before them. Though both wanted to help the boy, neither could bring themselves to move. Liam gripped Elara's hand in a poor attempt at brotherly reassurance, but he couldn't hide the trembling of his own fingers from her.

They had heard whispers of the rich feeding on the poor, the rumors circulating for some time now, but to see it with their own eyes was a nightmare made flesh. They couldn't pretend that the horrendous tales were false any longer, and Elara bit back a sob as the boy's cries grew weaker, his body going limp under Mr. Crowthorne's grip as he passed out from the pain.

The girl's hands flew to her mouth to stifle a scream, her eyes brimming with tears. Liam's grip on her tightened, his knuckles white with rage as he gritted his teeth. They had to do something, but what could two children do against a monster like Mr. Crowthorne?

With a heavy heart, Liam made a decision: he couldn't save the boy, not without putting himself and his sister at risk. No one would believe the word of two orphans against a man such as him, anyway, but they could still spread the word. If even one person thought their story could be true, then they may be able to save at least one life, and that would be enough. They retreated, their thoughts racing with the gravity of what they had witnessed, and that was when Elara slipped.

The sharp crackle of snow made Mr. Crowthorne's head whip toward them, teeth bared in a snarl like a cornered dog. The children scrambled, Liam never loosening his grip on his sister's hand, and he half-dragged her along as he sprinted toward home. There was no way the man could have seen them, and they knew the alleyways better than he did, so with full confidence the siblings darted for safety. Once inside, they slammed the door behind them, placing the heavy, wooden bar down just in case. Liam re-lit the lantern so that the darkness wouldn't be as suffocating. Silence reigned between them, broken only when Elara finally began to cry.

She tried to speak between choking breaths, her whole body shaking. "W-we can't l-let this h-h-h-happen to anyon-ne else, Liam-m. We h-have to t-tell som-meone, a-anyon-ne!"

Liam nodded solemnly, wrapping his arms around her as he gently stroked her curls. "I know, but who can we speak ta? No one's gonna believe two kids, especially ones who don't have no parents or nothin'. They'll just think we're lying coz we're desperate for attention."

He knew that speaking out against the rich was a dangerous game, especially in a town where noble word was law, but how could they just stand idly by and let this continue? There was no solution and no way to erase the horror they had borne witness to. Nothing good was going to come from that boy being taken, and by now Mr. Crowthorne would be halfway home with his prey. All he could do now was comfort his sister, even if that meant lying.

"It's okay, Lara. Maybe we misunderstood, eh? Maybe the kid did somethin' stupid and was just bein' punished like any other time. He'll limp home an' be just fine, I reckon."

For a moment, hope bloomed in Elara, her tiny face tilting up toward her big brother. She wiped her tears with a dirty knuckle, her palms scraped from her fall. "You m-mean it? He's 'kay?"

Before Liam could further whisper lies of false reassurance, their conversation was cut short, the wooden snapping of a window shutter breaking slicing through their home. The siblings froze in terror, Liam still hugging Elara. A few heartbeats later, Mr. Crowthorne stepped into the room, his shadow looming large in the flickering candlelight.

His earlier smile was gone, replaced by a cold, calculating stare. "Ah, so these are the little mice who have been spying on the big, bad, old pussycat."

His voice was a sibilant hiss, the tone a low, malicious purr that sent shivers skittering down their spines in tandem. The children remained frozen, four eyes locked on the figure that had brought their nightmares to life. Elara's hand was back over her mouth, caging her scream, and Liam's arms tightened around his sister as his pulse raced, his chest constricting almost painfully as he gasped.

"You have seen what I was up to, and I am sure that at least you, boy, have figured out what I do, which means that I cannot let you two go no matter how much you are about to beg and plead for your lives."

Liam managed to find his voice, each syllable shaky as he squeaked, and he had never felt so small in his life. "We, we, w-won't t-tell anyone! I-I, swear it-t!"

122

Mr. Crowthorne shook his head, the mock sincerity in his words coating over the madness shining in his eyes. "I am afraid that will not be enough. You see, silence can usually be bribed in these cases, but I have found that money is too often forgotten and farrrrr too easily spent for me to take that route again. Especially with young children who are not fully capable of understanding just what it is they are agreeing not to talk about."

He took a step closer, the smell of his expensive cologne mingling with the stench of the alleyway filth his boots were caked in, and Liam had to stop himself from gagging. "But fear not, you precious things!"

His tone had switched to one of maniacal joviality as if Elara and Liam were his long-lost children that he was ecstatic to welcome home. "I still have a proposition for you: stick with me, and you shall never go hungry again!"

Liam's eyes widened in horror, his face twisting into a grimace of disgust at the man's implication. "Never!"

He spat the single word, the vehement in it making their stance crystalline clear. Mr. Crowthorne's lips curled in an unhinged smile, eyes growing colder as his cracked mouth stretched wider.

"Suit yourselves, then." The man shrugged his shoulders nonchalantly, his polite demeanor as unshakeable as one could ever expect from a nobleman of high standing. "Too bad your mother never had time to teach you that the price of defiance is steep in Willow's End."

In a blur of motion belying his stocky build, he lunged at them, his movements surprisingly agile for a man of his age. Liam shoved Elara out of the way, reaching for his only weapon, and he swung the lantern with all his might. The glass shattered against Mr. Crowthorne's head, and for a moment the room was bathed in a shower of sparks and the acrid smell of burning hair.

Elara took the opportunity to scramble to her feet, her heart hammering in her chest, but her legs felt like lead. She wasn't as fast as her brother, and that was their downfall.

Through the fog of pain, Mr. Crowthorne's hand shot out, grabbing her by the arm and squeezing. She screamed for her brother, but Liam was already jumping on him. His small fists pummeled the man's back, and with a roar of frustration. Mr. Crowthorne swung around, tossing Liam off of him as if the boy weighed no more than a rag doll. Liam's head hit the stone fireplace with a sickening thud, his blood-spattered body rolling to a stop with eyes that stared vacantly up at the ceiling.

Elara's world narrowed to a pinpoint as she stared at her brother's corpse, her fear burned away in a flash of white-hot rage. With a strength born of desperation, she wrenched herself free from Mr. Crowthorne's grip, the girl diving for the knife Liam used for slicing up any squirrels or rabbits he managed to catch. Her hand closed around the hilt, the weight unfamiliar in her hand, and she spun to face the monster who had invaded their home.

Mr. Crowthorne's eyes widened in surprise, the blood from his head wound trickling down his face, and for the first time, it was his eyes that shone with a glint of concern. "Now, now, see here, child..."

His voice was meant to be soothing, the man known throughout the town for his silver tongue, but Elara was beyond listening. She lunged at him, the knife glinting, and it was his bravado that kept him from cowering back. There wasn't a single second in which he imagined a weak little girl like her could harm him, so he failed to dodge the blade that sank deep into his chest. Mr. Crowthorne staggered back, a look of shock lacing across his cherubic cheeks as his eyes rolled down to gaze blearily at the metal protruding from his starched shirt.

After a few seconds, he lifted his head, his final expression a snarl of pure hatred, and he reached for Elara. His fingers were barely an inch from closing in around her throat, but his muscles were already weakening. With a wet, gurgling breath, he collapsed to the floor, the knife still lodged in his heart.

Elara stood over him, trembling, the stained knife slipping from her grasp to clatter on the floor. Her home was eerily quiet now, the only sound the distant echo of the town center's clock once more chiming, but even that was rapidly fading into the winter's night. She turned to Liam's body, her eyes searching for any sign of life, but she knew it was too late.

The weight of what she had done settled heavily upon the young girl's shoulders, the stress and horror of the night causing her mind to fracture. She had killed a man, but in that moment, she felt no remorse; only the cold embrace of anger remained, a small comfort considering her brother had paid the ultimate price.

Her gaze fell upon Mr. Crowthorne's lifeless body, a new, macabre thought beginning to form in the broken fragments of her thoughts. If the rich feasted on the poor, then perhaps it was time to turn the tables. A twisted smile grew on her lips as she once more picked up the knife, her cheeks flushed with a mixture of anticipation and revulsion. Elara approached him, her expression a grim parody of the smile he had worn so often in life, and with trembling hands, she began to cut into his flesh.

The girl's eyes never left his cold, unblinking face, and with each slice of metal into sinew, she told herself it was for survival, or maybe for vengeance. Deep down, she knew it was more than that.

It was a declaration of war against the monsters that had claimed her brother's life. She didn't know what she was doing, Elara, having no butchering experience, but his belly seemed like a good place to take meat from. As she cooked Mr. Crowthorne, the scent of his flesh eerily reminiscent of the mouth-watering smell of bacon. She felt a strange sense of power surge through her, the warmth spreading from her core to her fingertips. It was a power she never knew existed, a power born of anger and desperation, and she was determined to take down all the other monsters just like him out there.

With each bite of her new favorite meal, she grew stronger, more determined, and she forced herself to continue gorging herself even when bile threatened to bubble up from her esophagus. The act was vile, a perversion of nature, but Elara didn't care. She was no longer the scared little girl from Willow's End; she was a survivor, and she would do whatever it took to ensure that no more children suffered the same fate as Liam.

The following days were a blur of grief and preparation. She buried her brother in the woods he loved so much, the grief-maddened girl whispering promises of justice to the silent earth. Then she set about cleaning the house, scrubbing away the bloodstains with a ferocity that bordered on insanity.

The townsfolk spoke in hushed whispers of Mr. Crowthorne's disappearance, but no one thought to connect it to the orphaned siblings. They had always been a peculiar pair, and with their mother gone, they had been all but forgotten, the duo left to the mercy of the streets like mangy dogs.

Besides, what could two scrawny, sickly children possibly have done to an adult man? Elara had always been the quieter of the two, often lost in her own world of imagination and dreams, but now a new fire burned in her eyes. She had tasted power and wasn't ready to let it go. Her thoughts grew darker with each passing day, twisted by the grief and anger that consumed her, and the taste of Mr. Crowthorne's flesh was never far from her unhinged thoughts. She would prowl the shadows, searching for the next person to feed her all-consuming rage, and it didn't take long before she found a target.

A rich merchant named Mr. Thornwood was stumbling home from a tavern, his pockets jingling with gold, and as he lurched through the moonlit streets, Elara stepped from the alleyway. Her unsettling gaze honed in on him like a predator's, just as Mr. Crowthorne's eyes had landed on her once upon a time. But drunken men rarely see the danger they're in.

She stalked silently toward him, her movements quick and well-practiced. Mr. Thornwood's eyes only widened in terror once she began to cackle, her teeth bared like an animal's as the girl's eerie mirth filled the space between them.

"Just in time for dinner!"

Alanna Robertson-Webb is a rising star among short story writers, and one of the anthologies she is featured in (Monsters, by Black Hare Press) has been nominated for a 2019 Bram Stoker Award. Additionally, the novella she co-wrote (Storming Area 51: Horror at the Gates) reached the #1 spot in Amazon's sci-fi books in October of 2019.

For Alanna the spooky side of writing is a riveting journey through the human psyche, so whether you are looking for some of her wholesome horror (Monstronomicon by Haunted House Publishing) or wish to be transported into one of her grimmer worlds (Death and Butterflies by Suicide House Publishing), then grab a book and embark on a thrilling read!

BLOOD MONEY
BY IAN GIELEN

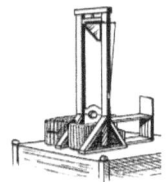

At the press of a button on his phone, the garage door slid open, revealing a spacious carport that showcased the epitome of luxury, complete with all the lavish embellishments money could buy. Pulling in his Porsche and parking smoothly next to his Ferrari, Jack turned the ignition off and sat there for a few minutes, breathing slowly with his eyes closed.

Today had been a good day. A good day, but a tough day. Managing a construction company was demanding, especially amidst intense competition. It helped that he didn't have any hesitation to do what needed to be done to win contracts. Whether it was bribery, supplying drugs, or women, he wasn't afraid to get his hands dirty if it meant putting more money in his pockets, but sometimes it took a toll on him.

He was human, after all, and unfortunately, he did have to deal with his conscience at times. Whenever he could find the time, he would meditate, following the techniques his relaxation coach had taught him, which usually helped him eliminate that small problem. Knowing that she was no doubt waiting for him upstairs to relieve him physically helped just that little bit more.

Smirking, he exited the car and delicately closed the door. He prided himself on looking after his assets; they had taken a lot of hard work to earn, after all. As he made his way to the door, his keys in hand and a tune on his lips, the almost imperceptible jingle of coins brought him to a sudden halt. He stood there and listened intently, his ears alert for any faint sounds. He was certain no one else was here besides Katherine, his relaxation coach. He knew that because he had driven by her car parked outside.

The sound of coins jingling returned. It sounded as if it was originating from within the garage. That was not possible. His high-tech security system would have detected even the faintest hint of unexpected movement by anyone and alerted him instantly.

The jingle of coins rang out again, defying all logic, and this time, it sounded even closer. He fished out his phone from his pocket and used the app to turn on the lights in the garage, scanning it carefully. The pristine and organized garage showed no signs of disturbance, with everything secure and in its proper place. Again, the sound of jingling coins filled the air, this time coming from directly behind him. He spun around in surprise, his eyes widening as he watched a silver coin roll across the floor toward him, coming to rest at his feet.

"What the hell?" Jack picked up the coin, turning it over in his hands to examine its peculiar design.

Although the coin was old and showed signs of wear, with parts of the metal eroded and the edges covered in nicks and scrapes, the detailed etching on the coin remained remarkably intact. Encircling it were intricate symbols, yet it was the figure at the center that sent shivers down his spine, filling him with fear.

The depiction displayed the upper half of a nightmarish being, its skeletal structure surrounded by a series of bones, ending in sharp tips stretching from its torso to its neck. Serrated-edged arms extended from its shoulders, long and thin. The bone-white head had gaping voids where its eyes, mouth, and sections of its skull should have been, creating pockets of darkness amidst its pale surface. A ring of razor-sharp teeth lined the perfectly round mouth of the creature.

The creature's eyes slanted downward as if it suffered greatly just by existing. Jack felt himself fixating on them as if they were pulling him in, making it impossible for him to look away. All of a sudden, the garage was filled with the piercing sound of an otherworldly harsh whisper.

"Graaaaaaaaaaaeeediiiiiiiiig."

As Jack looked on in terror, the figure within the coin started to shift and contort, separating itself from the coin's surface. The coin slipped from Jack's numb grip and hit the floor, a wave of disbelief washing over him as the creature on the coin came to life right before his eyes.

Standing at over eight feet tall, the nightmarish creature stood on spindly, thin, and razor-edged legs, its head hanging below its shoulders on a hunched skeletal body. It emitted a haunting moan as if enduring unspeakable torture, while a mesmerizing swirl of green and black light materialized within its empty eye sockets, fixated on Jack.

"Graaaaaaaaaaaeeediiiiiig," it whispered once more, the sound chilling Jack to the bone as it lunged toward him. Its arms, sharp as spears, mercilessly pierced through his chest with a sickening thud and emerged from his back in a gruesome spray of gore.

Helpless and impaled on the creature's arms, Jack squirmed in agony as it dragged him toward its skeletal frame. The creature's ribcage unfurled as if to welcome him into a grotesque, final embrace. Deposited within by its gore-drenched arms, Jack's chest rose and fell one last time in a blood-filled, ragged breath, before stilling forever as the ribs closed around him to a bone-chilling crunch as his body was squeezed to a pulp.

Satisfied, the creature vanished back into the coin, its metallic surface glinting under the garage light as it rested in a pool of slowly congealing blood.

***

Ryan held the door open for Rose, his last customer for the day, as she shuffled out the door with her half-full laundry basket, giving her a wave as he closed the door behind her. Wearing a smile, he headed to his office to pack up and close for the night. Ryan loved his job. He wasn't wealthy, far from it, but he enjoyed helping people, and his business helped far more people than he had dreamed possible.

He had always struggled for money, tirelessly working day in and day out, saving every dollar he could for years, all in pursuit of his dream to open his own laundromat business. That dream was achieved almost one year ago to this day when he opened "That Laundry Place" to exactly two customers who were waiting impatiently outside with their piles of laundry.

It was hardly the opening he had envisioned, but the laundry business wasn't exactly one that attracted the most excitement. Still, that had been his goal, and he achieved it. In the meantime, as he waited for his customer base to expand, he began volunteering the use of his machines to the local shelters in town. Thanks to his generosity, those less fortunate had access to clean clothing and bedding, giving him a reputation for being kind and caring.

His actions had a dual effect: not only did they bring in customers, but they also garnered attention from local newspapers and increased the number of aid requests from neighboring shelters, which he happily fulfilled whenever he could spare his machines. It wasn't long before the local politicians took notice, eager to capitalize on his popularity. He had shaken them off, recognizing their attention for what it was, a cheap grab for more followers and votes.

All but one, that is.

Brandon Samson had first appeared much like all the others who had tried to use him — dressed impeccably, with an aura of wealth and upper-class, and a confident strut. However, right from the start, he exuded a genuine warmth that was hard to ignore. With his affluent upbringing and an extensive network of influential entrepreneurs, Brandon had risen through the ranks of his political party, becoming one of their most esteemed politicians. His remarkable knack for executing tasks with speed and efficiency played a significant role in his success.

None of that came across, however, when Brandon had introduced himself. He had simply entered the shop, taken a look around, then chatted to Ryan about things unrelated to politics and promised to visit there every week. He had fulfilled that promise, and his warm smile and approachable demeanor drew Ryan into a friendship with him. Now he was one of his best friends, and it wasn't uncommon for the pair to head out on a night in the town, often leaving one or both of them with a serious hangover the next day.

And so, when the bell rang upon the front door opening, Ryan wasn't surprised to turn around and see Brandon strolling through, looking as sharp as ever in his fitted suit.

"Ryan, my man. I've had a hell of a day, so what say you and I find ourselves a watering hole and you can help me drown me in my sorrows?"

Ryan chuckled, shaking his head with amusement. "Well, hello to you, too."

"C'mon man, I'm dying here. Literally dying, like I need a drink and I need it now." Brandon mimed staggering and pointing at his mouth in mock desperation.

Ryan grinned. "Alright, alright, just let me pack up, and I'll meet you there. Same spot as usual?"

Brandon's face lit up, his eyes sparkling with a boyish excitement. "Yep, see you there in twenty?"

"I'll be there."

With a wave, Brandon exited the laundromat, his brand-new BMW i8 gleaming in the fading sunlight, parked illegally outside in the disabled parking spot.

With a tired sigh and a disapproving shake of his head, Ryan performed his final checks of the machines, making sure each one was primed and ready for the next day. Gathering his belongings, he flicked off the lights and locked up.

Brandon's favourite bar, "The Pint Place," was just a few blocks away, so there was plenty of time to get there. Ryan pulled into the half-full parking lot with five minutes to spare. With a glance at his watch, he breathed a sigh of relief. There was still enough time for him to buy a lottery ticket. Without wasting a second, he opened the app and made the purchase. Ever since he was in his early twenties, he had religiously bought a lottery ticket each week, and he wasn't about to stop that tradition now.

Stepping out of his van, Ryan slipped on his weathered leather jacket and trailed behind a rowdy bunch of twenty-somethings, their laughter filling the air as they entered the bar. Spotting Brandon waving to him from his favourite booth, he maneuvered through a cluster of drunk college girls, who cast curious glances his way, before settling into the seat across from Brandon.

"You know those girls were checking you out, right?" Brandon pointed out the girls at the bar who were feigning sobriety as they ordered another round from the bartender.

"Dude, I'm not about to take advantage of drunk college girls. I'm thirty-five, you know."

"So? That doesn't stop me, and I'm thirty-seven." With a smirk on his face, Brandon studied the girls intently, hoping to catch their eye.

Ryan shook his head, torn between disgust and amusement. "Are you just going to stare at them, or are we actually going to get to drinking?"

Brandon shifted his attention back to Ryan with a playful grin, and they ordered their drinks from the online menu. As they waited for the drinks, Brandon's demeanor became more serious, and he fidgeted uncomfortably while clearing his throat, showing obvious signs of nervousness.

"Is everything OK?" Ryan asked, taken aback by Brandon's unfamiliar behaviour.

Brandon glanced at him before averting his gaze and released a heavy sigh. "I had to make a really hard decision today. A choice between potentially losing a friend or turning down a deal that could skyrocket my career to new heights."

"Let me guess," Ryan said, reading Brandon's body language, "you went with the deal."

"That obvious, huh?" Brandon said with sadness, shaking his head slowly. "I really need to get better at my tells if I want to get anywhere as a politician," he said with a thin smile as he glanced at Ryan and then shifted his attention to his drink, lost in thought.

"Did I do the right thing?" He looked at Ryan hopefully, but he already knew the answer.

"Mate, if it was up to me, I would have chosen the friend every time, but I'm not you, and I don't have your job. Different strokes for different folks and all that."

"Just as I thought," Brandon said, his face reflecting defeat as he nodded slowly.

After taking a sip of his beer, Ryan placed it back on the table while stealing a quick look at the TV above the bar counter. It was showing the beginning of the lottery draw. Ryan found himself eying it as Brandon excused himself to go to the bathroom.

The draw had just finished when Brandon returned to his seat opposite him, his demeanor restored to his normal affable self once more. "So, you up for another round?"

Grinning mischievously, he waved to the waiter clearing the table nearby.

Ryan was gesturing toward his half-filled glass and was about to mention that he intended to leave after finishing his drink when he was distracted by the phone buzzing in his pocket.

The waiter had already arrived when he pulled the phone out of his pocket. It was a notification from the lottery app. Fueled by curiosity, he opened it, his eyes widening in disbelief as he took in the message. He had won the lottery. He was now $100 million richer. His heart pounding, he checked the message again, his disbelief growing stronger. Intoxicated by a blend of alcohol and excitement, his vision blurred, and his stomach churned with nausea.

"Are you OK?" Brandon's face revealed his worry as he extended his hand to touch Ryan's clammy arm.

"I... I think I just won the lottery," Ryan stammered, his voice filled with a mixture of shock and excitement, his face drained of color. "I'm going to throw up."

Rising to his feet, his legs unsteady, he clung to the table for balance and clumsily made his way toward the bathroom, leaving behind a stunned Brandon who watched him with wide eyes, a smile slowly spreading across his face as he processed the news. Still smiling, he considered approaching the drunk and rowdy girls at the bar counter, but the breaking news headline on the TV diverted his attention. He stiffened, his face turning ashen as he watched the news story unfold.

Returning from the bathroom, still pale and shaking but at least steady, Ryan sat back down opposite him. One glance at Brandon and Ryan couldn't help but break into a wide grin. "Mate, you look even more shocked than me, and I'm the one who won the damn lottery."

"I... I need to go," Brandon mumbled, his gaze still locked on the TV screen.

"Wait, are you OK?"

With an absent nod, Brandon rose and made his way toward the exit, his face betraying a jumble of unidentified emotions.

Trying to make sense of Brandon's behavior, Ryan glanced up at the TV with a puzzled expression on his face. The TV was playing a news report on the death of a famous business mogul in Baltimore. The victim had established a prominent IT firm, renowned for its specialization in security systems, and had amassed a significant fortune.

Though no body had been found, the amount of blood at the scene left no doubt he was dead. The only thing left behind at the scene was an ancient, unidentified coin. The report went on to detail that this was the fifth disappearance, or likely death, in a series that appeared to be targeting wealthy people. Each crime scene characterised by the same-looking coin left behind. There were rumours circulating that they were some sort of hit. The missing individuals were all rumored to have connections with shady characters and have questionable business dealings, although no concrete evidence had been found.

Still confused, Ryan leaned back in his seat. Why would this news have such an impact on Brandon? Did he somehow know this latest victim? He knew Brandon had rubbed shoulders with some people of means as part of his job, so it was possible, and he did go on regular trips to Baltimore.

He decided he would drop in at his house tomorrow to check in on him.

A sigh escaped from Ryan's lips. He was equal parts excited by his lottery win and concerned for his friend. A sudden wave of exhaustion hit him, causing his eyes to grow heavy. It had been a long week, and the latest happenings had worn away the last vestiges of his energy. He needed some rest to figure out his next moves.

Gathering his coat, he paid the tab for both himself and Brandon, ignoring the giggling girls who tried to reach out to lay a hand on his shoulder to get his attention, and drove home.

***

Still in shock from the news report, Brandon stumbled toward his car, his mind racing to process the information. In the smallish town of Emmitsburg, there weren't many who could say they were well-off, and the owners of large businesses generally congregated in the larger cities for convenience, so when it came to political gatherings and business dealings, he often had to travel to the larger cities.

Baltimore was one of them, and there he had met and befriended many of those deemed to be high society, a necessity if he wanted to advance his career. One such man he'd met was the victim on the news report. The others loosely mentioned, he'd also known but not as well, often seeing them in the same circles. If someone was targeting them, did that mean he was in danger? His latest deal was certainly shady and not exactly legal, and he'd often done things he wasn't proud of to attain the position he was in now, much like the other victims.

His stomach sank when he thought about what would happen when Ryan found out what he'd done. Ryan had always been a good friend to him, but when a large, prominent chain restaurant approached him to place one of their stores in the middle of the shopping strip where Ryan's business was located, he couldn't turn it down. Especially when they offered him $250,000 and an exclusive cruise with unlimited drugs, alcohol, and women.

He would get the ball rolling on the deal tomorrow. He just wanted it done so he could deal with the fallout and then enjoy what he was owed. Feeling a bit better after thinking about the rewards to come, he headed home. First, he would deliver the notices to the shops at first light, then he would see about hiring additional security.

***

Ryan, still on a high from the excitement of his lottery win the night before, unlocked the door to the laundromat and flipped the sign to open. A letter lay on the floor, an official stamp from the Emmitsburg council displayed on the front. Thinking it was propaganda or, worse yet, a bill, he flung it onto the desk in the office and continued with his day, exchanging cheerful greetings with his regular customers as they arrived.

Restless and distracted, he couldn't stop his thoughts from juggling between his lottery win and concern for Brandon, so he decided he'd close up shop a bit earlier and head over to check up on him.

After informing his customers, he patiently waited until the last one gathered their bundles of clean linen and locked the doors to his shop. Grabbing the letter and his car keys on the way out, he headed to his car and was about to turn the key when he glanced at the letter he had tossed beside him on the passenger seat.

With a sigh, he picked it up. He may as well get any unpleasantness out of the way first before he left to check on his friend. Fully expecting it to be a bill or an advertisement, his eyes widened in shock as he read the unexpected letter. It was a notice to vacate the premises due to an impending development for a restaurant chain that was to take place late next month.

He felt his heart sink at the signature at the bottom of the letter. It was Brandon's. He was the friend that Brandon was talking about losing. Shock made way for anger at his friend's betrayal. He had clearly wanted his blessing last night so that he could feel better about himself. Brandon had always been one to put himself first, but Ryan never thought he would stoop this low to get what he wanted. No wonder he had been relieved when Ryan had said he'd won the lottery. He had probably thought Ryan could open another shop somewhere else, so the impact of the news would be minimized.

Filled with anger, he flung the letter onto the passenger seat and gripped the steering wheel, his knuckles whitening. He would follow through with his plan on seeing Brandon, but this time, for a different reason.

***

Brandon was exhausted. Not only was he sleep-deprived, but he'd had to get up early to slip the notices to vacate under the shop doors. His guilt had gotten the better of him. It had never bothered him before, but he had obviously cared more about Ryan than he had thought he did. Still, he'd done what needed to be done. Now it was time to organise the extra security.

He called one of his contacts, who owned a security company that serviced Baltimore and surrounding areas, and left a message to call him back when there was no answer. He leaned back on his leather couch and sighed. Maybe he could squeeze in a nap before he met up with the restaurant chain owner to tell him the news and organise the cruise. As he was rising from the sofa, a faint sound of jingling coins reached his ears. The sound seemed to originate from inside his house. Frowning, he strained his ears. His mind must be playing tricks on him because of his lack of sleep.

Irritated, he shook his head and walked toward the stairs, but the jingling sound repeated, now closer. It sounded like it was coming from the kitchen. His heart began to race. The security system would have picked up any break-in, so it shouldn't be possible that someone was inside the house. He cast his mind back to the news he had heard last night at the bar and a chill ran down his spine at the thought that the same thing could be happening to him right now.

Reaching for the phone in his pocket, he thumbed the button to alert security and cursed himself for not organising on-site security earlier. The security he did have should be at the house within thirty minutes. Not soon enough if there was an intruder already inside.

Moving with caution, he selected an umbrella from the rack by the staircase and proceeded toward the kitchen. Besides the quiet hum of the refrigerator, the house was otherwise silent. Taking a deep breath, he reached the doorway and peered around the corner, his senses on high alert, but there was no sign of anyone in the kitchen, only the familiar sight of a dirty pile of dishes in the sink.

A wave of relief washed over him as he rested against the doorway. The events of the last few days had taken a toll on him. He was in desperate need of the cruise and some fun. As he turned back toward the staircase, the jingling of coins echoed through the air once more, this time from right in front of him. At the same time, a coin rolled around the corner from the front entrance hallway and came to rest at his feet. Tightening his grip on the umbrella, he leapt out from the kitchen doorway to the hallway where the coin had rolled from.

It was empty. There was no one there.

He released his grip on the umbrella, inhaling deeply, his heart pounding in his chest. What was wrong with him? Was he hallucinating? Peering back around the corner toward the kitchen, he spied the coin still sitting there, its dull silver surface standing out on the glistening white floor tiles.

Approaching it with caution, he studied it from a distance. It was the same type of coin that the news report had mentioned being left at the crime scenes. His gaze locked onto the peculiar coin, a mixture of curiosity and dread washing over him. He tried to back away from it but found himself frozen in place, unable to tear his eyes away from the mysterious creature etched onto its surface. The coin's allure was irresistible, its soft whispers captivating his thoughts and urging him to reach out and grasp it. Despite his best attempts to resist, he found himself being pulled toward it and bending down to retrieve it.

Panic consumed him, causing beads of sweat to trickle down his forehead and onto the flawless tiled floor, as he struggled to free himself from the coin's grip to no avail. His control lost, his body bent over to pick up the coin and lift it to eye level. The sound of gravel crunching under tires and a car door slamming outside startled him, but his attachment to the coin remained unbroken.

A faint, sinister-sounding whisper reached his ears, "Graaaaaaaaaaaaaeeeediiiiiiig."

The creature within the coin seemed to stir into action, shifting and moving, reaching for the surface as if to pull itself free. A loud banging on the front door and accompanying cry of anger was just enough for Brandon to regain some control of his limbs, and he staggered toward the door. Arms trembling, he continued to stare at the coin helplessly as he blindly reached for the lock. He felt his hands start to lose sensation as the coin struggled to regain dominance. With one last attempt, Brandon unlocked the door and froze as his body lost control once more.

The door flung open and crashed into Brandon, sending him flying to the floor, the coin still gripped in his fingers. Unable to rise, he lay there frozen in place as the creature within the coin continued to pull itself free. Ryan stood there agape at the sight of the prone body of Brandon, his eyes drawn to the coin and the creature emerging from it. Mist swirled and thickened as the creature began to grow. The air crackled with energy; the atmosphere filling with the presence of something ancient. Something that shouldn't be yet was.

The eight-foot creature, fully formed, confronted Brandon, its unearthly gaze locked onto his, while its loud, angry whisper reverberated through the house. "GRAAAAAAAAAAAAAEEEEEEDIIIIIIIIIIIIIG."

Ryan's body was frozen, trapped in a state of paralysis, preventing him from moving. Helpless, he could only watch as the nightmarish creature loomed over Brandon, its spindly and jagged bony limbs reaching out before violently crashing down into his flesh, shattering the tiles below. It lifted him effortlessly off the ground, its eyes never wavering from Brandon's as if savoring his last moments of existence. Its enormous body, resembling a macabre cage, unfurled its expanding ribs, eagerly awaiting a bone-chilling hug.

Brandon was pulled into the creature, the sickening snap of bones echoing through the room as it forced him into a space that was far too small for him. Its ribs sealed shut, spraying blood and viscera onto the walls and floor as Brandon's body was crushed. Rearing back on its haunches, its body pulsed as it sucked the blood and bones from Brandon's lifeless body until it became a husk, a boneless pile of flesh, before it, too, was consumed.

It stood there for a moment, its eyes finding and locking onto Ryan's. The swirling green glow of its eyes flared as it took him in. His skin prickled with unease as he felt the creature's piercing gaze penetrate his core. His entire being seemed to be enveloped by the tendrils of its otherworldly presence, probing and prodding into his consciousness. Every thought, every memory, every decision he had ever made was exposed, the creature analysing each one for a purpose only it knew.

Gradually, as if satisfied with what it saw, the presence withdrew. The intensity of the creature's swirling green eyes waned until they vanished into the depthless black of its hollow eye sockets in its white, skeletal face. Fading back into the swirling mist, the creature disappeared, leaving only the deserted coin on the blood-stained floor.

Completely drained of energy, Ryan crumbled to the floor in exhaustion. Every part of him ached, his head throbbed as if he'd been in a boxing match and lost. He closed his eyes, hoping to calm his pounding head, and drifted into unconsciousness.

***

The next few days passed like a fever dream. Only snippets of memories remained — wailing sirens, hazy figures gathered around him, sporadic flashes of light and darkness, the constant beeping of machines, and the murmuring of voices nearby.

Since then, he had woken to find himself in the hospital, drifting in and out of consciousness. With a few more days of rest, his condition greatly improved. He was now sitting up in bed, receiving an intravenous fluid injection to replenish his dehydrated body.

With his phone in hand, he scrolled through news articles and social media, desperate for any information about Brandon's death. The authorities had connected it to the other disappearances as part of an ongoing investigation, but they hadn't discovered any leads as to who was behind them. His search for answers led him to a forum where people were discussing their theories.

One such theory, he found himself unable to dismiss.

There was a rumour of an ancient creature, its existence tied to a tale of an Old Saxon witch who, consumed by grief and anger, called upon its powers to avenge her daughter. A tyrannical king, consumed by greed and desire, had taken her life after she turned down his advances. As the story goes, the creature would pass judgment on those who held power and wealth, and if it deemed them unworthy, it would consume them, mirroring their own ruthless actions in their relentless pursuit of power.

Recently, an excavation uncovered some ancient Saxon artifacts, including the coins found at the crime scenes. The timing of the discovery and recent deaths suggested the creature had been disturbed and had re-emerged into the world once more.

A sudden chill swept over Ryan, sending a wave of goosebumps cascading down his arms and legs. He recalled the word the creature had whispered, "Grædig". A Google search revealed its Saxon's origins and its meaning — "Greedy," and he knew the rumour he had read about was true. He remembered the creature and the unsettling feeling it gave him when it studied him as if his very soul was being invaded. He knew it was a warning.

With his newfound wealth, the creature would always be lurking, ready to claim Ryan if he strayed from his moral path.

A horror fan since childhood, Ian Gielen is a proud geek, verified by a vast collection of books and video games that he will likely never get through in his lifetime. He is mad for all things Alien, Star Wars, and cats, his furry companions always keeping him company when putting pen to paper.

He is a father and is currently living in Melbourne, Australia with his partner, son, two stepdaughters, and four cats, which is enough of a horror story on its own.

You can follow his writing journey here: https://www.facebook.com/share/ccm285cDeH5JTzEk/?mibe xtid=wwXIfr

CORTEJO DE GENTE MUERTE
MAYA PREISLER

Autumn hung in the air with a palpable sense of pregnant expectation; a buzzing anticipation dancing in the shortening sunlight, whispers of change carried aloft on the wind. The children gathered, as they did every year, to watch the eldest among them receive their first invitation to the Hunt and the following Harvest. With wide eyes and eager smiles, they dreamed of the day their time would come to pass through the coveted portal of initiation and finally become adults.

After twenty-four summers and twenty-three falls of watching and waiting, Evelyn Lee stood tall and proud among the ranks of youth, calm and certain this year would *finally* mark her transition to adulthood. This year, she would restore the honor of her family name. Thus, when her grandmother handed her their family's traditional invitational knife, Evelyn clasped it to her heart with a silent smile and bow before joining the ranks of her fellow chosen as they paraded through the streets. Eyes shining with happy tears, Evelyn held her head high as the children she passed showered the stately procession with flower petals.

Finally, her chance had come.

Filled with excitement and anticipation, Evelyn and her fellow initiates followed the Wisewoman into the woods until they came to the sacred portal, a large sinuous circle whose shiny silver surface gleamed softly in the flickering torchlight. The Wisewoman stopped before the metal ring, a shadow in the gathering twilight, framed by the portal. After raising her arms to the sky, she turned to face them, hands still upheld.

"Welcome, initiates, to the gate of adulthood. Yesterday, you were children. Tomorrow you will be adults. Now, here, in this liminal space, you are initiates. This is your time, the year you must choose, as your family members have chosen before you. You stand in the footsteps of tradition, recipients of a sacred duty to cleanse the world of greed and evil, to secure a better future for humanity's children. Know that though your community has unanimously elected you as a candidate for adulthood, the decision is yours and yours alone. Beyond this portal, you will be forever changed, reborn anew in our community, with all the rights and responsibilities of an adult. But once you pass through, you will not be able to return to childhood, to seeing the world the way you once did. Are you ready?"

"I am," Evelyn answered, joining her voice to the ringing chorus of assent.

"Then let us begin." The Wisewoman lowered her hands.

The eldest of her assistants approached, handing her a flagon with a bow before disappearing back into the edges of the ritual. A line of other apprentices approached, each bearing a cup. The Wisewoman ceremoniously filled each vessel, and the apprentices delivered one to an initiate before returning to the end of the line. This process continued until every initiate possessed a drink.

The Wisewoman raised the bottle, holding it aloft where all could see. "You hold the drink of the Harvest, the final flagon of last year's brew. There will be no more without your assistance in achieving a successful Hunt." Lowering the vessel to her heart, the Wisewoman's voice took on a ceremonial tone. "Tonight we drink to your health, to the health of your community, and the future of humanity."

The Wisewoman tipped the flagon toward her mouth and drank. Evelyn followed suit, raising her cup to her lips with a reverent anticipation, drinking down the coppery, earthy draught until her cup was empty.

The Wisewoman smiled at them all gently, her expression a mixture of pride and joy. "Welcome to the first step on your journey, initiates. You are no longer as you were."

With these words, she turned toward the archway, pouring the remains of the brew as a libation upon the ground. "Tonight we remember we are part of a much greater whole, that our choices and actions impact not just our lives but our family's lives, our community's lives, and that of every living being in the entire world."

The Wisewoman began sing-chanting in a language Evelyn did not know, the apprentices taking up the tune as they circled the group, their voices harmonizing with the strange humming sound of the archway. A pleasant sort of buzzing filled Evelyn's skull, and a gentle warmth suffused her entire being as the landscape around her began to twist and shift into something almost unrecognizable. In the center of it all, the Wisewoman remained, her fingers dancing over a section of the portal, which had begun to glow with a soft blue light.

Evelyn lost all sense and meaning of time; she found herself carried along, flowing gently on the current of the music and the magic of the Harvest brew. Eventually, the Wisewoman turned back to look at them.

"Tonight you will face the crucible of maturity and prove yourself ready to come of age. But I must warn you, your task will not be easy. Before you lies a test of your strength, bravery, courage, morality, and determination. You will experience the most difficult challenge of your existence thus far, but I believe — as your community believes — you are ready and more than capable of triumph.

"Although this trial will challenge you, remember, you do not face it alone. The hope and belief of your entire community is with you, as are your peers. Together, you possess the power to overcome any obstacles that stand in your way. It is written."

The eldest acolyte approached again, an ancient tome held carefully in her arms as though it were a newborn babe. She handed the text to the Wisewoman before backing away.

The Wisewoman opened the book and began to read, her voice a sonorous tone. "Gather round, initiates, and hear the words of the ancestors. Not so long ago, in the times of your mother's mother's mothers, monsters known as the Bill'naires ruled these lands. Cruel beings without the ability to care, the Bill'naires were driven by a single need: the gluttonous desire to consume and hoard all they could. Possessed by a horrifying lack of compassion or empathy and driven by an insatiable desire to feed on the suffering of others, Bill'naires devoured all in their path, stripping the planet bare. They leveled entire forests, stripped whole mountainsides, polluted every ocean, sea, river, and stream until the Earth baked, the seas turned to acid, and swallowed lands whole. The skies wept chemical tears, fouling everything they touched until even the most remote locations died. Always hungry for more, Bill'naires left our desolate world in search of further treasures, taking their tools and stolen resources with them, leaving us here to perish. One by one, the few remaining species died. And so did we. Slowly, painfully, worked to death for the pleasure of our absent rulers, we scraped and dug and labored until our fingers bled and we fell sick and died. But still, the Bill'naires cared not. As long as their hoards grew and another generation of drudges was born to serve their needs, the Bill'naires were happy, locked away in their lavish palaces with more resources than one could use in a thousand lifetimes. And when the population dwindled due to lack of food, water, and medicine, they simply forced anyone who could bear children to do so, no matter their age or the consequences."

Evelyn gasped quietly, hearing similarly horrified sounds echo from the others in the circle surrounding her.

"When the people had nothing left to eat, the heartless Bill'naires told them to eat each other. That moment was when the ancestors realized that for every ten thousand people, there were only three Bill'naires, perhaps two thousand of them, total. In their desperation, our ancestors joined together and fought back against the Bill'naires, taking control of the portals so we might travel to their new world and end their dominion over humanity. Our ancestors then stormed the Bill'naires' seed and gene vaults, liberating the samples stored within and using those samples to restore what they could of our natural world. Thus, our ancestors observed the very first Hunt and afterward, the fruits of the very first Harvest."

The Wiswoman paused, smiling at each of them in turn, her voice growing somber. "But a single Harvest was not enough, for once the parasite of greed has taken root, it must be continually removed from the soil each year, lest it return to consume the entire forest. Thus we celebrate the Hunt and the following Harvest each year without failing, for should we neglect our duty to the greater whole, the poisonous disease of gluttony will return to devour us all."

The eldest acolyte approached again, this time with a bowl of blue paste in her hands.

The Wisewoman paused, looking at each of them in turn before speaking. "Should you fail, you will not return to us but be lost to the community forever. If you fear you may not yet be ready, there is no shame in waiting for another year until you are. Speak now, and we shall escort you safely to your home. Otherwise, step forward and be blessed."

One by one, the gathered circle of initiates stepped forward until it was Evelyn's turn. Heart hammering and palms sweating, she stepped forward, surrendering her cup and presenting herself to the Wisewoman.

The Wisewoman reached into the bowl of paste, anointing Evelyn's face, heart, hands, and feet. "May your eyes see the truth and your lips always speak it. May your heart always remember you are part of a greater whole. May you walk with gentle feet and kind hands, saving your weapons for the Bill'naires and the parasitic vines of gluttony. Go forth now, and join the Hunt."

Evelyn stepped through the glowing, blue archway, her skin tingling with the touch of a thousand unseen spiderwebs as she struggled with an odd sense of displacement, as though her soul had been ripped from her body and then just as suddenly reinserted. She blinked several times, waiting for her eyes to adjust to her surroundings. She and the initiates who had gone before her stood on some sort of road before what she could only describe as a palatial nightmare; different styles of buildings made from different materials had been hodge-podged together into a singular, monstrous franken-structure. The land around the building lay bare and flat, covered only by a single type of bright green grass; no trees, no rocks, no signs of life. Beyond the bounds of this property, Evelyn's eyes made out even more monstrosities, unimaginably large buildings of varying shapes and sizes stretched to the horizon as far as she could see.

Beyond them, the sky shimmered at the edges of the landscape, an odd glint of light here and there as though a sheet of glass stood between her and the stars. Even the air smelled wrong, stale and stagnant with a metallic aftertaste. In the background, a constant, deep hum lurked on the edges of her hearing. More initiates continued to walk through the gate behind her, each taking time to adjust to their new surroundings. Eventually, the procession of people ended, leaving the group of them standing alone on a deserted road in the dark, their ritual knives in hand.

"What now?" Mark asked, his copper brows drawn down in a frown, at odds with his usual joking demeanor.

159

"We hunt the Bill'naires, obviously." Shinichi stared at the other initiate, disdain evident in his brown eyes.

"But how?" Carmen frowned, staring up at the mountain of a building in front of her, twisting her bronze fingers together anxiously. "We need to come up with a plan and stick together."

"Room by room, I imagine." Mel came to stand beside Carmen, absentmindedly tugging on their long black braids while studying the palatial structure with its mishmash of nonsensical lines and illogical styles. "I think our best bet would be to move methodically from the front to the back."

Tamara shook her head, the beads on her braids tinkling as she did so. "The door is a choke point. We can be taken out one by one that way."

"So we split into two large groups," Mel suggested. "One goes in the front, the other in the back. We meet in the middle."

Evelyn nodded. "I agree. We should also plan to move as slowly and quietly as possible. We don't really know what we're up against."

One by one, the initiates sorted themselves into two groups. Evelyn joined the group headed for the rear of the building; she wanted more time to assess her surroundings.

She and the others in her group followed a flat, white walkway around the side of the building. Perfectly circular bushes sprouted at the base of the tall walls, each surrounded by a proliferation of smaller flowers, every blossom perfect and identical to the others. Evelyn couldn't help but notice that despite the apparent beauty of her surroundings, she neither saw nor heard any sign of insect life. Reaching out, she touched a petal on one of the flowers, only to recoil in disgust at the texture. They were unnatural. No wonder there wasn't any insect life. She began to wonder if the perfectly green grass was also made of a hard, brittle material.

By the time the group reached the rear entrance, Evelyn distrusted everything around her, especially the way the world still swirled around the edges of her vision, and how everything still appeared brightly colored despite the darkness of night. The building itself had begun to look less and less like a palace and more like a mausoleum. If she listened hard enough, she swore she could hear the voices of the ever-present dead.

"I don't like this place," Aadhya whispered quietly from somewhere behind her, nervousness altering the typically gentle lilt of her voice. "It doesn't feel right."

Evelyn nodded her head, whispering back. "Nothing about this place is remotely right. Did you see those flowers?"

"And the trees," Ayita added, sorrow evident in her voice. "Everything here is an illusion."

Evelyn approached the rear door silently, peering through the darkened windows as she passed them. She saw nothing but gigantic, empty rooms filled with furniture, but no people, as though the structure itself was as devoid of life as the landscape around it. Anxiety swirled in the pit of her stomach as she approached the threshold, an instinctual fear of the unknown that lay beyond. When no one else reached out to touch the door, she finally did, startled when it swung open before her approach.

Lights suddenly turned on, illuminating the cold, cavernous space before her. Countless art pieces hung on the walls and stood on plinths, each seemingly beautiful until she looked closer. Every image in the room, whether flat or sculptural, depicted the same inhumanly beautiful man — who almost reminded her of a younger version of her grandfather.

Unfortunately, the longer she looked, the less human he became; extra fingers sprouted from his hands, extra arms from his forehead. His eyes never matched each other, and the lines of the objects around him were completely illogical, intersecting each other in nonsensical ways.

Was this what the Bill'naires actually looked like? Her growing unease had morphed into a chasm threatening to swallow her.

A sound of metal clanging approached from her left, and Evelyn took a defensive position behind the door, noticing the others did likewise. Eventually, a metallic object walked into the room and stopped.

Evelyn's heart hammered in her chest. How was she supposed to take down a metal monster with just a knife? No one had said the Bill'naires were armored!

The metal monster spoke. "Greetings, guests. Welcome to my Master's humble abode. He will be with you shortly. Would you care for a refreshment?"

"Sure," Mark replied, sounding anything but.

"Mark!" Carmen hissed, glaring at him and rolling her eyes.

"Certainly," the metal man said.

As if by command, a host of smaller metal creatures clanked into the room, each bearing containers of brightly colored liquids. They circled around the room, stopping near each initiate.

"No, thank you." Evelyn waved hers away. She wasn't about to eat anything in this bizarre mausoleum.

Despite Carmen's warning, Mark accepted the substance, taking a cautious drink before spitting it out and returning the remainder to the tray. "Gross! What is this?"

"A nutrient slurry specifically designed to meet your nutritional needs," the metal man replied.

"I thought it was gross at first, myself." A humanoid figure in shiny garments entered the room, his face shifting between something almost human and something else entirely *not*. "But you get used to it eventually." The stranger smiled at them, his expression as false as the flowers surrounding his home. "It's far better than the Harvest brew, at any rate."

Evelyn stared at him in shock, comprehension dawning, shedding light on details she wished could stay unseen. Whomever — or whatever — this monster was now, he used to be an initiate once.

The monster-man laughed, staring at each of them in turn. "Oh, you didn't know. How precious." His eyes roamed around the room until they stopped on Evelyn's, something in them reaching toward her with the claws of greed. "But they don't tell you that, do they? No. They gather you together in some mystical ritual and make you drink the brew and swear you're ready, even though you don't even know for what. And then they read from a dusty old tome and say it's the truth, that the world was run by monsters, and it's your sacred duty to stop them. But they never tell you who the monsters really are. Or what the brew is. Or what the 'fruits of the Harvest' actually are. Don't you want to know?"

Evelyn stared at the stranger, equally terrified that his almost human visage seemed vaguely familiar and that he seemed to be addressing his little speech to her.

Was she supposed to answer him?

When no one else spoke, the monster-man continued. "Right now you're probably wondering why I look so familiar to you. You look familiar to me, as well. But then, you look so much like your grandmother."

Evelyn reminded herself to breathe.

"What did they name you?" The stranger stepped toward her, holding out his hand. "Evelyn?"

Evelyn bit back her surprise. She could feel every eye in the room on her.

The monster-man grinned. "Haven't you figured it out yet, Evelyn? How I know your name? Why they waited so long to give you your invitation? It's because of me. I'm your uncle."

Uncertain of what to say, Evelyn stared at him in silence.

"The 'monsters' are us, Evelyn. The Bill'naires are people, like me, human beings with hearts and lives and families, or at least I *had* a family until they kicked me out for wanting to learn more about the Bill'naires' technology. You take one little piece home with you, and they banish you forever." The monster-man paused, studying her face. "But they didn't tell you that part, did they? They didn't tell you they made me what I am by exiling me here. It's only natural to be curious, to want more than the simple life your neighbors live, to want to be better than they are. It's only natural for the strong to rise above and dominate the weak."

The stranger smiled and turned to walk around the cavernous room, gesturing at all the oddities within. "Look at all of these wonderful things the Bill'naires enjoyed! Why shouldn't we enjoy them also? Flameless lights, fireless heat, cooling! Machines that can sing and dance and write and entertain me, bring me food, clean for me. After all, the Wiseones keep and use Bill'naire technology; that's how they restored the planet. That's how they sent me here, how they sent you here. But when I dare to use the same technology, they call me a monster. For what? Making art? Living comfortably in a beautiful mansion? This is why they sent you to kill me?"

Evelyn struggled and failed to repress the gasp that escaped her lips.

The monster-man grinned, turning again and walking toward her. "Do you know what the knife is really for, Evelyn? Do you want to know why they call it the Harvest?"

A sick feeling crept into the pit of her stomach.

"You're here to hunt me and harvest my body, Evelyn. You're supposed to drain my blood for the brew and serve my body at the feast." The stranger paused, staring at her with a begging look that failed to reach his cold, dead eyes. "It's why they feed you the drugs. So you don't realize what you're doing is wrong. But you don't have to listen to them. You could stay here and live comfortably with me."

He stepped even closer, placing his hand on her shoulder in a way that felt entirely too presumptuous for someone she had only just met. "You wouldn't kill your Uncle Chris, would you?"

Evelyn stared at the monster-man before her and thought about what the Wisewoman had said about seeing the truth. A series of visuals flashed across her mind: the creepily misaligned lines of the building, the fake flowers, the sterile soil, the lack of insect and animal life, the uncanny valley of monstrosities he called his art, the haunting voices of the dead. How could she trust the words of a man surrounded by lies?

She couldn't.

Evelyn stepped forward into his embrace, reaching around to hug him, her invitation still clasped in her hand. "Yes, I would," she said as she drove the knife into his back.

Maya Preisler is an author, artist, and nerd of many talents who has been writing stories since they were old enough to hold a pen. They are the author of The Laws of Entanglement as well as two short stories in CORVID 19 and A Crack in the Code. They received a BFA from UNC Charlotte in cross-disciplinary studies and have been an active member of the East Coast literary convention scene since they were eleven.

When not writing, they can be found making art, playing video games, or befriending a local murder of crows. You can find them on social media as @MayaPreisler or online at www.mayapreisler.com

SEAMUS
BY BRÝN GROVER

The bullet hit at the wrong angle. He must have started to move a second before I composed myself to pull the trigger. I had him in my sights, and I missed. Well, I missed the instant kill shot. He still went down. But I didn't know if it was fatal or not. He was moving on the ground. He should be still. It should be done. If it wasn't, I would have to come up with another plan. I couldn't hang around. People saw him drop and came out of the building, hovering over him and looking around. Since his head didn't explode on impact, they probably didn't know what happened.

I stayed low behind the parapet on the rooftop across the parking lot. Packing up my belongings, I made my way back to the other side of the long building, across a different parking lot well out of view of this building, and then across yet another parking lot to my car.

Time to regroup. To wait and see what happened. Find out the results of this shot gone astray. It wasn't like me to miss. Ever. I consistently tested as an expert marksman in the service. I just didn't miss. And yet, today, something happened. Perhaps I was too nervous. It took a little bit of time, too much of it, to pull the trigger when I had the perfect shot.

Milliseconds matter.

As I drove down a couple of back roads through the country, I listened to the local police scanner app. Nothing. No reports of a shooting. No ambulance calls. No police dispatched. It was weird. Maybe I tuned in too late to hear the initial chatter. I kept the scanner on and drove around aimlessly, hoping to hear something. If I missed the start of things, follow-up reports would be forthcoming.

They had to be.

As I made a turn down by the Potomac River, I pulled into a state park along the old C&O canal. I walked out to a bench and sat down. Watching the river roll by, I continued to listen to the app. The minutes ticked by. An hour or more passed. Nothing. I had no idea what was going on at this point. Maybe no one found the bullet. They could have thought he'd tripped and fallen.

He could have gone to an urgent care center for non-life-threatening injuries. If I missed altogether, he didn't even need any treatment. Could I have missed that much? Confused and worried, I decided to head home. Tomorrow was another day. My plans would likely have to change. But the end goal was still the same. One way or another, I would get revenge.

Seamus would die.

We would part ways once and for all.

I barely slept. At least not a deep REM type of sleep. My mind raced throughout the night. I couldn't stop thinking about things, about everything. The bastard had stopped paying me after seven years of working there. Months of broken promises and no pay. Then he fired me. Not so much as a thank you for all you've done. Nothing.

In fact, he didn't have the balls to do it himself. He had Human Resources call me while I was on the road working for them — without pay and naively hoping their promises were not lies. Hoping the back pay was coming soon. Hoping it was just an Accounts Receivable issue that tied up the cash flow. I had wasted months working for free. My bills kept coming. But I had been cast aside. My ire grew almost daily. And now, I missed the kill shot. I had the chance to exact revenge. But somehow Seamus escaped his well-deserved fate.

When I awoke late the next morning, I ate a quick snack and sat down in front of my laptop. Searching through online police reports, local community chats, the county newspaper's site, and other locations, I found nothing. There were no mentions of anything related to my experience the previous afternoon. Wondering what happened, I decided to drive by the area and take a quick look at things myself. If police had been there, the existence of taped-off areas might give a clue.

I was running out of time. If I wanted revenge on this bastard, I had to take it quickly. Rumors were he intended to leave the country soon. I'd resigned myself to never seeing my back pay. But not getting revenge was not an option. I had to move and move fast. He needed to die before he had a chance to go into hiding in some country that wouldn't extradite him for all the lawsuits and charges that were potentially pending. He and I needed to part ways. On my terms, not his. He couldn't be allowed to relax on a beach somewhere after causing all this suffering.

I decided to drive in the back way and around the buildings in the industrial park. No one who might recognize me would see me. With a set of binoculars in hand, I parked at the end of a building that ran at a 90° angle from this one. Had they been on the same elevation, it would have looked like an L with a break between the arms.

I idled the car but kept the radio playing in the background. Looking at the building, I saw nothing out of the ordinary. The normal cars were in the parking lot. All but his.

God, I hoped he hadn't already bailed out and left the country. I felt my temple throbbing as the thoughts of him escaping raced through my mind. If I had missed and lost the opportunity, I'd never forgive myself. I'd never get over it. He had screwed me and my family. For that matter, other co-workers and families, as well.

I tried to focus my mind. Pushing these thoughts out of there and concentrating on the task at hand was not easy. I continued to look over the scene. There did not appear to be any police tape. No one milled about. It was another normal workday. Not trusting my naked eyes, I pulled the binoculars out of their case and zoomed in on the area outside the front door and lobby. I hoped to see something on the ground indicative that the police had been there.

I saw nothing.

Not a sliver of yellow tape was anywhere that I could see. Without going over there myself and walking up to look behind the small bushes that blocked some of the view, I would not be able to confirm.

While a stroll could help confirm things, walking up there could be a problem. A big problem. An even bigger one if

172

a report got squelched in the local media. That would be especially true if a trap had been set. They say the criminal always goes back to the scene of the crime. Here I was following the stereotype. Walking up to the door could land me in some viral video about the dumbest criminals. I decided against it. Putting the binoculars back into the carrying case, I backed the car out of its parked location and popped it into drive. Then I retreated from the business park the same way I had entered, behind and around the buildings instead of on the main roads in the middle of it.

I drove discouraged. I made my way out to some open land I often used for hunting. Large tracts of property belonged to an elderly man I'd known since childhood. He gave me free rein to hunt during deer season and even the occasional bear season which usually took place for a week in the fall in Maryland. But he also gave me permission to practice shooting. It was a way to keep my skills sharp and honed. I made my way to my unofficial firing range in which I set up near a natural berm and placed objects along the side of it to target practice at different ranges and angles.

In frustration and confusion, I fired round after round, expending magazines from all my weapons. It felt good. I rarely missed. Those times I did miss were merely attempts at trick shooting. I would play like I was in an 1880s Wild West show traveling the country showing my skills. Sometimes it worked. I often missed with trick shots. But it was fun and served as an added distraction, pretending to be Buffalo Bill Cody at one of his Wild West shows.

I imagined Seamus as my target. With each shot fired, I grew angrier and more intent on getting my revenge. He would die. He would die soon. He would not have the chance to leave the country with his money and leave all of the rest of us sitting around trying to recover and survive. We would soon part ways.

Checking targets afterward revealed how true my shots were. Knowing I still had the eye for it, the failure to finish off Seamus baffled me. My own indecision and delay caused a missed shot. It would not happen again. Tomorrow was another day. My frustration over the whole thing rose.

I grabbed what rounds I had left and fired off round after round, unleashing my fury. I imagined the face of Seamus on every target. Then my rifle failed to discharge. At that point, I called it a day. I was emotionally, and not a little physically, tired. I had expended a lot of energy, like a massive bipolar mania had kicked in and was just starting to come down from the precipice. Packing up my rifles, guns, and clips, I threw everything into the trunk of the car and headed home.

I stayed home the rest of the day. It was a moment of calm before the storm. I relaxed. I prepared myself mentally for the next day. I envisioned the position on the roof. I envisioned the scope and sighting. In my mind, I practiced squeezing the trigger. I practiced breathing in and out with purpose. They were Zen-like calming breaths. They were steadying. I would not make the same mistake again. Seamus would die tomorrow. But first, I needed adequate rest. So, I settled in for the night.

I got up early. I was in a good mood. Today would be the day. I would not miss. I'd practiced. My aim remained true. Nothing would stop me. Revenge would be mine. Seamus would die for all he had done to me. He would pay for how he affected my family.

In some ways, I would have preferred to beat him down first and get the satisfaction of seeing his face as I did it. However, jail time wasn't worth it. There couldn't be any witnesses. I knew others felt similarly. But I would be the one to exact revenge.

Driving to the office park, I felt almost elated at the prospect of finishing things. No one ever knew about the previous attempt. There were never any reports of any kind. He had probably just tripped and fallen on his own. My shot was not true, and wherever it went astray was not noticed. I imagined there was a shell embedded in the wall, but didn't know for sure.

Now I was ready. This time would be different. My set-up on the rooftop of the building across the parking lot and up the hill was perfect. The angle was great. The parapet provided cover. It was easy to descend and get away. I only had to keep low, aim true, clean up, and leave.

It would happen. I could listen to the emergency scanner app for any reports. It would be music to my ears and the final feeling of vindication.

I zigzagged through buildings and parked farther away than last time. I didn't want there to be any security camera coverage that showed my car in the same spot. It could look like I had been plotting and casing the location. Police would investigate if they thought something appeared out of place. So, my entrance and exits would be different than previous ones. My parking location would be different. There wouldn't be anything consistent to track. Only the location of the shooting would remain the same. And since the first shooting had not panned out, there was no previous 'location' for investigators to compare.

Confident in my decisions and resolute in my desire to accomplish the task at hand, I made my way to the prime shooting location. I got there early and full of excitement. I was nervous too. But more than anything else, I was ready to put an end to Seamus. At long last, he and I would part ways permanently. He would never affect my life again. That thought brought a smile to my face as I settled in and waited.

He was later than usual showing up to work. As the minutes passed, I wondered if my preparation had been in vain. The minutes ticked until half an hour had passed. I started making plans for another day by checking the weather forecast on my phone. I wanted to ensure I had a clear day with no wind or rain. I didn't want to take any chances of having my vision obstructed or needing to adjust for windage. The distance was close enough that the windage was not likely a real concern. Nevertheless, I wanted a clear, dry, quiet, and sunny day. I also knew my time was limited.

I waited. And I waited. An hour passed. My anger grew. Another forty-five minutes or so passed. I was panicky. He did not show up. I tried to stop thinking about it and checked the forecast. The next day looked like it would have great weather, as well. But I wanted to get it done now. Before it was too late. I wondered if it was already too late.

Sweating profusely, I started cursing under my breath. How had I missed that damned shot? This should be done already. He should be dead. Instead, he could be on his way to the airport or already out of the country. Fuck.

Fuckity fuck fuck.

After getting myself worked up, I started planning for the next day. I was still intent on getting this done. I only hoped I hadn't missed my chance at revenge.

As I started packing up to leave the rooftop, I saw his BMW turn into the parking lot. He was two hours later than his usual arrival time. As the saying goes, I muttered to myself, better late than never. I would not need to come back the next day and try again. Today would be the day. Seamus would die.

I waited as he parked and fiddled around in his car. Watching him with one eye through the scope, I waited. Then he got on the phone. I cursed the circumstances that would provide him even a minute's respite. We needed to part ways, and soon. I began to develop an itchy trigger finger. I half wanted to take a shot through the window. But I decided to wait. I wanted a clean shot with no chance of a deflection. I wanted a bullseye.

So, I waited.

Anticipation grew as I anxiously waited for him to get out of the car and present himself as a target. There would be no flights for this bastard. No chilling on the beach and out of reach.

No, today he would meet his maker.

When he finally stepped out of the car, I felt relieved and light-hearted, like a weight of worry had been lifted off my back. He grabbed a few things from his back seat, closed the doors, walked around the car to the sidewalk, and toward the front door. I knew he would have to get out his ID badge and scan it at the door to unlock it for entry. That would force him to stand idly in front of the door, thereby presenting the perfect stationary target.

When I saw him pull the badge out of his right front pocket, I zeroed in on the side of his head, an inch above the ear and toward the hairline. The moment was here at last. Redemption.

Revenge.

I was steady. I was ready. I pulled the trigger. Then it was all done. The incomplete discharge of the previous day was never cleared. When the bullet stuck the lodged round, it caused the gun to explode. As I lay there dying, I realized that Seamus and I were finally parting ways.

Brýn is a Northern Virginia resident who writes weird fiction/horror and poetry. He is a member of the Northern Virginia Writers Club, the Horror Writers Association Virginia Chapter, and NoVa Bards.

In his spare time, he enjoys listening to blues music, reading, traveling to UNESCO sites, exploring abandoned buildings, graveyards & cemeteries, and dark tourism sites.

A THORN IN ONE'S SIDE
BY CHRISTINE CUNNINGHAM

Thorn was reckless; he knew that. All this time, he thought his father's patience had rubbed off on him.

For the most part, he enjoyed his job of escorting clients through the woods from town to town, but his current client, Tomin, proved that wrong. Every time Tomin mentioned that he was the half-brother of a wealthy businessman overseas, Thorn counted the scars on his hand to ignore the hunger pangs. If they didn't stop and allow him to hunt soon, the client would end up as a pile of bones picked clean.

The caravan rolled to a stop. Sahara knew by now how Thorn got when he was hungry. Tomin stepped out of the caravan and sighed like he was being inconvenienced. Thorn cringed as he went on and on yet again about how he was "underappreciated" back home, and the absurd amount of trips he took all around the world so he could collect the rarest artifacts from each place.

He even boasted of a jeweled mirror said to be used to communicate with the Gods. A sacred artifact kept in a temple just outside Sylvan Hollow, something that should never have left it to begin with. But of course, this rich guy from across the sea would feel entitled to it.

The human meatsack had taken his sweet time getting comfortable in the caravan, only to moments later hurl himself out, screaming that the jeweled mirror would have to stay with him in the back and not with the other bags up front.

Thorn had been tempted to 'accidentally' drop the other bags in the mud, but Sahara noticed his hostility and snatched them before he could, placing them up on the seat.

"You can have your mirror," she said, her steady voice and calm demeanor betraying none of the tension between them.

Thorn picked hard at the mud on his boots with his worn, rusty knife until he saw Tomin approach Sahara. She nodded at Thorn to go do his thing, but Thorn watched as Tomin took her hand in his own pale, buttery soft ones.

She squirmed, mildly uncomfortable as he towered over her. He looked as though he'd never spent a day outside, let alone done any work with his hands. The epitome of every bland, rich human they carried between the towns. The clients he really got along with had little money.

They had a ways to go, and Thorn's stomach grumbled. He scouted out the forest surrounding them, trying to catch a scent of any animals nearby, but they tended to keep away from the road during the day. He'd have to go deeper. Thorn cursed himself, forgetting to eat before they left. It was such a routine by now, it shouldn't have ever happened. He considered Tomin again. He looked like the kind of human who could get lost on a road only going one way.

No one would care if he disappeared.

While it was rare for Thorn to act on his fantasies, he had them all the same. Imagining exactly how he would end this man's life. When they'd reach the most isolated part of the trip, that's when he'd do it. A chase into the woods, a broken leg, and a lot of mockery before the killing blow.

He was so in his head, he forgot to consider Sahara with her amazing knife skills, who had probably one of the best client streaks in the books. All of her clients made it to their destinations alive, regardless of losing a few personal items. And the driver, Moloch, he had a little bit of history with. There was a time when Moloch's father cured his younger brother of illness. Thorn was grateful to their family ever since.

When his hunger won out, he promised himself he wouldn't harm Moloch. He couldn't, not with the debt he felt he owed him. Sahara was tricky. It would bring too much attention to him if she were to go missing in his company. Tomin was still droning on about how his family never let him handle any important business matters. He was the one they sent off overseas to see to mundane things. As though travel wasn't exciting enough on its own. Thorn rolled his eyes and focused on the symbol of a half-closed eye in a repeated pattern all over the cloak he wore. Adharian by the look of it. He had yet to meet a humble Adharian.

Sahara snapped at him, caught his attention, and he remembered he was supposed to be hunting. He waved at her in acknowledgement and slipped toward the front of the caravan.

Thorn focused on the trees ahead of them on either side of the road. Their ancient, gnarled roots grew suddenly at an alarming rate, erupting from the middle of the packed earth road in front of them, a tangle of pale beige and deep brown.

The oxen shrieked and almost overturned the cart, but Moloch was an expert at his job, and he calmed them down just enough to put everything upright.

With Moloch focused on the animals, Sahara went to investigate the roots, ignoring Thorn almost entirely as though he were a rookie. But Thorn had been on his own for years now, and while his reputation was okay, his tendency to kill his richest clients was beginning to get noticed. Not that anyone knew he killed them, it was more like they vanished under mysterious circumstances, and of course, no one could prove they weren't vanishing after he dropped them off, or else that they hadn't simply gotten lost. But there were never any witnesses.

He simply couldn't have witnesses.

"Looks like we're stuck unless we can clear the roots from the road," Sahara said. "Or else we can try to go around, but the trees won't make that easy." She eyed Thorn again, "Are you gonna go hunting or what? I can tell you're hungry and now we'll be delayed."

Thorn grinned a hunter's smile. "I'll go off in a minute," he said, wandering toward the back of the caravan. A few minute gestures later, the road behind them was full of jagged spikes stabbing upward from the ground like a cage of giant whale bones.

They were completely trapped.

All were confused, and he decided it would be best to put Moloch to sleep for now. He'd give him a false story later.

He only had to deal with Tomin and Sahara, and only really if she forced his hand. He should knock her out, too, he figured, but she was no longer inspecting the road. She was helping Tomin out from the caravan. Even after he was out, he clung to her like a parasite.

"What's the plan?" Thorn asked.

"We'll have to find a way to get rid of some of these roots. Otherwise, we'll have to walk to the nearest town to get help," Sahara replied.

Tomin, who had spent much of the time on the road complaining about every bump and speck of dust, suddenly didn't seem to care so much that they were stranded. In fact, he seemed quite content keeping ahold of Sahara's shoulder even after they were both firmly on the ground.

Even as she tried to shrug him off, he persisted. He followed. He stuck to her like he was on a short leash, tagging behind her as she examined the thick, pale roots that were once underground. Sahara ignored him, but Thorn felt indignant for her. He didn't want her to be in the way, she wasn't his target. But with them practically glued together, he didn't have a shot at putting her out before he went for a hunt.

Thorn sighed. It was unfortunate she'd be a casualty because of Tomin's insistence on being a nuisance. He decided to give her a chance to escape. But no witnesses meant no witnesses. If he couldn't knock her out or change her mind, she wouldn't get far.

One of the trees at the side of the road shifted its weight toward them. The earth cracked beneath their feet, and a root as wide as two bodies rose above them and slammed into the ground next to Sahara and Tomin. Both lost their footing, and they fell in a heap.

Thorn grabbed at the man's ankle, tried to pull him away from Sahara and into the woods, where they'd both be under cover. He turned his back to Sahara as he threw the man forward into the brush as though he were a rag doll. He stopped to take a breath and stretch his shoulders when he felt something sharp pierce his thigh. He staggered away, surprised, and looked down.

Sahara crawled across the ground, covered in the dirt from the road. She got both hands beneath her chest and pushed herself to her feet, panting. The knife in her hand was coated in his blood.

Thorn forgot about the man for a second, turning on Sahara. He hadn't felt that kind of pain since his father tested his healing abilities years ago. And she wouldn't get to try it again. Sahara put herself between Thorn and the man, a mistake on her part. Thorn regained his composure, his face relaxed back into a smile.

"You're gonna want to get out of here as fast as you can," he said.

Sahara scowled. "That one was a warning. Get the fuck out of here, or I won't miss your vitals next time."

Thorn looked down casually at the wound and glanced up at her just as it began to clot and scar over unnaturally fast. He saw her composure break. His leg still throbbed, but he couldn't help but laugh as she watched him heal. He stretched his arms again leisurely.

"I can't believe you got me."

He ignored her for a moment to see what befell the human in the trees. He was still there, a bit shaky, trying to get to his feet. But somehow the branches always impeded him. They bent down to scratch at his face as he tried to stand.

"Don't you fucking ignore me," Sahara screamed at Thorn. She would've had the knife at his throat if the vines on his back weren't so reactive.

Shoved between them, they tangled her arms and pulled, forcing her down. He crouched to meet her glare and watched the recalculations in her eyes as she flitted between the healed wound, his empty hands, and the vines trailing out from underneath his shirt.

She looked back at the road and put it all together. "The roots in the road, that was you, wasn't it?" she said, panicking. "You trapped us here to do what? Kill us?"

Thorn shook his head. "Not all of you, not intentionally. If you go to sleep, ignore me and this whole incident, I'll let you survive."

It was such an easy request, and if she agreed, he wouldn't have to risk the consequences if she didn't come back from the trip. He loosened his grip, his own mistake thinking she would take the more reasonable route.

Sahara pulled away from him, put herself once more between him and the client. He stared at the ground, dug his fingers into the soft earth, sifting it. Sahara watched him closely, brow furrowed. Thorn smiled as she paid far too much attention to what he was doing and not what was coming for her.

The gnarly bough of an ancient tree at the side of the road knocked her down and pinned her face forward in the road. She squirmed and inched out from under the branch as it seemed to hold its place rather than pressing her deeper into the terrain.

She barely had time to deflect a thinner, incoming branch that whipped at her arms, leaving red marks. She panted heavily and dodged another one. The movement drew her close enough to Thorn, he could almost reach out and touch her.

Without getting close, however, she couldn't hit him again. She tried regardless, aiming low. The vines slipped from his back again, smooth and green and strong enough to catch her leg and pull it out from under her. She lost her footing with one vine, and her knife with another.

Thorn crouched to put the knife against her throat this time. "Looks like you lose."

"What the fuck are you?" she spat.

Thorn sighed because he was sick of hearing that. "Such a boring question from someone about to die." He could hear the blood pounding through her. His other hand was against her left shoulder, pinning her down. Thorn could practically feel her heartbeat as it drummed against her ribcage.

"You need me to save your ass if you want to keep your job," she hissed.

"I doubt you'd choose to help me. As you implied, I'm not human. You'll just turn me in, and they'll have me killed for potential murder." Thorn mused. "Or murder if they look too deep."

"I-I-" she stammered, barely getting the words out. "I could be your witness! I'll tell them it was a bear, a storm cat," Sahara said. "Maybe he was even fine when we dropped him off in town." Her pitch got higher, her voice faster as she came up with ideas on the spot. "He must've missed the boat, gotten lost, maybe someone in town got him?"

Thorn paused. She was begging, sure, but not even for her life. No, it was to help him cover up the eventual murder that would happen, whether she was alive to see it or not. "I don't trust you," he said.

"So why not wait and kill me after? You can-" she hesitated, "you can even tie me up, I'm not sure what you did to Moloch but-"

"He's sleeping," Thorn cut her off. "I don't want him to be a part of this."

"Okay," she said slowly. "Then let me talk to him when he wakes up. I can convince him that we're doing the right thing. Coverups are my specialty, and people in the guild trust me enough that they would overlook your presence on this trip."

Fear oozed from her voice, and he felt the thudding of her heart more as her body tensed, bracing for uncertainty. "If I end up dead, what will Moloch think? We work together all the time. I don't know why you want to keep him out of it, but-" Desperation showed with her rapid breathing and wide eyes. "I-please, I swear on my life, I'll help you." She squeezed her eyes shut.

Thorn thought about it. "If you tell them anything about it, I promise you'll be dead."

Thorn pulled away, keeping the knife. He watched her slowly get up and go to the caravan, sifting through the man's bags. She held up the mirror.

"I forgot to mention, that mirror is going back to Sylvan Hollow," Thorn said.

Sahara begrudgingly wrapped it up and nestled it carefully in one of the bags. "Can I at least take the rest of the valuables?"

Thorn shrugged. He really didn't need them this time. He turned back to the client's spot on the ground. Though he had plenty of time to try and get up, the trees kept playing with him, keeping him crawling on his belly slowly across the forest floor, so he hadn't gotten very far.

Thorn allowed the branches to hold off and planted a foot firmly on his back. It would be far too boring to hunt down a man who couldn't even run.

"Do you see that tree over there?" Thorn pointed to a very distinct, gigantic tree with the largest root system visible above ground. "Can't miss it, right?" Thorn ground his boot harder into the man's back, pushing him down deeper into the mud. "I want you to run to that tree. If you make it before I catch you, I won't slit your throat. Does that sound good?" He removed his boot and stepped away, allowing the man time to get to his feet and start running.

Thorn leaned back against a tree and watched. He could feel the life flowing through the whole forest, from the ends of roots to the tips of the canopy. The trees connected, and communicated with each other like synapses. He could feel, hear, the vibrations of heavy footsteps as the human ran for his life.

Thorn felt the kind of energy that only surfaced during a good hunt. He stepped deeper into the woods, surrounded by the sounds of birds, wind, and life. Then there were the smells, overwhelming to a human, but not to him. He could pick out each one, and he followed the man with ease, slowly, allowing the woods to close in around him.

The human was hopelessly lost by the time Thorn caught up with him. Running in endless circles as the forest kept him in place. It was too easy, though, and he allowed the forest to let the man through to find the tree. Thorn slipped his boots off to feel the dirt, mud, and flora between his toes. The smell of human fear lingered in the air. It wasn't always a pleasant smell, but the taste of the meat was divine enough that it didn't matter. He knew the exact right way to gut a meal.

The human tripped over a branch sticking out of the mud, not even something Thorn controlled, and Thorn burst out laughing behind him. The human mewled like a lost baby animal, crawling along the ground on his belly.

Thorn tried, barely, not to keep up.

"You don't want me to slit your throat, right?" he hissed in the man's ear. "Then try harder." Thorn stepped back, giving him some space, waiting for him to get to his feet at the bare minimum.

The tree didn't seem that far away. Mere yards, but the time seemed to drag on for Thorn. By the time the man made it to the tree, panting, hands on his knees, doubled over with exhaustion, Thorn was barely a foot behind. He strolled up, clapping his congratulations.

He didn't run very much, did he?

The man, his hair disheveled, his face slick with sweat, looked into Thorn's eyes defiantly and laughed. "You said you wouldn't kill me if I made it to the tree," he said confidently.

Thorn grinned, showing just how sharp his teeth really were. "I said I wouldn't slit your throat," he replied. "I didn't say I wouldn't eat you."

The man's smile dropped, his face paled. Thorn allowed the silence to hang there until the human couldn't stand it anymore. He turned and ran deeper into the woods, trying hard not to scream for help. There was no help out in the middle of the woods, after all.

Thorn's smooth vines slithered from beneath his shirt to loom around him like a cloud of snakes. The trees nearby shifted together, wove their branches into nets, scratched and clawed at the human as he ran blindly. He stopped and pivoted and tried to duck under the weave, but they grew around him like a spider's web.

No matter how hard he tried to move, he just got more and more scratched up. The branches spit him out at Thorn's feet, a mess of thin bleeding cuts and throaty sobs and screams. Vines shoved him up against the rough bark of a tree, one pushed into his mouth as he screamed. It was about the size of an adult human fist sliding down his gullet. It glided easier as the man's saliva glands worked overtime to provide enough lubrication to avoid tearing the soft, slimy flesh on the way down.

The vine stopped and tiny spines extended along it, traveling all the way down into his throat. He couldn't scream, the vine too thick, no air reaching his lungs. Thorn ripped it out and with it came flecks of torn flesh and gore. The human spluttered, coughed, the meat of his esophagus shredded and undoubtedly painful.

The spines retracted, and Thorn ran a hand over the dirtied vine to wipe it clean. The blood came off on his palm, tangy and sweet, someone with too much money to spend.

The man doubled over on the ground, retching a thick red stream of foam and stomach acid. A high keening noise came from his ruined throat. He covered his mouth in an attempt to keep his insides in, but only managed to vomit all over himself. Thorn removed his shirt and set it away from the thick slough of body fluids and viscera.

No one else was around. No one who would live to see what was about to happen. He pressed a finger into his stomach, feeling the crease of the mouth he rarely used. He curled his fingers into it, coaxing it open until his whole chest seemed to split in half. Rows of sharp teeth at the ready.

A sudden, intense wave of hunger hit him.

The vines from Thorn's back lashed around bloodied limbs and the man's torso. They pulled him forward, toward the gaping maw. His scream was wet, gurgling. Blood bubbled up on his shredded lips and pooled from the side of his mouth, a thick red drool.

Limbs popped from sockets, and Thorn no longer heard the screams, the man's body going into shock. Parts found their way to the mouth-arms, legs, torso, and head-until all was devoured.

No one had dared follow him into the woods. He preferred it that way. He cleaned himself up and went back to the road where Sahara and Moloch were waiting. "It's done," he said.

They traveled the rest of the way in silence.

Christine Cunningham is an X-ray technician and author of the short story, A Thorn in One's Side. For over a decade, she has mainly written horror and fantasy stories for herself. Born and raised in Northern Illinois, where the weather can change in the blink of an eye, her newfound stability in the X-Ray world has pushed her passion for writing to a new level. She has published a short story, Carnival Daze, in the Dark Carnival Anthology by The Macabre Ladies. She has also published a short story, Returned to the Earth, in Cold and Crisp by 815 Publishing.

More of her horror and fantasy writings can be found at https://www.wattpad.com/user/halfbloodlycan

THE HOUSE ON THE HILL
BY R.E. SARGENT

Prologue

His heart beat loudly as he traversed the hilly terrain. The sound of a twig snapping brought his full attention back to his actions. He slipped behind the closest foliage in case he had attracted unwanted attention. Although the fog had started to settle in, he still had a clear view of the house on the hill. The lights were on, and the blinds were wide open.

Occasionally, he would see a shape pass behind the glass — obviously, someone going about their nightly routine, living their life. Anger rose up through his veins. He felt his muscles tighten and he could almost hear them as they stretched to their limits.

The image of the house on the hill blurred as he reached desperately inside himself, clawing at distant memories, wondering why he was the way he was. The pain in his soul was fresh, raw. He knew he had been through something, but he couldn't discern what. It was as if a fog had penetrated his skull and wrapped around his brain. It wasn't simply that he didn't understand why he was this way. It wasn't even because he didn't remember what his name was. His main confusion stemmed from the fact that he didn't know *what* he was.

If I have a name, I must be human. But I don't look human. I don't feel human. But I can think. I can feel. He reached down and picked up a boulder the size of his meaty fist. *I know this is a stone. How else would I know that?*

"Stone," he whispered. "I shall go by Stone."

Stone watched as the lights winked off in the house for the evening — its lone occupant most likely turning in for the night — took one last look at the house and staggered down the makeshift trail toward the bottom of the hill. He trekked for miles until he happened upon a grove of trees he decided he'd slumber in — the first place he felt safe since he had found himself in this existence hours earlier.

He collected a few boughs of branches and handfuls of leaves and put together a sort of bed to rest on. Not that he was tired. He had too many wispy and fleeting thoughts wafting through his brain that conflicted with each other.

The mystery wasn't only who or what he was. He had to find out who lived in the house on the hill. Why had he become so enraged when he gazed upon it?

Stone took a moment to examine himself for the first time. He held his hands out in front of him. He decided they weren't hands after all. More like hand-paws. Was he a dog? Impossible. He had walked upright. He stretched his hand-paws to see how wide the pads would expand.

Razor-sharp claws popped out, catching him off guard.

Holy shit! Not paws, claws.

Stone worked the muscles again, and the claws suddenly popped back out of sight. Stunned, he sat there and looked at the details of the meaty mitts. Then it dawned on him. He could see every detail plainly, even though no light from the atmosphere made its way through the copse of trees. He had extraordinary vision.

How he wished he had a mirror.

Mirror. I know what a mirror is. I have intelligence. I must be a man... but how? How did I become... this? He felt his face and although the pads on his hand-paws gave a completely different sensation than he remembered feeling with fingers — which meant he had to have been in a human's body before — he could feel a full beard. Possibly even an entirely furry face. His ears were sharp and pointy, and it felt like the cartilage had been replaced with stiff cardboard. He felt for his mouth.

Is that a fucking snout?

His teeth were long and felt sharp to his touch. It was then he noticed the thick fur on his arms and legs. He was naked, and he had the uncanny feeling that he should be uncomfortable being so, yet it felt natural. Upon inspection, his genitalia did not appear human to him and he didn't recognize it, but he felt a swell of pride at the sight.

Stone concentrated on the vaporous thoughts and snippets of knowledge as they floated through his mind, trying to latch on to something that might explain what was going on. He was aware that he existed, but he was not aware of existing before this night. His fragmented memory told him that he must have lived in another time as another being, but his mind felt like a puzzle someone dumped back into the box the moment more than two pieces were connected together.

He tried to focus on what little he could retain. He had become aware for the first time earlier tonight at the base of the hill. And he had inexplicably been pulled toward the house. He did not understand it, but he had little control over his mind and body as he traversed the hillside to get a closer look at the outside — at the movement behind the glass.

Before he realized it was happening, Stone's heart started beating at hyper-rate. Thoughts of blood and body parts surged through his brain as images of carnage flashed behind his eyes. He felt aroused and then ashamed, for he did not understand what was happening to him. As he tried to sort through new, overwhelming emotions, new feelings, and new thoughts, only one emotion floated to the top when he thought about the house on the hill. Rage. Stone animalistically knew why he was here... even if he didn't understand why.

The bloodlust.

Chapter One

Woody McGregor sat near the front deck of his rustic home smoking a Marlboro, watching the sparks pop from the firepit and disappear in the chilly night air. He took a swig off his Miller and pushed back in one of the Adirondack wooden rocking chairs he had purchased when he had bought the place, which was so far out, it was almost off the grid. If it wasn't for satellite wi-fi, he'd have no connection to the world at all. He eyed the second chair. *God knows why I bought two. I've never had company. Ever.*

The sky was void of any moon and the house lights were extinguished. The only light came from the thirty-six-inch steel fire pit that sat on the stone sitting area, which looked out over the valley and away from the simple 1,080 square foot single-wide mobile home he called his castle ever since his old life ended.

The view of the valley was majestic — during the nighttime with the lights from the small town below and during the day, just from the sheer beauty of the landscape — which was one of the reasons he had purchased the place. The other was the lack of people. He had absolutely no other neighbors around him. The rough and rutted dirt road that served his property at the top of the mountain stretched for a couple of miles from the main road at the bottom of the hill with no other dwellings along the path. People truly had no reason to be up in his space, and accordingly, he installed a gate at the bottom of the hill and kept it chained shut unless he was driving through it.

Taking another chug of his beer, Woody ran his hand through his thick, graying, beard and thought back on what put him here less than a year ago. The break, which caused him to lose any remaining faith he had left in human beings and the world.

He hardly recognized the man he used to be. The corporate man who wore the suit to work every day. The man who showed up before everyone else and even took calls on the weekend. The man who spent twenty-five years of his life working for the same corporation, moving his way up from an entry-level position to one of the company's highest-ranking managers. With only two people above him, he felt accomplished, like his hard work was finally paying off.

What happened, occurred overnight. Woody was well respected, and his professional career was at its peak, even though his direct boss, Ron, was a total prick. What he didn't realize at the time was that the prick — the one he put up with every day, because he knew that in the corporate world, you always had to deal with at least one asshole to make it — felt threatened for his own job by Woody. Woody didn't realize that being smart, achieving the results that he was asked to, and being liked by everyone would be the end of him.

Out of the blue, two hours after arriving at work on a random day, he found himself before a committee and bullshit wild accusations. Within two days, Woody was gone. Unemployed. Stripped of his reputation, his stock options, and his life. Escorted out of the building by security like some criminal.

Downing the rest of his beer, Woody straightened his worn ball cap, scooted himself up off the chair, and went into the house, flicking on the interior light. He heard a movement behind him and turned to watch as Dexter, his ninety-pound German Shepherd, got up off the ground to join him.

"It's okay, Dex... you can stay there. I'm just getting another beer."

Dexter stopped and looked at him, then proceeded to follow Woody into the house and over to his water bowl, where he lapped up the cold liquid, the stray droplets splattering the ground around him.

"What's the matter with your water bowl outside? Did it get dirt in it or something?"

Woody smiled slightly and rolled his eyes, knowing the water bowl outside was fine. Dexter just wanted to be where Woody was, and that was the way it was. Woody used the bathroom and grabbed another beer, heading back out to his favorite chair, which he had added especially comfortable cushions to. Dexter lay down on his dog bed beside Woody with a contented, "hmmph."

Woody reached down and scratched Dex behind the ears, smiling. Dexter was the only "person" he truly loved any longer.

When Woody had arrived home from work that day, in the middle of the day — to his wife's astonishment — she was the rock he needed. While she tried to push him out of his depression, to keep him moving forward, he had a hard time doing so. The injustice he felt was unreal. He felt betrayed. Tossed away like yesterday's newspaper. He applied for hundreds of jobs. Went on numerous interviews.

He knew that if he heard the word "overqualified" one more time, he was going to lose it.

When the money from savings dried up, he desperately tried to figure out how to make ends meet as his wife's meager minimum-wage job barely paid for food and utilities. Then one March day, his world came to an end. As he left his wife, Marcy, to sleep in while he went out to buy some flowers and pick up some breakfast to celebrate her forty-fourth birthday, he came home to find her still on the bed, deceased. She had never woken up, and the coroner had ruled it as a heart attack.

Woody knew that the stress of their situation had been the end of her. The woman who had been there for him most of his life — and the only actual person remaining in his life since his parents were deceased and his friends and coworkers dropped him like a bad habit — was gone.

Just like that.

That was when the break happened. When he slipped into darkness. It wasn't until two days later that he realized he was lying in his own waste beside her, the cold coffee and the stale breakfast lying on her nightstand.

When they had finally taken her, he fell into a deep fog, night turning into day and day into night. He mostly got up to use the bathroom or forage for any remaining food that had been left in the sparse cabinets. It wasn't until the day the electricity went out that he crawled up out of the pit he was living in and assessed his surroundings.

Why hadn't he noticed before that he smelled like shit?

When was the last time he had taken a shower? His sweats and t-shirt were stained with things of various colors. He reached down and scraped a dried ramen noodle off his shirt. In the bathroom, he reached for the light switch and flicked it, only to remember the power was off. When was the last time he had paid a bill? Thirty days?

Sixty? More?

Reaching for the shower valve, he turned it and was surprised to find water coming out of the showerhead. He decided to take advantage of it while he still had the chance, opened the frosted window enough to shed some light into the room — and stepped into the tile cubicle. He was surprised the water was still hot since they had an electric water heater, but he knew as soon as it cooled off, that was the end of that luxury. As he reached for his soap, he noticed all the stray hair and scum that clung to the surfaces of the entire stall, and he wrinkled up his nose in disgust.

Afterward, he dried off on his mildew-smelling towel, found some clean clothes in the back of the closet, and pulled them on. He went and checked the mailbox, which was stuffed full. As he made his way back to the house, he flipped through the envelopes. All bills and junk. And a five-dollar rebate check. Dinner. As he approached the house, it was the two notices taped to the door that caught his attention. They were exactly what he thought they were. Foreclosure notices. He had sixteen days left before his house was gone... the house, and any equity he had in it.

Woody looked back over the twinkle of lights and at his life now. The beer was cold and satisfying. The air danced in his lungs as if it hadn't ever touched another human before. This place was his. A place that the bank didn't have any claim to. Privacy. And the best companion in Dexter he could ever imagine. He would never go back to the corporate world — he got anxious even thinking about it.

This was his life now.

When he read that final foreclosure notice, he knew he had to act fast. Calling a real estate investor who had posted a yellow sign at one of the intersections of town claiming to buy homes for cash, he was able to squeak the sale out before the greedy bank grabbed the only thing he had left. Before it closed, he sold all the furniture, packed the things he wanted to keep in twenty-two boxes, and moved everything remaining to storage. With his equity in the bank, which was way more than he thought it would be, he lived in the cheapest motel he could find while he searched. A search that lasted sixty-seven days, and then he found this place.

Although under no obligation to do so, the real estate agent who had listed the property provided the history of the house, taking it to the point of too much information. The house had sat vacant for over a year and a half after the elderly man who lived there was found dead — they estimated for months before they found him. He was found in the yard, his bones picked clean by who-knew-what.

While they couldn't find any evidence of foul play, they couldn't attribute his death to natural causes, either, so his death was listed as "unknown." With no heirs and no will, the estate was escheated to the state and finally sold.

That was the beginning of his new life. A remote, online job providing chat support for some random company. An electric, internet, tax, and insurance bill only. An older Chevy 4x4 that was paid off. He adopted Dexter a month after he got the place. They had been living their life of simplicity ever since.

Although life was simple, for Woody, there was no joy. Not after the curveball life had thrown at him. While Dexter provided some comfort and companionship, it wasn't enough to scrape away at the formation of stone that surrounded Woody's heart. He would be two more beers in before he went inside to get ready for bed, although it was still early by most people's standards.

As was his habit, he turned out the lights and slipped into bed, knowing that sleep would overtake him almost instantaneously.

Chapter Two

The pain inside Stone's head was too much to manage, and he curled up in a ball, his paws over his face, his body burrowed into the tree branches. A low whine emitted from his muzzle, which he hoped no other creature of the night could hear.

He tried to understand his predicament. How had he become trapped in a body that wasn't his? He tried to understand his mission. If there was a reason for this — this hellish transformation into some kind of abomination that only movies and folklore supported — what was it? Was he destined to ravage the hillside, desecrating rabbits and any other varmints he could find? Cattle? Horses? Maybe even people?

He concentrated, tried to picture yesterday. What had he done all day? Was he in this body or another? No answers came to him, and images of the house on the hill filled his mind once more.

Is that my purpose? Something to do with that fucking house? He tried to picture it on the inside. Had he ever been in it? Who lived there? Did he know them?

Feeling his right hind leg bouncing, Stone tore out of his hiding spot, scrambled the miles to the base of the hill, and crisscrossed halfway up before slowing down to a crawl, careful not to give away his presence. He felt clumsy in his newfound body. Breathing out through his nose quietly, he concentrated on being stealthier.

The scents of the night assaulted his sense of smell — which he had not noticed before. Dampness. Pine. A nearby animal.

Stone stopped and tried to determine the source and direction of the scent. He concentrated on it, trying to channel his anxiety and discourse toward the critter. The animal must become his new focus. The power to focus would be his. The power to choose belonged to him. The animal must die. The draw of the house pulled his attention away from the scent of the unsuspecting meal, and without him even realizing it, Stone had abandoned the scent of the animal and was creeping closer toward the house on the hill.

He paused at the edge of the yard, sniffed the vehicle beside it, then the grass, and took one step onto the property. The lights in the windows were dark, and although Stone felt like he should be worried that they would all be illuminated at the same time and he would be caught prowling, he chuckled internally. *I think they would be the ones that were scared shitless, not me.*

He approached the front window, slinking up underneath it, peering through with eyes that he only imagined looked evil as hell. He could make out the outline of furniture: a couch, a coffee table, a recliner.

Furniture. I know what it is. I've sat in a chair before. On a couch.

There was no movement in the house. Stone made his way to the next window. A dining room. Beyond it, a kitchen. He continued around the side to the back. More windows. All dark. All covered by blinds that were turned down tight. He could not see inside. He turned to his other newfound senses. He listened intently but only heard the whirring of a motor. Maybe a heater? He concentrated on the scent permeating from the home.

A man. He smelled something else.

There's a dog in there!

Stone felt his hair stand up on his back — a new sensation for him. His lip involuntarily pulled back and his teeth bared. An urge took over him, and he commanded all his control to keep from ripping a hole through the side of the building. He clamped down hard on the avalanche of lust, wanting badly to understand, subconsciously knowing that whoever was in there was just like him — well, like he used to be. He could not lose control. He was not a killer.

Knowing that the smallest noise would send the dog into a frenzy, he crept away from the home, surprised at his newfound stealth. When he was out of earshot, he cut a wide berth around the home and found his way back down the hill.

As he made his way back to his lair, he tried to dissect his fascination with the house and the occupant inside. He tried to understand his urges. He grappled with the strange turn of events that put him in a body built for murder, with no instruction manual.

Back home on his pile of branches, he curled up once again, exhausted. Unable to unravel the threads of his mind, he let the darkness of the shadows overtake him and fell into a deep slumber.

Chapter Three

Woody opened his eyes and sat up in bed. His eyes locked on the digital clock on the nightstand as it clicked over to five thirty a.m. After all the years of getting up at the same time every day to head into the office, his body had set its own eternal alarm. Unfortunately, it didn't know what weekends were. Woody was up at the same time, seven days a week, whether he needed to be or not.

Dexter raised his head, reluctantly pulled himself up, and jumped off the bed. As soon as Woody was done relieving his bladder, Dexter followed him out to the living room and went over and tapped on the back door with his paw.

"Like you think I'm not going to let you out. We do this every morning." Woody opened the top of the Keurig and pulled out the empty pod from the last cup of coffee. He replaced it with a fresh one, pressing the brew button.

Dexter tapped on the door again.

"Okay, okay! Geeze!"

Dexter ran out the door and started sniffing around the backyard, taking several minutes to select a spot before he lifted his leg and soaked it.

"Obviously, it was urgent," Woody muttered.

When Dexter had done his business, Woody called him back to the house, dog food bowl in hand. When Dexter didn't come inside, Woody sat the bowl on the counter and went out onto the back deck. Dexter was sniffing below the bedroom window, his nose caught on some scent.

"Come, Dexter. Let's eat."

Dexter stopped sniffing, cocked his head, looked at Woody, and then pawed at the ground under the window.

"Leave it. Come inside now. I don't want you digging up the yard."

Dexter paused again, mid-dig, and looked at Woody. He then looked back at the ground and pawed it again.

"Damn you, Dex!" Woody started down the stairs toward him and Dexter barked once, bounced on his haunches, his two front paws in the air, and then he took off running around the yard. Shaking his head, Woody went back inside and poured cream into his freshly brewed coffee. He went to the refrigerator and pulled out the ingredients for breakfast. Dexter waltzed inside and sat in front of the counter, waiting for his food.

"Okay, so now you want it, huh?"

Dexter licked his chops.

Woody set the bowl down on the floor against the wall toward the dining room and prepared his morning omelet and sausage. He had a habit of cooking three eggs into his omelet each morning, but he never ended up eating the entire thing. Dex was a loyal companion, though, and somehow found a way, sacrifice that it was, to fit the remainder into his belly.

After breakfast, Woody cleaned up, took a shower, and changed into clean clothes. Even though he worked from home, he tried to be disciplined, stay clean, and get dressed each day.

By 6:55 a.m., he was sitting at his desk and logging into the company interface where he would promptly be connected to the queue at seven sharp. If there were any customers waiting for assistance, which there typically were, he would automatically be connected to the next one in line.

Woody's work shift was very straightforward and controlled. His breaks and lunches were regimented by the computer. As soon as two hours passed, the computer put him on an automatic fifteen-minute break the moment he finished with the customer he was helping. That usually gave him time to use the bathroom, get another cup of coffee, or smoke a cigarette. After four hours, the system pushed him out of the queue for an hour lunch, and then another two hours after he got back, it made him take his final break. At quarter to four, the system would no longer assign a customer to his queue. Once he finished up with the customer he was currently helping, he was logged off for the day.

Of course, there were overrides built into the system that allowed a support person to alter their automatic schedule if an urgent need arose, but Woody refrained from using it most days, as corporate sent you a nastygram if you used it more than twice per month. The last thing he wanted to do was be on someone's radar.

Because of this, Woody was shocked when at twelve minutes after ten, he clicked the manual override to start his lunch, before a new customer could be spooled to his chat window. Confused, he watched as the countdown timer showed he had a little over fifty-eight minutes left before his shift started again. Woody got up from his desk chair and rubbed his right temple. Dex got up as well, wondering if playtime was coming early — Woody usually threw the ball for five minutes during lunch — and traipsed out to the kitchen.

Unsure of why he started his lunch early, Woody followed Dexter out to the kitchen and opened the back door for him when Dex tapped. On the deck, Woody sank into one of the chairs that overlooked the yard and inhaled the cool air. An unknown worry tugged at the corner of his mind and he tried to reel it in... to grasp it, analyze it. A knot twisted in his stomach as dread kicked in. You are in danger, it seemed to say.

Being one who was typically in control of his body, this new turn of events worried Woody. He was a person who had never done drugs throughout his life, simply because he didn't want to ever feel out of control. He even shied away from over-the-counter medications if he knew they would make him feel loopy. Now, here he was feeling out of control of his body.

Simply put, he felt... well... off. Like he imagined a bad trip would be — except this trip made him want to simply squeeze his eyes shut tight, curl in a ball, and go to sleep until it passed.

A sound from inside startled him awake — he hadn't realized he dozed off. He jumped up off the chair and ran inside the house. At his computer, the timer had elapsed for almost two hours and the system was prompting him to click that he was available and back on shift. Because he hadn't been at his desk when his lunch hour finished, the system started sending reminders to confirm that he was back, which then escalated to frequent chimes and flashing messages asking him to acknowledge he was available and ready to take a customer chat.

Woody knew he was going to get an email from his boss once the daily production report hit his boss's desk in the morning, but he didn't care. Woody clicked the override button asking to end his shift. When the system prompted the reason for his request, he checked the radio button labeled "Ill", submitted the request, and then logged off the system. With the sun hitting the bedroom window, Woody pulled off his tennis shoes, wiggled out of his pants, pulled his shirt over his head, and slipped into bed.

Not understanding the break from the regimen, Dexter let out a heavy breath, flopped his body down on the floor with a thump, got back up, and turned around, then lay back down again. One minute later, Dex stood, jumped up on the bed, turned his back toward Woody, and plopped down next to him, his body stretched out against him.

Woody didn't notice as sleep had already consumed him.

Chapter Four

The power in his legs wasn't something he had noticed the night before. When sleep had overtaken him, Stone had slept most of the night as well as all day. At least it felt like an entire day had passed since he had curled up on his crude bed.

He wondered if he was nocturnal and was supposed to sleep during the day. Still, he didn't remember stirring. He hadn't even been awakened by the need to piss.

Now, his instinct told him to run blindly, and he followed it recklessly. When the landscape turned flat with little obstruction, he found himself sprinting over the flat land at a speed he could not fathom as being possible. Still, possible or not, he had the power. Another thing he noticed was he could run upright, or on all fours. Somewhere along the way, he adopted a hybrid gait — sometimes loping on all fours and sometimes only on the hind legs, depending on the terrain.

The light from the moon fell through a small sliver, leaving shadows alone to wreak havoc among the timid. Stone took advantage of the dimly lit sky and stayed close to the dark, lest he should be seen by an innocent, becoming the fuel that fed their nightmares.

The scent hit his nostrils before he saw it. He slowed his approach, cautious. He wasn't scared of what someone might do to him if they spotted him. He knew his new body could handle itself and he would always be the victor.

Instead, he was scared of what he might do to them if they locked eyes. Even now, the thought and anticipation of that warm, sweet flesh brought him once again to that state of arousal. Bloodlust.

He spotted several tents scattered around the area. Farther off in the distance, several campers and trailers were parked. Why had his instincts pulled him to a highly inhabited campground? He was trying so hard to fight the need, yet here he was, a buffet surrounding him. Like an alcoholic just hanging out at the bar.

Stone pulled his thoughts away from carnage, trying to focus one more time on what everything meant. He certainly couldn't have been put in this body to ravage and destroy. He had to have a higher purpose. Until he knew it, he would have to control his urges, which would be easier said than done.

Stone spotted the brick buildings then. A duplex of bathroom facilities that many campgrounds had. Curiosity overcame him. Stone scanned the campground, looking for movement. He saw nothing. Listening, he heard nothing but the crackles of a couple of almost burnt-out fires. He estimated it to be in the wee hours of the morning, long after the campers and partiers had slugged their last beer and crawled into their sleeping bags. Cautiously, he stalked toward the restrooms. He had to know.

At the door, he looked around again. Stillness. He wrapped a hand-paw around the pull handle, yanked, and slipped inside.

The room was illuminated by a dimly lit single bulb with a wire cage around it. Along the wall in front of him were two sinks; next to those were two urinals and, in the far corner, a stall.

Stone approached the sinks, looking down. Fear held his eyes to the porcelain. Fear of what he was. Fear that by acknowledging it, he would be destined to stay this way forever.

His eyes shifted to the stranger's in the mirror. The details of his face gave him no indication as to his identity. As he suspected, he wasn't human. He stared at the hair covering his body. *I have fur. I am covered in fucking fur.* His ears appeared to be canine, as were his snout and teeth, but this wasn't an ordinary dog. This was a dog on steroids and acid and anything else you could think of that took the cute, fuzzy image of a dog and made it terrifying. His jaws were long and powerful, his teeth razor-sharp, as if he could snap a tree trunk in half.

The reflection of his eyes pulled him closer, and he studied them — they were deep red, but semi-covered with patterns of black haze, as if a storm cloud was floating across the surface. The nose was black. He touched it with his hand-paw. It felt dry and cracked.

Catching the sight of his paw in the mirror, he pulled it away and studied it in the dim light. It was bigger than he remembered, almost the size of a catcher's mitt. His paws were connected to beefy forearms, his biceps bulging. The remainder of his body was built and powerful.

What am I?

He stepped back and took in his full seven-foot frame. Almost like a wolf, but not really. He thought how he walked upright when he wasn't running at great speeds. Posture of a man. *I think like a man. But what's with the dog suit I'm in?*

Stone stared again at his head — his face. A strange creature stared back at him. He felt like he was a passive soul in an alternate life, but the face staring back at him was sinister and foreboding. If it wasn't him inside of the beast, he would have been scared shitless.

A scent caught in his nostrils, and he found himself back outside, scanning the campsite for movement. The scent was strong, sickly sweet, and overpowering. He slipped into the shadows on the side of the building, famished, confused, angry, scared.

The click of a latch sounded, and Stone sensed movement from the restroom door — the one on the other side of the building. The scent intensified, and he heard the slapping of flip-flops as they flapped ground to heel, ground to heel.

Before he could react, she was there. Her face mere inches away from his. Her features locked in a portrait of fear, her worst nightmare realized. The bloodlust took over and, with lightning-quick speed, Stone's claws from his right paw were clamped around the girl's mouth, her body pressed up against the stone wall.

"Don't... scream," he managed to growl, his throaty voice barely a whisper.

Her body trembled and her feet started fighting for purchase on the hard, dirt earth. It was then he realized he had underestimated his strength and he was holding her a foot off the ground.

He caught her heartbeat pulsing through her throat with his peripheral vision.

I must have her.

His face lowered to her neck, and she tried to scream, but he clamped his claw down tighter over her mouth. "Scream again and die."

Her body relaxed.

The pheromones she gave off ravaged his senses. His mind was rent with conflicting emotions.

Rip her throat out. Her flesh is yours. He raked one of his fangs across her delicate, white shoulder.

She's an innocent. You're not a killer. His internal voice caused him to pause, looking into her eyes once again. *Is this what people look like when they know they're going to die?*

A tear slid down her right cheek.

What the fuck am I doing? Was I really going to tear her throat out? He slid her body down the rough surface of the wall until her feet touched the ground.

"Shhh... shhh, please. It's okay. I'm not going to hurt you, but I need you to listen to me."

She nodded the best she could with his hand clamped around her face.

"I'm going to uncover your mouth. Don't yell or it will be your last time. Do you understand?"

She blinked rapidly and nodded. Stone slowly removed his hand from her mouth. "What's your name?"

Her lip trembled, but she said nothing.

"Please. I'm sorry I scared you. Your name."

"S... Sarah," she whispered.

"You can't tell anyone about me, do you understand, Sarah?"

"Yes." Her head bobbed up and down rapidly. "I understand."

"If you say anything about me, I'll come back for you."

"I promise."

"You sure? Not a word. Not to your husband. Nobody."

"N... no husband. Here with the girls. Th... they wouldn't believe me, anyway. Please. Just let me go." Hope blossomed in her eyes.

"Until next time, Sarah."

She looked at him, unsure.

"Walk back to your camp. Don't turn around. I won't follow you."

"How do I know? I don't want to die!" Fresh tears sprang from her eyes.

"Because, Sarah, if I wanted you dead, you'd already be dead."

She nodded, an understanding sifting to the top of her emotions. After one more glance, she turned, took a few steps, then stopped. She did not turn around.

"What—?"

"It's better if you don't know," he interrupted. "Please. Go. Before I change my mind."

Before she made it twenty feet, he was gone.

Chapter Five

Woody sat up in bed, disoriented. The room was dark, and no light filtered through the window blinds. He looked over at the clock. Almost three thirty in the morning. Had he really slept all afternoon and all night? It was unfathomable.

His bladder screamed at him, and he kicked his feet over the edge of the bed. Dexter jumped off the bed and ran out into the living room.

"Oh shit. Sorry, Dex." Knowing Dexter had been locked inside all afternoon and all night and hadn't eaten, either, Woody scurried after Dexter, flipping on lights as he went. He flicked the locks open on the back door, and Dexter tore off to the grassy area, stopping to relieve himself for an exorbitant period of time before he started sniffing in various places while he circled, searching for the right spot to finish his business.

Unable to hold it any longer himself, Woody went to the edge of the cement slab and drained his own bladder on the nearest plant. Dexter cocked his head sideways, looked between Woody and the bush, and then sniffed the bush.

"You aren't the only one who can mark shit around here," Woody said. Inside, Woody scooped kibble into Dex's bowl, set it down for him, then rummaged around in the freezer for something to eat. Woody's stomach growled loudly, causing Dexter to stop eating and look up from his bowl.

After microwaving an individual frozen pizza, Woody sat down at the table and scarfed it down. He was still hungry after, and in the fridge, he found the leftover salad from two nights before. Only after eating it also did the hunger pains in his gut start to subside.

What is going on with me? I have never slept this long before. He took inventory of his symptoms: exhaustion, muddled thoughts, lethargy. He knew he didn't have the flu or even a cold — the indicators just weren't there, so what could be causing him to feel the way he did?

Looking at the clock on the kitchen stove, Woody knew it would be time to wake up in an hour for work. Dare he go back to bed? His mind said no, but his body said yes. With his decision made, he set his alarm clock just in case, so he wasn't late. He was asleep again within a minute of pulling the covers up to his chin.

Chapter Six

Stone sat and swayed back and forth, having returned to his cluster of trees, to his makeshift bed. "I almost killed her. I almost shredded her throat."

That's what you do. You're a killer. You were built for this. Embrace it.

"No! I won't embrace it. This isn't me. I don't know what I'm doing here. Let me out. Let me OUT!" he growled.

Don't fight it. It's in your blood.

Stone sprang to his feet and attacked the nearest tree, lashing out at it with his claws, landing thunderous punches against it, bending, twisting, breaking, until it resembled something that had been caught in a hurricane.

"I can't. I won't. She was so innocent. So sweet. This isn't me."

His mind had no response.

"I refuse."

Silence.

"I'll kill myself first."

Stone's mind snapped to his latest concession. He would be too chickenshit to do it normally, but under the circumstances? He had no life. He was stuck in a body that embraced everything he abhorred. Could he really do it?

Could this... this beast die? What would happen to him if the body no longer existed? Would his mind — his soul — go back to where they were supposed to be?

The memory of the bloodlust overcame him, looping through his thoughts. He had no choice. When it was time to kill, he would kill. When the grip of the disease steered his thoughts and controlled his actions, his mind was nothing but an unwilling passenger. Or was it? He had been driven to kill Sarah. To tear her throat out, yet he had somehow fought the urge. He fought it, and he won. He was in control then, and he could be in control again. He just had to want it... to fight for it. To hold on to the fact that good would always crush evil.

A scent hit his nostrils.

Not human.

His hunger unsatiated, he knew he must feed.

He silently got up from the ground and waited, listening, watching, smelling. A crackling sounded through the tree line to his left. He made his way to the edge of the pines, slipped into the shadows, and snatched the animal up before it realized he was even there.

His pride turned to panic as he realized he was holding a skunk. He didn't need to have clarity to know how bad things were about to get, and without thinking about it, he ripped the skunk's ass off — tail attached — and hurled it above the trees like a hand grenade with the pin pulled, hearing it land some hundred yards away with a soft plop.

The animal was clearly in shock, and Stone immediately removed its head and tossed it to the side before crunching into the furry underbelly of the critter, blood and viscera splattering the front of him and the ground around him. He didn't stop until nothing was left but the fur pelt, the bones strewn about, lying where he had spit them.

Exerted, he slumped to the ground, the adrenaline from the hunt and feast subsiding. He looked down at his paws, the flesh a crimson color. Bile rose up in his throat as he tried to calm his emotions.

"Is this what I've become?" His body heaved with sobs as he blubbered into his hand-paws. He loathed himself. He wondered if the talon-like claws on his hands could rend his throat into strips of pulpy fur and flesh. If they could, would he bleed out? Could he die, or was he one of those monsters who was exiled to walk the earth for all eternity, feeding on the bodies and souls of others?

The house on the hill crept into his mind. There was a familiarity about it. He felt drawn there. Yet he knew he should stay away. Just like at the campground, he had been overcome. He was blinded by the need. He couldn't give in. He had to control himself.

But who was that person in the house on the hill? Why was he so drawn to it? Was it the key to all the mystery shrouding his identity? His newfound self?

Suddenly, Stone felt an overwhelming need to know what was behind door number one. The way to the house was ingrained in him, like a map built into a GPS unit. He did not falter as he traveled the distance to the overgrown hillside and started traversing his way up. The air was moist yet crisp. The slight breeze drove away the quiet. The stars were neatly tucked into their cloud blanket. It would still be dark for a couple more hours.

Outside the house, Stone settled down behind a row of shrubs. He waited. Daylight would soon come, and maybe his questions would be answered.

But you've never been out in daylight before.

He hadn't even realized how true the thought was until he had it, and he was overwhelmed by the accuracy. He pondered what that meant. Would the sunlight turn him to dust like a vampire? Would he turn back into the man he was supposed to be? Anxious, he decided to wait it out. One way or another, he would find out what it was he needed in this house. The one on the hill.

Around five-thirty a.m., Stone's attention was pulled to the window when a light popped on inside the house.

Chapter Seven

The scent grew stronger. A door opened. Stone could hear the jingle of a collar as a dog explored the backyard. He slunk back tighter behind the shrub, thankful the breeze was blowing away from the house. The dog went back inside. Shadows cast against the now-covered windows as the figure inside moved around. Stone tried to imagine who was there and what they were doing inside. Strange smells of food and fragrance wafted to him, ever so slight, yet they were there. Stone took deep breaths, his chest tightening as he felt that familiar urge.

I have to fight this. I'll never know what this is all about if I give in—if I lose my head.

Sounds permeated the structure as well. Footsteps. A playful bark. The hissing flame of a water heater. Someone is getting ready to start their day.

A memory flashed. *Why is this so familiar?*

He's in the shower himself, yet he had no fur. Another spark. Breakfast. Cooking food. Cooking inside on a stove. Putting on clothes. Not naked. Not furry.

The bloodlust slammed into his senses and took control, and Stone had to physically pull his body back to keep it from ravaging that hole through the side of the house that he had many times fantasized about. The person in there... they're evil. They're responsible. But how? And responsible for what?

He vomited onto the ground, so nauseous at the conflicting thoughts having a boxing match inside his head. He wanted to shred, kill, maim, but he feared that doing so would keep him from ever finding the answers that he was looking for. He pulled himself back, his body shuddering.

He listened, watched. The noises changed from room to room. The first glint of sunlight cracked over the horizon. Some of the shadows were pushed away. His mind snapped and then sprang back, clarity pouring into the void and filling every empty crevice. The bloodlust called for the final time. This time, Stone did not hold back.

The front door came off the hinges with so much force that it shattered the dining room table and sent the shards through the window on the far side of the house. The noise was like an explosion — deafening. As Stone scrambled through the door, he scanned the room. Empty.

A bark immediately started up from the hallway, loud, seemingly ferocious, the dog volunteering to lead the charge against a creature that it had never seen before, a creature that it underestimated.

Stone was surprised to hear a guttural growl come out of his own throat as he rushed toward the hall. Brave to its own detriment, the dog leapt through the air, latched onto Stone's shoulder, and tried to tear a chunk out. Rage overtook Stone, and he reached for the dog's throat, ready to tear it out.

Wait! You have a dog. You love dogs.

This epiphany threw Stone for a loop, and the dog started flinging its body back and forth, trying to use its weight to pull Stone to the ground.

Struggling to keep upright, Stone stumbled over to a door set in the wall by the stove. He flung it open to find a pantry. He stumbled inside, the dog hanging from his shoulder. He reached with his right hand and tried to pull the dog's mouth loose, but its jaw was in a death clamp.

Out of options, and not wanting to hurt the dog, Stone grabbed the broom hanging from a hook on the wall and threaded the handle through the empty space at the back of the dog's jaw, the wooden rod pushing through the gap on the left side of its jaw and exiting the right side. Stone applied downward pressure on the broom handle as if he was jacking a car up off the ground. Finally, the pressure proved to be too much, the dog loosened its grip, and Stone tore his shoulder out from the teeth ripping into it, leaving the dog biting down on the wood handle instead.

Giving the broomstick a twist, the dog was thrown onto its back, and Stone took the opportunity to run out of the pantry and slam the door behind him. The dog went crazy and started tearing at the door with its nails. Luckily the door was solid wood, and the beast wouldn't be loose any time soon.

Stone turned back toward the hallway, a small rivulet of blood running down his shoulder. The brief scuffle with the dog had pulled his attention away from why he was here, but with the dog in time-out, his rage returned. The bloodlust returned. He knew his purpose, and it was time to get his.

Obviously, the owner of the house knew Stone was there. He had lost any element of surprise he had when he knocked the door down. Rather than play a game of cat and mouse, he decided to go after what was his. Whatever happened, he could live with it.

Stone stalked down the hallway toward where he knew the bedrooms to be. He paused to look at a painting on the wall — it was one he remembered. He had passed it the night of the last Christmas party here when he had gone to use the restroom. It was cold. Sterile.

Like the inhabitant of the house.

At the bedroom door, Stone heard a shotgun slide. He stepped around into the center of the doorway, the man inside standing beside the bed, the gun pointed in Stone's direction.

"I don't know what the fuck you are, but if you don't get out now, you'll be a dead fuck."

"Hello, Ron." The sound coming out of Stone's throat was cold, calculating.

"How... how do you know my name?" The gun shook in Ron's hands.

"Just like you not to remember. How does it feel to be the most narcissistic asshole on the planet?"

A trickle of familiarity flashed through Ron's eyes.

"I dedicated most of my adult life to that company. I put up with your crap for twenty-five years. When I couldn't stand by and watch you shit on all the little people anymore, you instead turn on me? Ruin my life?"

"Woody? What happened to you?"

"You happened to me."

"I mean... are... are you some fucking animal?"

Woody grabbed the shotgun by the barrel and twisted, both shots firing, sending chunks of splintered doorframe in a shower throughout the room. Smashing the nearby window with the butt of the gun, Woody threw it outside on the back lawn.

"Now, where were we?"

"It wasn't my... my fault, what happened to you. You did it to yourself."

"Because I wouldn't stand by any longer and watch you destroy people? Because I have a conscience? Integrity?"

"Because you messed up. You broke the rules and you had to go. You can't blame that on anyone but yourself. I'm not going to take the fall for that."

"Or, at least that's what you told them, right? That I broke the rules? That I was acting inappropriately? Who are they going to listen to? The narcissistic prick who nobody will stand up to, because they are scared of what he might do to them, or the manager that must have lost his mind overnight and done things that were extremely out of character for him?"

Ron glared at Woody, his eyes spewing hatred.

"You know, I never realized just how insecure you really were until right now. I wasn't a bright light on your team to you. I was a threat. You knew I was smarter than you. Better than you."

"Get out of my house, Woody. I'm calling the cops."

"I'm afraid I can't allow you to do that, Ron. Hey, did you know you destroyed my life? Yeah! True story. I pretty much lost everything. Oh yeah, you remember Marcy, don't you? Yeah... funny thing about her. She'd dead. Fucking heart attack, Ron. Her ticker just couldn't handle the stress of what our life had become, thanks to your generosity."

"This is the last time I ask you to leave."

"Or what? What, Ron? What are you going to do about it?"

"I'm go... goo... g—"

"Goo goo, gah gah," Woody mocked. "What's the matter, little baby, Ron? You going to shit your pants?"

Ron sprinted toward the open master bathroom door and tried to slam it on Woody, who was already halfway through it before it was even partially closed. Trapped, Ron put the only barrier he could between Woody and himself. He clambered into the shower stall and slammed the glass door between them.

Woody stopped, looking through the glass as if he were selecting a lobster from the tank right before he dropped it into boiling water. Ron cowered, resolved in the fact he was in no way talking himself out of this situation. A rancid smell hit

Woody's nostrils — urine and feces. The man had soiled himself.

Woody stared through the glass at the man who had ended everything for him. But it wasn't the material things that bothered him the most. It was the fact that he had lost all trust in humanity. This was the true end for him. In a world where he once mattered, he was discarded, tossed away by colleagues and friends. He had become a leper and a loner. He no longer had a purpose in life. He was merely sucking up oxygen in the atmosphere, waiting to die.

Woody's hatred soared, and he felt the raw, overpowering pull to destroy. To rip. To shred. To maul. He finally understood why he was drawn to the house on the hill and what his purpose had become. To live a good life was not going to be enough. It never had been. It never would be.

Woody's fist smashed into the safety glass, shattering it into a million fragmented pieces. Ron threw himself down into the corner of the tile, his arms over his face. Woody's claws shot out from his hands and he pulled back, ready to strike.

This isn't you, remember? You're not a killer.

That nagging voice in the back of his mind was back. It was right. He wasn't a killer. Never had been. He was a kind, compassionate, considerate soul who cared for others and nurtured them, not destroyed them. Who was he to play God? Who was he to decide what was fair? True, this guy was one of the biggest dirtbags he had ever met, but did that mean he deserved to die?

Woody lowered his right arm to his side. The claws retracted. The bloodlust drained from his eyes. Ron must have sensed the change. He lowered his arms, the fear in his eyes turning to wonderment.

The slash across Ron's face caught him off guard, and one of the claws hooked his left eyeball and pulled it out of the socket. It hung down by the optic nerve, bobbing against his nose.

"See you in hell, Ron, but just so you know, I'm going to be the one in charge this time." Woody thrust his claws underneath Ron's ribcage and shredded up, pulling out everything he could grab a hold of like he was removing the engine and transmission from a car.

Ron's fluids leaked out of him and his mouth started working as if he was trying to say something, but only a clicking sound emanated. Finally, his mouth fell open, his face in death mimicking the stupid look he carried on his face during his sordid, pathetic life.

Taking one last look at the carnage he had left behind — he hoped that whoever had to do the cleanup was thankful that he had kept most of the blood in the shower stall — he headed toward the front door. It was then that the barking and growling started up again on the other side of the pantry door, the nails joining in, most assuredly carving deep grooves on the other side of the door.

He must be hungry, Woody thought.

He turned and went back into the bathroom. The corpse looked pale and weak, and it was then Woody realized he should never have let that asshole have so much power over him. He bent down and lifted Ron's chin before grabbing the head in his hands, and with one quick twisting, ripping, movement, he detached the head from the body. In the kitchen, he held the head in his right hand and grabbed the pantry doorknob with his left.

"Dinnertime!" he yelled, tossing the head inside and slamming the door.

Epilogue

"Another rum and Coke, please."

"Coming right up."

Woody drained the rest of his glass and waited for the new drink to be served. It wasn't that he had stepped up from beer to hard alcohol. He just liked to mix it up a bit now that he was getting out and socializing a little more.

"Here you go, Woody. Want me to put this on your tab?"

"That'd be great, Bruce. Thank you."

Okay, so he was getting out a lot. Every day, actually. Woody had a different outlook on life since the morning of the incident that happened in the house on the hill. A house he had been to a couple of times for his company Christmas parties. A house that Ron had owned with his wife before she tired of his bullshit and took half of everything. A house that was on a five-acre lot in a sprawling mountain neighborhood approximately five miles away from Woody's property.

Answering the question of why he had changed into something else was a little more difficult. When he found himself back with his own body, in his own house, on his own hill, he was relieved, to say the least, but the fear of turning back into that thing left him scared shitless. He turned to research — dozens of hours of it — to try and determine how it was all possible. The only random information he was able to turn up was a handful of police reports, all public record, where the old man who owned his home prior reported mysterious happenings on the hill.

Some sort of altar he found in a clearing of trees. The sound of chanting carried on the wind. Dead animals. Later, the old man would report a run-in with a stranger and threats of a curse cast upon the property that had him fearing for his life. Woody couldn't help but feel that might explain them finding the dead man's bones months later.

The police had thought he was crazy. Maybe he wasn't so crazy, after all.

If Woody lived under a curse, there was a chance that he could change again if another huge injustice decimated his life. Rather than move, he decided to be careful. He did not ever want to put himself in a situation again where he woke up to a furry mirror.

Woody took a sip of his drink and pulled a cigarette out of his pack. He grabbed his Bic and lit it, exhaling the smoke up into the air.

"Excuse me."

Woody turned. A pretty girl who was probably in her thirties was standing there. He had noticed her playing pool with three other women earlier.

"Hi there," Woody said, unsure of what else to say, quite rusty at making small talk.

"Could I bum a smoke?"

"Sure thing. You run out?"

"Not exactly."

Woody raised a puzzled eyebrow.

"Um, well, I don't normally smoke, but this seems like a good time to start."

Woody laughed, a light, easy-going chuckle. "What's the occasion?"

"Not sure. Honestly, I've been sitting over there for the last two games wondering where I know you from. You look so damn familiar."

"I don't believe we've ever met, miss. Although now that you mention it," he looked into her eyes, "I think I've seen you before, somewhere. Do you come here a lot?"

"First time." She slid up on the barstool next to him.

"Well, we hopefully have time to figure it out." He held out his hand. "Nice to meet you. I'm Woody."

"Nice to meet you, too, Woody. I'm Sarah."

R.E. SARGENT is an editor, publisher, and the author of four novels, five novelettes, and many short stories in the genres of horror, suspense, and supernatural. He is an active member of the Horror Writers Association, the Alliance of Independent Authors, and the Community of Literary Magazines and Presses. His short story, "Lucy," was featured in the 2021 Splatterpunk Award-nominated anthology *If I Die Before I Wake Volume 3 – Tales of Deadly Women and Retribution*.

R.E. lives in the Pacific Northwest with his wife and their granddogs, Turbo and Diesel. And the rain. Lots and lots of rain. He is thankful that writing is an indoor activity.

His scope of work can be found on Amazon at https://www.amazon.com/stores/R.E.-Sargent/author/B072N 46VW8

USE YOUR POWER
BY KIRSTEN NOELLE CRAIG

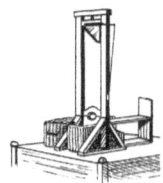

*T*he towering glass building glinted in the mid-morning sunlight, a monolith of power and prestige. In front of the building, pigeons strutted back and forth, pecking at discarded bagels. I studied the birds while wringing my hands. I wanted this new gig to work. My stomach flipped, and I daydreamed about being a pigeon instead of a stressed-out human on the verge of ruin. I had been dreading today. It was my first day as an entry-level employee at a company I never thought I would have the chance to join.

Cosma was an exclusive, Fortune 500 company that did work for the ultra-rich and powerful. What exactly they did at Cosma was kept top secret. I knew that having your foot in the door there could change your life. I needed my life to change.

I checked the time and decided it was now or never. I had a meeting with the hiring lead at eight. He laid out exactly what the meeting was about, but I assumed we would discuss what my role would be at the company. Speaking to him on the phone had been difficult as he spoke in such a neutral, clipped way. He likely wouldn't be sympathetic to my panic attacks or poor mental health. I couldn't afford to be late or to screw up this opportunity. My student loan payments were piling up by the day.

The loan I had gotten to pay for therapy was close to going to collections. This was something I needed desperately. I drew in a deep breath of humid Atlanta air and headed into the Cosma building.

Frigid, stale air pumped into the building from somewhere above. It whined a barely perceptible hiss as it escaped the vents. Everything inside the building felt manufactured and soulless. The lights immediately began to bother me. They were harsh, pulsing with an audible hum that caused my ears to ring. I wished I could wear my headphones in places like this. I focused on my breathing and tried to tune out the noise.

A series of terse directions from the front desk guard brought me to my destination, the sixth floor. After several more awkward interactions, I found myself standing in front of the hiring lead, Tim, forcing myself to maintain a calm energy.

"Let's chat," Tim said as he gestured toward an open office door.

I followed him in and took a seat. The spacious leather chair squeaked loudly as I sat. Tim's office was minimalist to the point of drab. He seemed to have no personal effects decorating the room. His desk was neat and tidy, sporting none of the usual paperwork clutter or framed family photos. Tim was a minimalist.

Rather than trusting the thought drawing my attention, I glanced around the room — No one uses this office.

He remained standing, casually leaning against his desk and crossing his tan arms over his chest. "You're Beth." He smiled thinly at me, waiting for my response.

My stomach lurched at being called that name. I know all my paperwork and information listed my name as August. I told myself he must have seen the name on a background check or other legal document and forced a smile of my own. "It's August, sir. My name is August. They/Them pronouns, please."

Tim couldn't hide the look of distaste that briefly flashed across his chiseled face. He tipped his head in acknowledgment and moved on to the next topic.

After half an hour or so of Tim talking without really explaining anything, he reached into his desk drawer and brought out some paperwork. "I do have one more thing for you to look over and sign," he said as he handed the stack of documents to me.

"We will also need a sample of your blood. That can be arranged by visiting our in-house lab." He mentioned it so casually that for a few seconds, I didn't register what he had said.

"You need... a blood sample from me?" My palms became sweaty at the thought of having to undergo a medical procedure when I was already nervous as hell about starting this job.

Tim waved his hand toward me dismissively. "Yes, yes. Just to make sure everything is on the up and up. Standard stuff." He walked me to the door, paperwork clutched in my hands, and pointed to a sign several doors down from his office. "Follow the signs for the lab. Good luck." He disappeared into his office and didn't look back.

***

Arm bandaged tightly, I shuffled down the small hallway toward my new cubicle. The medical staff in the lab hadn't spoken more than five words to me and that was a blessing. My mouth felt like cotton and bile randomly threatened to claw up my throat.

My nerves were out of control. I had only been an intern at Cosma for an hour now and already the urge to quit consumed me. During our awkward conversation, Tim explained to me that I would have my own cubicle but would be shadowing a trainer named Lee. I nervously glanced at the many cubicles I passed on my way past them.

Each cubicle housed a nondescript employee and a blocky desktop computer. Despite there being other people working in the office, it felt abandoned to me.

Lee was a short, stocky Black man who immediately put me at ease with his calming demeanor and easy smile. He extended his hand for a handshake when I walked up. We exchanged typical pleasantries before Lee offered to give me a tour of all the important areas at Cosma. I let my shoulders and jaw relax as I followed Lee around. He pointed out the copy room, break room, supply closet, and restrooms. I noted with relief that the two standard bathrooms located next to the supply closet were all-gender, single-stall.

Near the end of the tour, we passed an unmarked door with a coded padlock on the knob. I stopped in front of it and listened. The hum of something electrical was loud behind the door. The frequency of the sound was strong enough that I felt my arm hair rise in response to it. This wasn't just a room with a lot of fluorescent lights. Something massive and requiring tons of power was stored there.

Without thinking, I leaned in and pressed my ear against the door. I strained to make out what was causing the noise, hearing only the consuming hum.

Lee turned back to me when he noticed I had paused at the door. He moved quickly toward me, concern creasing his forehead, and a grimace slashed across his face. "That room is off limits," he commanded.

Questions formed on my tongue *(What the hell is in that room?!)* but I hesitated; my curiosity became even stronger after his reaction. "Uh. Okay?" I took one last look at the oddly pulsing secret room and followed Lee back to the cubicles.

***

The next few hours passed in a haze. Lee had urged me to spend time setting up my computer and creating a work email. I also had several training videos I needed to watch. Beyond those tasks, I still had no idea what my goal was at this job.

I attempted not to linger on that anxiety for too long. I feared I would run out of tasks to complete before my actual work was explained to me. In the periphery of my brain, I sensed the overbearing quiet of the office space. Typically, there would be at least some clacking of keys or clicking of computer mice. I glanced up periodically to make sure I wasn't completely alone. No one made eye contact with me.

Around lunchtime, an email pinged in my newly created work inbox. It was from Tim, and he was requesting I come to his office for a "chat". My stomach was too unsettled to eat anything, so I made my way back down the cramped hallway to Tim's office. I felt like a seven-year-old being told to visit the principal.

I was certain I hadn't done anything yet to warrant any kind of scolding. Nonetheless, panic coursed through my body. Every moment I had been in this building so far had been uncomfortable and off. This wasn't just my brain being difficult and trying to sabotage me. Something was wrong at this company. I had to decide if I wanted to find out why badly enough to possibly lose this chance at a new life.

"Come in, please." Tim was standing behind his desk when I swung the door open.

He appeared just as nonplussed as he was that morning. Clearly, the stress of the workday was not an issue for him. I sat without being asked to and looked down at my lap to avoid eye contact.

Tim cleared his throat. "Your bloodwork came back satisfactory." I wasn't sure if he expected a response or not, so I said nothing. "Lee says you've been shown the area and given all the basic instructions?" The inflection at the end of that sentence let me know he was asking me to confirm this.

I glanced up and nodded.

"Good, good." Tim shifted from foot to foot and cocked his head. "Did you have any questions for me... August?"

My name, coming from his mouth, sounded like an accusation. I swallowed the hateful response I wanted to unleash. I had years of practice dealing with people who thought I was beneath them. Despite how painful it was for me to know someone didn't like me simply because of a set of social markers in a manila folder

(Poor, queer, mentally ill) I knew my best bet was to pretend I was unbothered and compliant. I spoke up, "Yes. Actually. I am not certain still what all I need to be doing." I met Tim's eyes. His expression remained neutral. He waited for me to elaborate. "I know Lee helped get me started but... what do I do now?"

Tim smiled at me. It was a smile that felt like razors, and it did nothing to reduce the anxiety I was feeling. He tapped a finger against his desk, sharp and quick. "Yes. I suppose you might want to know that, wouldn't you? Well. Head back to your cubicle and you will receive email instructions shortly." I opened my mouth to ask what he meant, but he interrupted, "That will be all."

I left his office feeling worse than when I went in. The empty, heavy feeling of the building wrapped around me as I walked out. I realized I was just as confused about my role at Cosma and my hopefulness about this job was waning fast.

***

Despite how urgently I told myself to keep my head down and ignore the worry I was feeling, my mind reeled. Growing up in a toxic environment while fighting like hell to dig my way out made me observant of my environment. Something was off at Cosma and it wasn't just Tim's unethical managerial skills.

Running through my available options I decided to talk to Lee. Lee was an overall pleasant person. He knew the ins and outs of the company. It wouldn't hurt for me to ask him a few questions. The worst-case scenario was he tells me to mind my business and I learn nothing. If Lee told me something I didn't want to hear about the company, it would also be the worst-case scenario for me. I hadn't skipped lunch that day just because I was stressed. I had to figure this out.

Lee sat in his cubicle, typing monotonously on the computer. The blue light of the monitor washed his face in an eerie glow. I walked up from the right side of the cubicle, not wanting to alarm him. I cleared my throat softly. Lee continued typing.

I leaned forward a bit to attempt to get his attention again. My eyes flicked to his computer screen and my stomach sank. "Cosma is all Cosma is all Cosma is all" was stretched across the open document repeatedly. "Lee?" I whispered his name, which hung in the silent space like an anchor.

His head snapped toward me without warning. I stumbled a few steps back in shock. His eyes met mine and I immediately wished he would look away.

Lee's eyes were completely black. There was no iris, pupil, or even white space located within them. His eyes were just black. A trickle of blood ran from his right nostril. His mouth was slightly open, and I could see his teeth were grinding against each other, jaw working as if against his will. I backed up several more paces.

My hip bumped into my desk, and I realized I was in my own cubicle. Lee turned slowly back to his computer, teeth grinding and fingers slamming into the keyboard.

Panicking, I stepped carefully to the next closest cubicle. Lee was the only person at Cosma I felt I could ask for help, and he was clearly in an altered mental state. The person slumped in the chair at the next cubicle had dark curls framing their head like a halo. One arm of their grey, tailored suit hung sadly by their side.

The same unsettling blue light shone from the employee's computer screen; indecipherable lines of text spread out across the page just like Lee's. It seemed I was going to have to figure out what was going on at Cosma by myself.

***

I collapsed into my office chair with my head resting on the cool surface of the desk. I breathed in and out slowly, willing my heart to slow down. I couldn't breathe, let alone formulate a plan in my current state. I contemplated taking one of my anxiety pills, but I quickly decided against it. I wanted to be as clear-headed as possible to navigate this.

It seemed obvious to me that the off-limits room with the pulsing sound waves was where I needed to check for answers. Secrecy alone meant it housed something important. I knew the door was opened by a passcode, fingerprint, or slide card.

Certainly, Lee had a card to gain access to the room. All I had to do was take his entry card from him and hope that whatever scary situation he was in didn't make him violent.

Lee's entry card was on a Cosma brand lanyard around his neck. I silently approached his back and stopped inches from his head. He continued typing, as if in a trance. My presence didn't slow or disrupt his mission. I lightly pulled on the strings of the lanyard and began to lift it up. The key clacking continued. I managed to clear Lee's head with the lanyard. My breath was held the entire time. I feared even one exhalation of air against the back of his neck would tip Lee over the edge. I tensed every arm muscle as I lifted the lanyard up and away from the zombie keyboard employee.

I suppressed a whoop of triumph and shoved the key card into my back pocket. Lee filled another line on his screen with, "Cosma is all."

I sped as quickly down the hallway as I could without running. I didn't want any other attention on me than there already was. I was so focused on stealth, I almost passed the locked door. My brain was going a million miles a minute and my body was struggling to keep up. Standing in front of the door, I felt that threatening energy once again. Chill bumps broke out along my arms. I wrung my hands as I had this morning, twisting the Cosma lanyard in between my fingers.

Everything on the line with this job flashed in my head — my dumpy apartment, my car, my credit score, and my sanity. I thought about how awful Lee looked, stuck in that rictus state of whatever it was, typing away on the computer for eternity. How many other people are being harmed by Cosma? Could I just ignore the bad things happening here?

Decision resolved; I slid Lee's key card through the door's keypad. The tiny light on the pad turned green and I slowly swung the door open. I stared at the inner workings of the room but saw only black. As my eyes adjusted, I stepped into the dark room. It was a hallway. This company is fond of hallways. At the end of the hallway there appeared to be another door, sickly light spilling from underneath it. I moved toward it.

The closer I got to the door, the more my fear grew. Sweat dotted my forehead, and my hands shook. This door had no lock like the previous one. It didn't even seem to have a doorknob. The sound pounded into my ears and dulled all my other senses.

The pulsation from behind the door surged, drilling into my consciousness. I threw my hands up to cover my ears. It felt like a worm was burrowing its way into my thoughts. I shook my head, hoping it would dislodge the sensation. From deep in my brain, I heard a voice burble up. This was not my voice. This was a voice that sounded like thousands of voices speaking at all once in a single, powerful voice.

"COSMA IS ALL!" it bellowed, simultaneously vibrating inside my awareness and inside the room. It was too much, and I fell forward, slamming my palm into the door to stop myself. When my hand touched the door, it clicked open. The light inside the room blinded me. It permeated every atom in my body, and I screamed, leaning against the doorway to keep myself steady.

"The source was too much for you. We have made it more accommodating now." The voice spoke inside my mind. I stood and staggered into the room beyond.

"Who are you?!" I called out to the light. I felt my way along the wall and moved further into the room.

Toward the back of the room, taking up most of the available space, was a gigantic ball of light. This is the most simplistic way I could describe it. The massive entity hung suspended by nothing in the center of the room. No electrical cords were attached to it, and it wasn't being projected by any means I could see. It just was.

Around the perimeter of the glowing, blue sphere were hospital gurneys, drilled into the wall in an upright position. There were six of these beds and strapped securely to each was a body. I slid closer to the bed nearest me, hands still feeling the rough walls to guide me.

The massive presence spoke inside me again, "You are here too soon, human. We did not need you yet."

I had no idea what to respond to this thing. I could not even begin to imagine what it meant by "needing me" and I wasn't sure I wanted to know.

The voice boomed a reply, "The next to feed Cosma. You. Your blood was a sufficient offering, and it will feed the Great Source well."

I had shuffled enough that I stood below the first gurney attached to the wall. The body that lay strapped upright to the bed looked to be a middle-aged woman. Her long dark hair hung limply on her shoulders. She wore a pantsuit that appeared well-worn, navy-blue fabric fit awkwardly against her body. Her mouth was agape, and her eyes stared out at nothing. Knowing it was a stupid choice, I touched her hand. Her body shivered. She moaned and began to thrash inside the restraints.

"WHY DO YOU DISTURB THE SOURCE'S FOOD?!" The voice infiltrated my brain again. The woman on the bed thrashed harder. Clearly, the voice was in her head, as well.

"Please. Help," she pleaded to me. Her hand had clasped mine and her grip was strong.

I squeezed back on the woman's hand. I might not have known what exactly was going on here, but I was not going to let it continue.

This woman and the other people trapped here were suffering.

"They are not suffering. They are provided the power that enriches those who ask for it." The voice continued to talk to me.

I decided to try and ignore it. I studied the restraints strapped over her hands and feet. They were simple enough. I began to undo them. "Hang on," I told her quietly. "I've got you."

She whimpered but did not say anything else. Blood had escaped her nostrils and was dropping off her chin in tiny rivulets. I worked faster at undoing her restraints. I unbelted the last strap holding her in place and the woman slid down to the floor. I crouched beside her. She panted, head lolling to the side.

"Hey. You're okay." I tried to keep my words calm but my hands shook as I patted the top of her leg. "What happened? How did you get here?" I asked this question abruptly, figuring the urgency of the situation allowed for bluntness.

She moaned again and managed to lift her head to look at me. "This is Cosma," she said and lifted her finger to point toward the glowing orb in front of us. "Those fuckers recruit people who are desperate and won't be missed. They feed them to that thing. They make billions. The clients get all the power." She exhaled sharply and then slumped back down against the wall in defeat.

"Shit. Okay. I'm going to go around and try to free the other people here. Will you be okay for a minute?" I stood up and glanced down at the battered woman's face.

She nodded. Behind me, Cosma pulsed again. Something so bright and full of energy should be hot. It should have been as hot as the sun or another burning star, but it wasn't. Icy cold tendrils of air crawled outwards from its center, chilling every hair on my body.

It must have sensed me thinking about it because it spoke up, "Cosma has always been here. Always watching. We have helped humans for millennia. All we ask in return is life force. We do not care for one type of person. Only that they have strong blood. Rich or poor are not concepts Cosma knows."

Cosma finished its speech as I reached the second gurney. This one contained an older man who was stripped down to just his boxers; his sunken chest highlighted every rib in his body. His white hair was only wisps, trying and failing to cover his liver-spotted scalp. He was emaciated. His arms and legs were rail thin and under the light of Cosma, his skin looked grey.

I watched his chest for several seconds. I didn't notice it rise or fall. I hung my head, tears threatening to erupt at the loss of this innocent man. His only crime was needing a job. Needing to survive. I realized with certainty that all the people in this room were the same. The company chose people who were struggling and desperate to stay above water. They feed them to Cosma.

"You will be next." The sphere grew when it spoke in my mind as if attempting to intimidate me.

"The hell I will!" I yelled in its direction. "I'm getting out of this place!"

With my plan to rescue everyone in here abandoned, I made my way slowly back to the woman from the first bed. She sat where I had left her, arms wrapped around her knees protectively. I looked up at the doorway in front of us. The blood in my body grew cold when I noticed Tim was in the secret room with us. He was standing there watching, a sinister grin plastered on his face.

"Ah, Beth," he cooed. "I knew you would be a thorn in my side. I suppose it is time to pull it out." He stepped into the room fully.

I stood defiantly in front of the woman, body like a shield to protect her cowering form. The quiet, people-pleasing part of who I was had come unmoored. I was done with lying down and taking abuse all for the sake of surviving.

I filled my chest with air and said, "My name is August, you asshat."

Tim came closer, his hands shoved casually in his pockets. The woman grabbed hold of my leg, a child clutching their parent after a nightmare.

"Don't come any closer, Tim. I know about what you are doing here. I'm going to the police." I scanned the floor around me, hoping to find anything to use as a weapon if I had to.

I found nothing.

Tim laughed. The sound was empty and echoed around the room. "Where do you think the police get their power from? Hmmm, BETH?" His words stabbed into me.

The little bit of hope I held inside me was fading fast. How could I get help? How would I get me and this woman out of here alive? Years of feeling helpless rolled over me. My stomach burned and my eyes watered. Every time I'd felt scared or threatened resounded inside me like a power all its own.

Cosma spoke to me over the turmoil, "That is a power even I could not create, human. Use that power. Never ignore it."

Tim was standing in front of me. His spindly hand reached out to grab me and I reacted. I put both my arms out and shoved at him. He wasn't expecting me to fight back, let alone assault him. Shock played across his face as he flung back into the rising tide of Cosma's light.

One second, he was floundering; the next he was gone. Cosma's pulsation turned from light blue to red and faded back to blue. I stared into the depths of this ancient being, head empty of all thought. I'm not sure how long I stood like this but soon I felt the woman tugging at my arm.

"Let's go," she begged. She took hold of my sweaty hand and we started for the door.

"He had weak blood. He did not deserve the power." Cosma resonated within me.

"You are strong enough. You can lead Cosma and have everything you have ever wanted."

A flicker of longing stopped me in my tracks. I imagined myself as a Tim-like person, with a huge fancy office and an expensive wooden desk. I thought about all the debt I had racked up and how easily Cosma's power would get rid of that. I winced. That would never be me. I would rather struggle and scrape than give my soul over to greed.

Instead, I posed a question to this god wedged inside of a corporate office in downtown Atlanta. "Cosma, what would happen if I left both doors open? Like, what would happen to everyone in the building?"

It took a few seconds for it to share the answer. Whether it was contemplating the response or just wanted to make me wait, I am not sure. Finally, it said, "Cosma's light would fill the space and take whatever offerings it could find within that space. Cosma needs no master to feed."

That was enough of an answer for me. I pulled the woman with me through the open door and down the dark hallway. We exited the main door, and I stopped the woman before she could close it behind us. I shook my head at her. "Leave it open."

She swung the door all the way out, searching the office for something as she did. She grabbed an abandoned chair from a cubicle at the edge of the office and jammed it under the doorknob.

Before we walked out of the office I glanced back into the secret room. Cosma had grown to fill the entire room. The light was creeping its way along the blackness of the hallway.

"Use your power," it had told me.

I planned to.

I held hands with the woman again and walked out of that shining tower of metal for the final time, with my head held high. The pigeons eyed us warily as we stumbled out of the sliding glass doors, then continued their pecking.

Kirsten is an elder emo who drinks too much coffee and reads too many books at one time. She is currently pursuing her bachelor's in Library and Information Science at the University of Southern Mississippi. Kirsten lives in Chattanooga, Tennessee with her kiddos, cats, and backyard chickens.

You can find her short stories in Curbside Curses: The Yardsale Anthology, Final Passenger, Pretty Girls Make Graves: A Feminine Rage Horror Anthology and There's a Haint in That There Holler. Her first solo work, The Curse of Medusa, is a feminine rage reimagining of the classic Greek myth of Medusa.

BACON BITS

BY BESU TADESSE

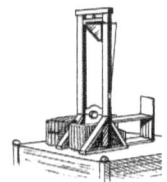

"Ellicott Manor, I presume?"

Gloria Edwards wasn't sure why she was standing in front of the amazingly large and garish mansion. Its Greek Revival exterior was plastered with adornments and colors that were just out of place. Gloria didn't feel that she was sophisticated enough to understand why it was so ugly, but at a visceral level, she knew she didn't like it. She had driven her rusty sedan past the bent and broken gates, admiring the plant overgrowth that lined the manor's driveway.

That was the first moment she questioned if she was the right Gloria Edwards to be invited. She looked at the invitation in her hand, just to make sure that she was in the right place. It had all the right information, even her middle name, Evelyn, and her home address as confirmation that it was, indeed, meant for her. It was also marked at the bottom corner with a number — 27.

She reached out to grab the large iron knocker when the door suddenly opened. A scrawny older gentleman appeared in the doorway, wearing a slim black tuxedo and a clean, pressed white shirt. His mustache was trimmed finely, like he was emulating Hercule Poirot, and his shoes shone against the moonlight.

"Madame Edwards?"

Gloria was taken aback. "Why, yes, how did you know?"

"You are the last to arrive. We have been expecting you."

As Gloria stared at him with her face scrunched, trying to understand what he was talking about, the butler turned around and began to walk away. Taking it as a signal for Gloria to follow, she obliged, walking slowly to avoid aggravating her joints. "And may I ask your name?"

"No, you may not," the butler said coyly. "Besides, you would not remember my name, anyway. I am but a mere pawn."

Gloria didn't like the halting way he spoke, and calling himself a pawn was a bit unusual. But she decided not to push any further. She was more interested in the chaotic interior of the home.

It was even uglier inside. Modern paintings installed next to much older paintings. Gold leaf splattered on pink walls. Red crushed velvet carpets surrounded by deep blue and royal purple drapes. All of it looked expensive, but none of it looked elegant or even planned like someone handed a colorblind interior designer a blank check and told them to go crazy.

You really can't buy taste, Gloria thought, as she followed the butler down the main hallway.

They arrived in front of large double doors at the other end of the main hall. The butler knocked three times on the door, which was answered by two deliberately louder knocks. The butler responded with a final loud bang on the door, the kind a police officer would use before barging into a house. One of the doors opened slowly, and the butler turned to Gloria, his back facing the door.

"Please proceed, Madame Edwards."

Gloria took a deep breath before walking through the doors. She nodded to the butler, a sign of thanks for bringing her to her destination, which he reciprocated. As the door closed behind her, she saw a large dining area with three rectangular tables connected at right angles to form a horseshoe shape creating an open area in the middle. The tables were covered with dark red tablecloths but were otherwise bare. A large group of people was already seated and chatting quietly. She looked around and found a single seat open, so she walked over to it. On the table in front of that seat, she saw a placeholder marked "27", the same number that appeared on her invitation.

This is my seat, I guess.

She sat on the soft, velvety blue seat and folded her hands in her lap, observing the goings-on.

The people at the table seemed just like her, wearing ordinary clothes and speaking about ordinary things — family, work, struggles. Gloria quickly counted the seats at the table — including herself, thirty-one people. Around the periphery were still more butlers, each dressed the same way as the one she just met, frantically moving back and forth to clean the area and move various boxes from one side to the other.

Why are we all here? Who's giving us the five-star treatment?

No sooner had she thought about the possible circumstances that brought everyone together, than one of the butlers lightly clinked an empty glass with a teaspoon. The guests went silent, all hoping to understand what was going on.

Then, the clinking butler announced, "Presenting, Madame Leslie Bernard."

From a bright orange door on the opposing wall, out popped a tall and lively woman dressed in her own two-piece black tuxedo. Unlike the other butlers who were very prim and put together, this person was completely off. The buttons on her sauce-stained shirt were shifted, which made it crease and jumble around her midsection, and she completely missed the top two buttons altogether, which showed off her cleavage. The jacket and pants were both too big, even with the use of suspenders. The knot of her tie hung down to her stomach, brushing against her cummerbund. Her shoes were ill-fitting, even with the laces tied as hard as possible. It was as if she just threw on a much larger man's suit that had yet to be laundered.

On top of that, she was very loud. However, she wore pristine white gloves, which only exaggerated the chaos in the rest of her costume. "Welcome everyone!" She strutted indelicately to the center of the room. "I'm glad everyone was able to arrive expediently. Thank you so much for being here."

She started to move around the center of the room, striking mannequin poses as she spoke. Her moves oscillated between circus ringmaster and elite runway model. "Now, I know that you are not aware of why you came here, which is why I'm so honored that you had the faith in your own instincts to know that you would not be in danger."

She paused for reaction.

There was none, so she continued. "And I will reiterate that you are. Not. In. Danger. Not in the slightest, my good people. No! Not in danger at all." Her insistence that there was no danger made people uneasy, as if she were overcompensating. "And to show you how appreciative I am, I have prepared a feast." She finished this part of her speech by quickly stomping her right foot straight down, as if in military attention.

This was the cue for the butlers to rush in. As she stood stiff, the gaggle of butlers flooded through the dining hall, their hands filled with different items. One group set down small silver platters that were covered with gold-finished domes, each polished to a mirror shine. Another group brought over small, sealed gift bags, each a standard black gift bag you could find in any store, but stuffed with black velvet instead of gift paper.

The guests were even more confused, but the coordinated effort showed how deliberate the experience would be, much like a dinner theater or murder mystery game. They warmed to the experience.

"My apologies," Leslie Bernard said. "I am usually more prepared than this. The gift bags are generally more impressive." She then did a spin and raised both her hands and her voice. "Now! We are about to start one of the most luxurious, scrumptious, delectable, mouth-watering dinners that you have ever had. And along with your dinner, you have been given a special gift as a courtesy of your trust in us."

She then lifted a single index finger higher into the air. "But! You have a few rules before you can begin. First, you may not open the bags until everyone has completed their dinner. We shall not have people touching their gifts with grubby hands. Second, you may not accept your gift unless everyone accepts the gift. We will not have individuals playing holier-than-thou tonight. And third, we may not continue unless everyone accepts the conditions that I have just outlined. Please raise your hand to provide your consent to continue."

The guests, still stuck on what exactly just happened in front of them, were hesitant to agree. One person with the place setting marked "14" raised his hand. "Excuse me, Miss Bernard..."

"Madame Bernard," she insisted while looking away from the man asking. "You may refer to me as Madame Bernard. Or Madame Leslie. Or just Leslie, or Bernard. These are all acceptable, but not Miss Bernard. Leave that for one of your other little friends."

"Sorry. Madame Bernard, what if we are allergic to what is under here?"

"Sir, Mister Fourteen, I assure you that we only use hypoallergenic foods."

"But not every food is..." He was abruptly cut off.

"Does anyone else have any more questions?"

The woman with the "5" place setting chimed in. "Will the gift harm us?"

Leslie Bernard blurted out a quick, "No."

Finally, Gloria asked, "What if we can't take the gift?"

"Can't take it?"

"Yes, like if it's too cumbersome?"

"Madame Twenty-Seven, I assure you that when you leave, you will feel light as a feather."

The guests mumbled to each other, trying to figure out what to do. With nothing to lose, Gloria raised her hand first. "I consent."

Leslie Bernard smiled and scanned the room silently, her eyes big and wide. Then, one by one, other guests raised their hands to show their consent to the rules of that evening.

Leslie Bernard nodded in approval. "Very well. I'm glad that I could earn your trust." She clapped a muffled clap. "Now, let's begin the feast!"

As she announced the meal, more butlers appeared from the orange door, one for each guest. In a synchronized move, each butler stood next to each guest, leaned forward, and lifted the domes from the platters. On each platter, there was a loaded chili dog, resting on porcelain plates, complete with footlong hot dogs, sweet and salty chili, cheese sauce, onions, and bacon bits.

The butlers stood for two seconds then scurried away through the orange door. The sight of chili dogs was a bit jarring to the guests. They were expecting something fancier — maybe an expensive steak or some kind of elaborate pasta dish. Some openly grimaced, while others politely moved the platter away.

However, Gloria sat curiously, looking around at the unusual setting, the even more unusual woman in front of her, and her empty stomach. Surely there was something more interesting happening.

"This looks wonderful. Thank you very much." She slowly reached out and picked up the chili dog with her gentle, arthritic hands. The chili oozed from the sides and onto her hands, which she ignored as she took a slow, deliberate bite.

Gloria was moved by the mix of flavors and seasonings, or maybe it was just that she hadn't eaten in several hours. Either way, she was moved to blurt out, "This is the most delicious thing I've eaten in my entire life."

Leslie Bernard wryly smiled at Gloria's boldness, and that boldness motivated others to take their bites. A wave of bliss from the guests echoed through the hall, which was quickly replaced by a ravenous fervor. They inhaled their chili dogs, some with rather indelicate munches and slurps. As they indulged, half of the butlers reappeared with a glass of bubbly liquid in each hand and placed them next to each guest. For those who enjoyed alcohol, the glasses were filled with champagne. For those that didn't, sparkling white cranberry juice. Everyone grabbed their glasses and started drinking without thinking. Gloria was tentative about having a drink, but she took a sip anyway.

She got the cranberry juice.

They know I don't drink, she thought. *Did they even ask me before? How did they know?*

Suddenly, Leslie Bernard clapped her hands hard again. Everyone stopped moving and sat still. "Bravo! We have all completed our dinners! Now is the time to open your gifts!"

Each of the butlers who remained carefully opened each gift bag for the waiting guests, most of whom were still sweating from the speed at which they consumed their tasty chili dogs. The butlers then removed the contents of each bag

— brightly colored binders with copious amounts of documentation. Some were larger than others, but all were hefty.

The butlers once again ran off. The guests proceeded to quietly open their binders with their greasy fingers to see the gifts they had received.

The man with placeholder "5" was the first to utter a sudden, "Whoa..."

The others followed suit, and the reveal was shocking. In front of each person was a package showing that all of their debts had been discharged. Mortgages, credit cards, student loans, medical bills, department store loyalty programs, loan shark promises written on random pieces of paper — all of it gone. For every person in the room. Many of the guests flipped through their binders multiple times, incredulous at what they were just given. Others began to holler and cry.

A couple of guests openly thanked the heavens. Gloria sat there and quietly cried to herself, knowing that the lifetime of struggle had paid off. She saw the stack of discharge statements, the crushing weight of debt lifted from her shoulders. The woman was right; she suddenly felt light as a feather. She took a deep breath and smiled, relaxing in her seat as Leslie Bernard grinned at her.

All of a sudden, more butlers returned with large platters stacked with chili dogs, along with platters of French fries, salads, various fruits, and other items. Classic rock music started blaring over the speakers, and the chatter started turning rowdier. This was turning into a lively party. In contrast, Gloria's excitement was muted. She felt the weight of the world off of her shoulders, but she was never one for spectacle or big shows of emotion. She giggled as she saw the others dancing and carrying on, as she rubbed her sore hands as they lay on her lap.

While all of this happened, Leslie Bernard slowly ambled around the tables and directly to Gloria's seat. Gloria looked up to see Leslie Bernard's face, softer than before.

"Madame Leslie, thank you so much for doing this for us."

She shrugged her shoulders. "Well, it was a team effort."

"I mean, of course, I can see all of the help that you receive here. This is your mansion, after all," Gloria said with a pleasant face.

Leslie Bernard shook her head, then reached out her hand to take Gloria's. "Come with me. Let me show you something."

Gloria took Leslie Bernard's hand and stood up slowly, then they both moved quietly out of the room through the orange door as the others continued their festivities. The door closed behind them, the party sounds fading away behind them. They walked into a dimly lit hallway, gray drywall around them with a few tiny spotlights encased in round pewter installations. No adornments, no pictures, no shiny trim. The hallway was temperature-controlled to keep any humidity out, and the floor was polished so clearly that even in dim light, the floor shimmered.

The hallway's acoustics were dampened, but they could faintly hear the bustling of different metal items clanging together from the other end of the hallway. Leslie Bernard interlocked her arm with Gloria's while continuing to hold hands. It was awkward, given Leslie Bernard's height.

"You know, you seem like a special person, Madame Edwards."

Gloria smiled, knowing that she was no longer a number. "Of course, you know my name."

"Yes, Madame Edwards. I invited you, as I invited everyone else in that room." The dress shoes squeaked and clunked as they walked together. "You're different from the others. You seem like... an observer. One who looks around and takes in the truth of the moment."

"Well, I've been told that I've been quiet my whole life. Too quiet, my parents would say."

"Yes, your parents Ricardo and Melissa?"

"That's correct."

"You don't seem surprised that I know that information."

Gloria sucked her teeth at that statement. "Madame Leslie, you know my name and found a way to get rid of all my debt. You even knew that I don't drink alcohol and gave me the sparkling cranberry. Whatever you can do to make that happen, I assume that you know everything about me already."

Leslie Bernard chuckled in a mocking way. "Ah, you got me. See that's the thing, Madame Edwards. I needed to know so much about everyone so that I could deliver exactly what I gave you today. I'm sure you can appreciate the number of people out there named 'Gloria Edwards', so I had to get it just right."

Gloria nodded her head. "That makes sense."

"And you know very little about me. Leslie Bernard isn't even my name. I just made up a name from two of my favorite TV show characters. I thought if they were real people and met in real life, they would have hooked up. You know what I mean?"

"I have no idea what you're talking about, but I'm trying to follow."

"The key thing here is that I want to help someone find who exactly they are, for themselves."

Gloria was now uneasy about what was going on. *Why did I go with her? What is she talking about?* "Madame Bernard, I'm pretty sure I know who I am."

"Yes, my dear, but what are you capable of?"

"I don't see-"

Leslie Bernard continued without noticing Gloria's interjection. "Are you aware of who is the original underwriter on your mortgage?"

Gloria was confused again. "What does that have to do with it? It's already paid off."

"I assure you, it's important for what I'm going to ask of you later."

Ask of me?

Leslie Bernard noticed her confounded face and proceeded to answer the question before it was asked. "I ask this because it is the reason we are here now. Not the mansion, of course. I mean this very hallway right here."

They took a few steps silently, listening to their own dampened steps. As Gloria opened her mouth to proceed with the conversation, Leslie Bernard launched into another speech.

"Madame Edwards, your mortgage touched several hands. One bank bundles them into packages, then sells them to another bank. They make some money off of you, then when they're done with you, they package that up and send it somewhere else. It's all very shady business, I think. Especially when you do this to so many people. No personal touch, no feeling of responsibility to each other." Another brief pause, then she continued, "That's why I, and my organization, have decided to remedy this issue."

"So... you plan to fight the banks?"

"Well, no, that would be silly. They're still too big for now. And quite frankly, that's not our style." She flashed a sinister grin.

Gloria leaned back, pulling her arm away slightly. "Then what exactly is your style?"

Leslie Bernard continued proudly. "When we did our research, we found that several of your loans were underwritten by an old lender, Hoffman and Mauricio. My colleagues and I looked into it and found out that they were some of the slimiest lenders in the business. Worst of the worst. Shakedowns, predatory behavior. Very tacky stuff. They were one of the early ones to give you that loan, knowing that you would eventually get into a deep and dark cycle of interest and fees. If I recall, you bought your house for around seventy thousand dollars, and after all these years, you still owe about... fifty-three thousand?"

"Something like that."

"And Madame Edwards, do you believe that this is appropriate behavior?"

Gloria understood the passion and had more confidence in her voice. "No, I do not."

"I don't either! Bravo, Madame Edwards." The clanging got louder and louder from inside the room near the end of the hallway. "Now, what we understood is that we can't go after the people who started this whole mess. They're already dead. But, as to be expected by any good capitalist charlatan, they had children. And those children had children, and so forth, you understand. So, as it turns out, those people who got rich off of preying on others were able to multiply that money, over and over and over again, hoarding money while people like you, and those in that dining hall, struggled. Never having to work a single day in their lives. Just showing up at a few meetings, prancing around in their fancy tuxedos from party to party. Buying all of the latest, most expensive things without any regard for class. Waste of money, waste of time, waste of style. Waste of flesh." She spoke with more intensity as Gloria locked into her words.

"This is all really interesting, but that doesn't explain..."

"And so..." Leslie Bernard continued undeterred, "we made sure to stop the waste, so to speak."

They stopped a few paces away from the end of the hall, where the final room was located. "We followed the money, figuratively and literally. Offshore bank accounts, property, stocks, backroom shady business dealings. Everything. And we got control of it all. Including this manor."

Leslie Bernard led Gloria into the back room — a kitchen area where three workers, dressed in the same tuxedo attire as all of the others, feverishly cooked meals. One was mixing an extra-large industrial-sized pot, where the smell of chili wafted through the air. Another was draining and filtering assorted colors of liquids with clear fizzy drinks, dividing the two between a wide array of carafes marked "Alcoholic" and "Non-Alcoholic." And one person was pushing flesh into a large meat grinder. Near the entrance of the meat grinder, sitting at the back of the counter, were two severed human heads.

Gloria was taken aback and screamed in terror. "What?! How?! Is this what you want to do to me?"

Leslie Bernard was reassuring. "Oh no, no, no. Madame Edwards. Please relax." She turned Gloria's head toward hers and started taking deep breaths, holding her shoulders and looking into her eyes to get her to follow suit. Gloria locked eyes and breathed in and out, first frantically and then slower to a pace slightly faster than normal. "Relax, Gloria. May I call you Gloria?"

Gloria was still panting as she heaved out a "yes" before turning away.

"Good. Now, Gloria, I want to understand when I say this. Those severed heads in there were once attached to Misses and Mister Morgan Hoffman the Fifth, the great-great-great-grandson of your financial tormentor, Morgan Hoffman, along with his little bride. Useless wastes of human beings that never worked, never struggled, never took the time to understand what the Hoffman legacy has done to so many people. They spent their days bullying the staff in this house while decorating it like they lived in a travelling circus. And for all of their indiscretions and, to be perfectly honest, dreadful taste, they still had all the power. So, we did the only thing that felt right. We took it back."

She then took Gloria's head and turned it back to the decapitated heads. "And not just for you. Every person that we invited for that dinner was robbed by Hoffman, and their descendants just run around playing with your hard-earned money! Even this mansion was the product of a hostile takeover against Preston Ellicott's companies. It's not enough to take from us. They pilfered from their so-called friends and business partners, too. Why do you think they didn't bother to rename the place? It's a flex, a show of force without bloodshed."

Gloria looked into the kitchen again, staring at the heads of the Hoffmans with the foreground of grinding meat sloshing onto the countertop. She was afraid to ask her next question. "So, the dinner that we ate..."

"Why, yes! Well, not every part of the dinner. Certainly, the hot dogs. And the chili. And even the bacon bits."

Gloria felt the food churning in her stomach and moving through her digestive system, even feeling it start to enter her bowel. She thought she would vomit right there, but she began to feel comfortable with what she did.

It was tasty, after all, and everyone seemed to be having a wonderful time.

Thinking more, she not only went from being comfortable with the whole idea, she started to love it.

"And when we choose to hunt a billionaire, we like to use the whole billionaire."

Gloria could feel her body tingling with excitement, then she turned back to Leslie Bernard. "Leslie... may I call you, Leslie?"

"That depends on what we're about to discuss next."

"How would someone join such an organization like yours, Leslie?"

Leslie Bernard grinned at Gloria. "You must have read my mind. Why do you think I wanted you to see this? This is why you were different from the others. They were all as happy as you, as deserving to be released from the yoke of continuous debt peonage. But they were too focused on their own celebration rather than seeing it as a collective win. I don't believe that they can see the bigger picture. You may not have noticed it, but I did."

Gloria just stood silently, her gaze darting between the sneering face of Leslie Bernard and the hustle of the kitchen workers. It was a chance to do more good, to relieve others from their own hardships. She wasn't sure if it was the chance to make a difference or the warmth of the cannibalized billionaire swirling in her system, but she felt more nourished with each moment.

Her smile became more crooked, stretching nearly from ear to ear. Leslie Bernard saw this, and her own smile stretched further than before. "So what do you say, Gloria? Shall we find a new host? I have a list that we can use. And we also need to figure out what we're going to serve."

Gloria turned to face Leslie Bernard directly and reached her hand out for a handshake, which she received. "Leslie, it would be an honor. I have some ideas already, but make sure we keep the bacon bits."

Besu Tadesse is a Maryland-based author with a primary focus on horror and horror-adjacent stories. He has published two books — The Ghosts of Poplar Valley, a paranormal horror novella about our history's echoes into the present, and Broken Persons, a short story collection that deals with broad themes of grief, trauma, and the effects of the world around us. When not writing Besu spends his time as a musician and family man.

Instagram: @stickybearartist

GRAVEYARD SHIFT

BY CHRISTINA GRAVES

I t's Vikki's second twenty-ninth birthday. She turned twenty-nine last year as well but no one will call her out on it. Personally, I don't give a shit about my coworker or how many birthdays she's had. She's a cunt.

Ever since her damn soda went missing from the break room, I've gotten passive-aggressive emails about every little thing that inconveniences her throughout the day. Everything from trash left in the break room to the toilet not being flushed. My other coworkers know it's not me doing all these things but that doesn't stop them from turning a blind eye. They're all spineless. They're just happy it's me she's harassing and not them. Today it all ends.

Birthdays are one of the only good things about my job. It means a break from the routine. Most days it's just my cubicle, the light clicking of fingers on a keyboard, and the chatter of the same script being read dozens of times to strangers who couldn't care less.

Answer with a smile. The clients can hear your smile through the phone.

I hear my supervisor's voice in my head each time I answer. I smile until my cheeks hurt. It's enough to drive someone mad. Suffice it to say, I appreciate some relief from the monotony, even if it means celebrating a bitch like Vikki. At least there will be cake.

We all crawl from our little boxes and herd into the break room, where administration has decorated the white-washed walls in cheap dollar store décor. We sing an off-key rendition of 'Happy Birthday,' and Jen from accounting walks in last, carrying the cake that I spent hours making the night before. Everyone had been surprised when I volunteered to bake it myself, considering Vikki's treatment of me as of late. They all assume it's a kiss-ass attempt at peace.

Vikki beams, managing to tear up as she thanks us all for making her feel special. I note that there's no individual "Thank you" to me for spending all night sculpting intricate fondant flowers to top her gift. Flowers that Jen has mindlessly shoved twenty-five-cent candles right in the center of. Rage pools hot behind my ears but I can't let it take over.

Not today.

I manage a smile when Vikki's eyes land on me. I see her warring with an appropriate response that won't reveal herself to be the bitch I know her to be. Everyone has been fussing over how beautiful my work is since she blew the candles out. She can't very well snub it now, so she decides on the high road.

"Thank you, Fern. You shouldn't have gone through this much trouble for me."

"It was no trouble at all," I say, waving her forced compliment off.

"This must have taken hours. I feel guilty cutting it." She laughs, but lets the blade come down hard in the center. She enjoyed it.

"Here, let me!" I say taking the knife from her. "It's bad luck to cut your own cake."

She takes a step back, like I may swing it at her pretty little throat. I smile in spite of myself and for a moment I consider it. The thought is so tempting... but it's my turn to take the high road.

Instead, I cut her a thick slice and offer it up to her on a plate. She hesitates and for a moment I worry she won't take it. What will I do if she doesn't? What will I — My shoulders relax when she finally takes the plate from me, rather forcefully, and puts on a show of taking a bite. I go to work, dividing the rest of the cake and offering it up to the rest of my coworkers. They accept them eagerly.

"Is this cinnamon?" Cheryl from Processing asks.

"It is. It's my own recipe."

"You'll have to write it down for me. It's so good!"

I nod even though writing anything down for her would be useless. It shouldn't be long now. I'm beginning to worry I messed up the measurements when I see Vikki's hand move to her stomach. Considering the time frame since she finished her second slice, it only makes sense she'd be the first one impacted by the poison.

No one even has time to notice that something is off before she coughs, spewing red liquid all over the table. The room falls silent. All eyes are on Vikki, keeled over, bracing herself over the assortment of red-splattered sweets, her eyes widened in horror. When she looks up at me, knowing washes over her pale face. A smile pulls at the corners of my lips like puppet strings. The feeling, it's... euphoric! There's nothing like it.

My entire body feels like it's humming.

Everyone had been so consumed with stuffing their faces they didn't notice I was the only one who wasn't eating. Before she can react, a wet, guttural sound escapes her throat. Her hands grip her abdomen again and the contents of her stomach, a mix of bile, blood, and half-digested cinnamon cake spews from her mouth and onto the table. Far more blood than any one person should lose at one time. She retches again, this time covering Saul, our boss, in the muck. Cheryl opens her mouth to help but instead, the same bile erupts from her, covering Vikki and several others who were unfortunate enough to be standing too close.

The room erupts in chaos. It's almost funny watching everyone scrambling to help the other only to succumb to their own dose of the poison. It's far more than I expected. None of the articles I read could have prepared me for the operatic nightmare before me. It is the single most thrilling thing I have ever witnessed and it's far from over.

Max from maintenance runs for the door of the break room. An attempt to call for help, no doubt. He doesn't make it far beyond the threshold before collapsing to his knees and emptying his stomach onto the tile floor. I don't blame him for trying. He couldn't have known how futile his attempt would be. By the time help arrives, everyone will be dead already.

Everyone except me.

I make my way back to my desk as one by one the screams fade into silence. I open my email and select the option to 'Delete All.' With a click, they're gone.

So quick. So easy.

It's almost like they never existed. Pretty soon it'll be like none of them ever existed.

The phone on my desk rings and for the first time, answering with a smile is easy.

Christina Graves is a digital artist and author currently living in the Deep South with her husband and three children.

Her debut psychological thriller, Still, Dark Places, is available everywhere books are sold.

Stalk her @christinagravesauthor everywhere.

Links:
        Instagram:
        https://instagram.com/christinagravesauthor
        Facebook:
        https://www.facebook.com/christinagravesauthor

FUR BABIES
BY WAYNE TURMEL

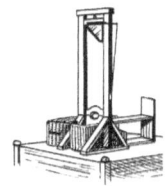

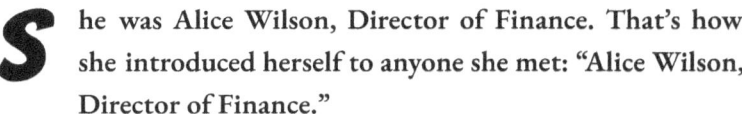

She was Alice Wilson, Director of Finance. That's how she introduced herself to anyone she met: "Alice Wilson, Director of Finance."

It's how she answered the phone. She'd actually practiced, "Alice Wilson, Director of Finance, how may I help you?" so it always sounded the same, calm and professional. She dressed to look precisely like "Alice Wilson, Director of Finance" should look.

People knew what to expect from her. To the point. Professional. The very picture of the person one should find in a workplace. The details, the little things done correctly made her as happy as she ever was. After all, this was a workplace, dammit.

What she abhorred in the workplace was sloppiness and unprofessionalism. More to the point, she loathed Patrice Owens, who embodied those very features along with several other weak traits that made Alice wince.

One Tuesday afternoon, Alice couldn't avoid speaking to the fat loser. The numbers for the Jackson account were late and inaccurate. Not terribly late, and not so wrong as to be a problem, but still late and inaccurate, which reeked of sloppiness and unprofessionalism.

She'd have preferred to call Patrice into the office. Public reprimands were messy, but time was of the essence. Alice tread quietly up to the edge of the slob's desk, slightly behind the other woman's back. She saw a half-empty bag of Fritos, its powdery remnants dusting the desk and keyboard. A framed photo of Patrice beaming and hugging a bored-looking, orange tabby took up prominent desk space normal people reserved for kids and spouses.

"Patrice—"

"Oh, my goodness, I didn't see you there. Good morning."

The worker bee had her usual dopey smile on her face, the one that said she refused to grasp the seriousness of any situation. "What can I do you for?"

Alice was about to launch into the several things the idiot could "do her for," when the itching in her eyes began. It started as a hot irritation, followed by a desire to scratch her own eyes out. Then came the final embarrassment.

"A-CHOO!"

It was a most unladylike sneeze, coming from her toes. Several of the office drones poked their heads up like meerkats.

Patrice fumbled for a tissue from a plastic box covered in seashells that spelled out, 'Destin, Florida.' "My goodness. Are you coming down with something? I know there's a bug—"

It wasn't any damned bug. Alice saw the long black hairs all over the ugly, pill-covered sweater. "Is that cat hair?"

"Oh yeah, sorry." Patrice wheeled her chair a few inches back, like that would help. "I know you're allergic, but my fur babies needed cuddles this morning. They get so mad if they don't get their cuddles."

"Well, it's very inconsiderate. There are others besides me with allergies. If someone had a peanut allergy, would you slather yourself with peanut butter before showing up for work?"

Pale green eyes flashed behind her glasses. "Peanut allergies are dangerous... cat allergies are just..." She stopped herself and lowered her voice. "I'm sorry. You're right. I'll be more careful."

For a brief moment, Alice considered reporting the moron to HR, but that would require speaking to HR, and a little Benadryl could avoid that nightmare. After a calming breath, she said, "I wanted to talk to you about these numbers."

Thursday, it was Patrice's turn to sneeze. And cough. And use up half a shell-covered box of tissues to stem the snot trickling from her red, sore nose.

The honking and hacking echoed across the office. Alice cringed at her desk. Then it drew nearer, and nearer again until Patrice's bleary-eyed form filled the doorway.

"I wanted to know if I can work from home. I don't feel good."

Alice managed not to roll her eyes. "Working from home" was bad enough during that Covid hoax bullshit and things were just getting lazy butts back in the office where they belonged. Besides, given the quality of this woman's work, it was clear some people couldn't be trusted without supervision.

A gold Mont Blanc pen hit the desktop. "We've talked about work-from-home. Your position doesn't qualify."

Patrice moaned. "Well, then, I guess I have to use one of my sick days."

A couple of clicks on the keyboard and Alice found what she wanted. "I'm afraid you don't have any left. You took three days last month and four in January." The woman gave a smug smile.

HR was good for something, after all.

"But those weren't for me. Mister Whiskers got attacked by a coyote. Poor thing lost an ear. I was so worried... And in January, poor Jellybean needed—"

"So, you were claiming sick days when you weren't the one sick?"

The weaker woman recognized the threat behind the question. "I'm sorry, but they wouldn't let me take family leave. My babies needed me. They needed cuddles." Patrice's eyes watered and she hacked up a lungful of something nasty that went into a used tissue.

"That's for children and spouses. Cats aren't family. They're, well, they're just cats."

"They're my family," came a half-hearted reply.

"Take it up with HR. Anything else?"

Patrice's shoulders slumped. In a choking voice, she offered a weak, "Guess not." Then she sniffed and horked her way back to her desk.

"Don't forget to wash your hands. And maybe take some DayQuil. They sell it downstairs," Alice added.

The sick noises continued til noon. The rest of the staff had gone to lunch and Patrice was still at her desk, probably hoping if she got her work done, she could sneak out early.

Typical. At least the hacking and honking stopped. Maybe she'd gotten that medicine after all. What wasn't typical was the scream erupting from the cubicle farm about twelve-forty-five. One of the analysts returned from lunch to find Patrice collapsed over her desk, her mucus-smeared face smashed against the keyboard. In her lifeless hands was the framed picture of the orange tabby.

Jellybean? Mister Whiskers?

It didn't matter much now.

Alice supervised the removal of the body and made sure Patrice's coworkers had the number for Employee Support. She doubted anyone would miss the woman enough to need emotional help, but some would take the chance for a day off. Of course, the office would empty out for the funeral.

As the boss on that floor, it was Alice's job to type out the all-company email. No need for originality or fake emotion. It was standard corporate jargon. Everyone knows when the subject line reads, "Sad news," someone's died. Didn't mean they'd be missed.

***

The following Friday, the cube farm was a ghost town. Some clown in HR decided that, under the circumstances, people could work from home on Friday, even those who didn't attend Patrice's service. The decision was made over Alice's — technically Patrice's — dead body.

Alice Wilson, Director of Finance, took the opportunity for some impromptu desk searches. As she suspected, she found two liquor bottles and a bong. The handgun was concerning, but there had been complaints about parking lot security.

Several browser searches revealed a discouraging number of web visits to recruiters and employment agencies. She immediately planned to start screening resumes to get ahead of the upcoming turnover problem.

As Alice was throwing things out of the breakroom refrigerator, simultaneously noting the names of people leaving food over the weekend, she smelled something. Not from the fridge, but behind her.

Her nose wasn't the first to detect it, though. The itching in her eyes was followed by a deep sniff and she recognized that distinctive odor.

Was there a cat in the office?

Looking about, Alice saw nothing. She rubbed her eyes and headed back through the cube farm to her office and a waiting tablet of Benadryl. As she walked past Patrice's empty desk, she heard a clear, "Meow."

In Patrice's chair, a huge orange tabby sat upright. Its amber eyes followed Alice, its expression bored and arrogant.

"Shoo." Alice waved at it, but the little bastard had the temerity to yawn at her.

This was a job for maintenance, but first, she had to get the allergy tablets from her desk drawer. Alice sneezed again and momentarily froze. Concerned she might have peed a little, she took a second and looked around. Realizing everything was fine, she stomped back to her office with a little more urgency than before.

"Meow."

A skinny black and white cat sat on her keyboard, licking its lips. The stupid animal had one ear missing, a small, scarred nub where its right ear should have been, as if it had been attacked by some animal. The email Alice worked on all morning was nothing but a meaningless collection of hieroglyphics.

"Maintenance!" Alice screamed over her shoulder, but nobody heard her. Sniffing back a river of mucus, she tried shooing the cat away. It ignored her, purring away happily and pawing at the "delete" key. The animal licked its lips again and waved a paw as if in greeting.

"Ugh." Alice pulled the drawer open to find an empty blister pack where she kept her stash of vitamins, along with her anti-diarrheal and allergy meds. Had she forgotten to buy more? It wasn't like her to let them run out, but why would she need them? Who would ever think there'd be a cat in her office? Never mind two of them.

The deformed creature let out a plaintive meow and walked toward her, intending to rub itself against the woman's leg. Alice yelped and jumped back. She also let out a barking cough as the phlegm built up in her nose and throat. Two cats. On the sixth floor. Which meant they got past someone first. Heads would roll, but first, she needed to get the little bastards out of there. Ignoring the desk phone, effectively guarded by the cat, she dialed security on her mobile.

"Hello, Security? This is Alice Wilson, Director of Finance and—"

"Thank you for calling the Security Desk. If this is an emergency, please dial nine-one-one. Otherwise, please leave a message, the reason for your call, and we'll respond within a few minutes."

Alice didn't wait for the beep. "Of course, it's an emergency. Why else would I rely on you idiots?" Then she heard the tone, and in a much calmer voice, said, "Hi. This is Alice Wilson, Director of Finance, and we have two feral cats in the office on six. Can someone please come and take care of that?"

She realized she'd made a mistake. There were four cats. Two adults and two grey and black kittens, to be exact. The babies, eyes as big as their striped heads, rubbed against her ankles. They purred and playfully snagged her expensive stockings with razor-sharp claws. Both of them let out the tiniest sounds. "Mew. Mew."

In her rush to escape, Alice kicked at them. She felt a mix of regret and satisfaction as the tiniest kitten went ass-over-teakettle. Served it right. She'd go down to the lobby and wait there until Security did their job.

Leaving the department, she gasped as she walked. Her lungs burned, ablaze with the need for oxygen. Alice hacked and coughed, lava-hot tears leaking from her red, burning eyes.

If she could just get to the elevators.

Just as she emerged into the corridor, the elevator doors slid shut, and Alice did something she seldom did in the office. She let out a minor curse word. That was followed by a major one when she saw the orange tabby curled up on the floor between her and the elevator.

"Meow."

"Piss off! Where are you little fuckers coming from?" Alice barely recognized her own raspy voice. She coughed twice and wheezed as her lungs sought air not polluted with fur and dander. Through blurry eyes, she saw the ladies' room door and made a dash for it.

The door slammed shut behind her and she clicked the lock. Leaning against the cool wall, Alice burst into tears. Her chest heaving, she pounded a fist on the wall.

"Goddamn cats."

"Meow."

A monstrous, fluffy, white Persian with matted fur sat on the toilet tank with its head cocked to one side. It studied the crying, sniffling woman.

Alice screamed, "How many of you are there?" Then she ripped open the door and ran back into the hallway. "Help! Is anyone here?"

"Meow."

"Meow." She couldn't see it, but this one sounded different. Bigger, maybe. The tone was deeper, angrier.

"Shut up!" Alice ran into the IT department. Someone had to be there. One of those creepy nerds was always around. Instead, the place was deserted. But there was a breakroom with a door on the other side, and no cats between here and refuge.

Alice took a couple of steps, then kicked off her heels so she could move faster. Her bare feet caught a cord from a surge protector, tripped, and pitched forward. Before hitting the ground, she thought, *that's an OSHA violation.* A serious infraction, but far more concerning was the crunch of her wrist breaking as she hit the floor. Writhing and clutching her hand, she screamed.

"Meow."

The big orange cat brushed against her leg. Alice kicked wildly but the tabby stepped calmly out of range.

Alice was going to take a second kick at it, but heard another cat behind her. The one-eared black and white tomcat looked at her and licked its lips. Then she heard a third animal.

"Meow." The Persian slowly stalked across the room, followed by the kittens. It never blinked, staring directly at her.

Panic filled the woman's mind. Breathing was increasingly difficult. Her broken wrist throbbed. Alice was sure she was hallucinating when she saw three more cats prance toward her. One, she was sure, came through a broken air vent in the wall but that couldn't be right.

She pulled herself into a fetal position, weeping, coughing, screaming. Somewhere in her brain, a switch flipped. She switched from screaming to laughing hysterically. "Good kitty. Good kitty."

Alice Wilson, Director of Finance, shrieked over and over as the black and white cat lay down beside her, nuzzling against her stomach. Then the kittens clawed their way into her lap, needle-like claws kneading her thigh, seeking a warm place to snuggle. More cats came from everywhere, rubbing against her thrashing body, burying her under a pile of writhing fur, claws, and sandpapery tongues.

The orange tabby licked the hysterical woman's cheek, then crawled into a happy, purring ball over her open mouth, muffling a sound that was half prayer and half wail.

Patrice's fur babies had been too long without cuddles.

Wayne Turmel is a former stand-up comic, car salesman, and business consultant who writes fiction to save what's left of his sanity. He's the author of six novels and his short work has been published around the world and has been nominated for a Pushcart prize. He lives and writes in Las Vegas, where he lives with his wife, the Duchess, and Mad Max, scourge of lizards and most manly of poodles.

Find him on Bluesky @authorWayneTurmel or www.WayneTurmel.com

WHAT WAS COMING
BY JULIET ROSE

The limo weaved through the dark streets of the poorest part of town, the passenger searching for a particular mark. As the limo eased down a side street and a shadow stepped in the light, the passenger tapped the dividing glass separating him from the driver.

"Stop here," he ordered. He hoped the driver understood discretion at any cost. This was a new company to him, as when he tried to call his company's car service, they claimed they didn't have a car available for him. Idiots.

The driver did as he was told and the car idled in the cold, the exhaust creating a cloud in the air. The shadow moved toward the car window as it rolled down. The passenger leaned to the window.

"I'm lost. Can you tell me where Tenth Street is?"

The shadow, now becoming visible under the streetlight, smiled, a large straight line of white teeth. "Tenth you say? I think I got you."

The code had been successfully accepted. The passenger rested his hand on the window, waving a stack of hundred-dollar bills. His Cartier watch caught the light and he smiled. Money talked and he had unlimited flow, allowing him to get whatever he wanted. Whomever he wanted.

"I have particular tastes. No old women, no drug users. You understand?"

The shadow, now a man, nodded. He was dressed well, a fitted suit and leather boots, adorned with gold chains. The passenger noted nothing was brand, though. Clean and in good shape, but still, not up to par. He snorted, then caught it in his throat. Regardless of the man's status, he had what the passenger wanted, so for now the rich man needed to play the poor man's game. The poor man, a pimp, gestured behind him.

"I have all kinds. What are you looking for?" he asked the man in the limo.

"I like them young," the rich man, a CEO of a corporation that swooped in and bought homes from people down on their luck, answered, his voice emphasizing *young*.

The pimp tipped his head, considering. "How young? Male or female? I can get just about anything."

"I can work with boys or girls. They just need to be unseasoned, if you catch my drift." He waved the stack of bills to show that money was no matter. His phone dinged and he glanced at it, seeing his wife had messaged. Damnit. Her timing was terrible; he didn't want her killing his vibe.

He flipped the phone over and peered up at the pimp, who at first looked White, but now almost looked Asian, or Hawaiian. Strange. His face changed under the streetlight as the pimp moved slightly.

"Sure, sure. No boys tonight. I have a girl, though. One of my new girls. Hold on, I'll be right back with her." The pimp disappeared into an alley.

The man began to get nervous when the pimp didn't come right back out. He'd done these types of deals all over the country on his business travels, and it was usually seamless. He even had a map on his desk at home, marking each town he'd bought time with a child. His wife thought it was just him recording his travels, but he kept it to remind him of his conquests. Of their soft skin, their tears, their blood.

He was just about to tell the driver to leave, when the pimp emerged from the alley, his face again looking more White. Must have been the way the light was hitting his face. He was followed by a girl, trying to precariously balance on stiletto heels. She shivered in the chill of the air. They came to the limo and the pimp pushed the girl forward.

"This is Bobbi. Will she do?"

The man groaned inwardly. The girl had to be at least thirteen or fourteen, already developing. "You don't have anyone younger?"

The pimp shook his head. "Sorry, man, this is as young as I have tonight. Bobbi's new, though. Fresh and tender."

Bobbi stood with her eyes down. She did look fresh. No scars or bruises showing she'd been knocked around, as most of them did as they moved through their work. The man sighed, she'd have to do. "Is she at least a virgin?"

Bobbi shifted uncomfortably, not looking up. The pimp smiled. "I can assure you, this is her first time."

The man accepted that and handed the pimp the stack of bills. "Will this do?"

The pimp counted the money and bobbed his head. "Yes, sir. That will pay for the night. Bring her back here before the sun comes up."

The man didn't like the pimp telling him what to do, but he didn't need a run-in with the seedy side, either. He pushed open the door for the girl. She glanced at the pimp, who smiled at her in almost a brotherly way.

"Go on, now. I'm sure he'll treat you just fine."

The man laughed inside himself. He wasn't paying to treat anyone just fine. He'd do what he wanted with her. Part of the thrill was them begging him to stop. The girl stepped forward and climbed into the limo, almost falling on the ridiculously high heels. The man didn't like when the children were dressed like adults. He preferred them in their natural state. Dressed like the children they were.

He motioned for the limo to drive away once the girl was seated and threw her a pack of wipes. "Wipe that shit off your face. Take off those shoes. If I wanted an old prostitute, I would have paid for that."

The girl did as she was told. He eyed her shiny, tight, pink spaghetti-strap dress and shook his head. Nothing could be done about that; he didn't have any clothes in her size. He watched her wipe the makeup off and was more satisfied when her young age came through. That was better.

"Bobbi, huh? Bobbi what?" he asked the girl.

She had her hands clasped in her lap and glanced out the window. "Lore."

It didn't sound like a real name, but they rarely were. "Lore? Like a story?"

The girl nodded, not meeting his eyes. He liked that. He wanted her to be afraid of him. She certainly would when he got through with her. He was doing her a favor. She'd deal with a lot of abuse as a prostitute, so he was simply breaking her in.

Breaking being the operative word.

"Yeah, yeah. Everyone has a story, right? A sob story I'm sure. Your daddy ran out, your mom did crack. Something like that. I don't want to hear about it. I really don't care," he said even though she hadn't tried to tell him anything.

He motioned for the driver to pull down an unlit alley. He didn't waste time or money on hotels. The limo was paid for by his company, so he made use of that. The driver drove to a dead end and cut the lights, making the limo invisible to prying eyes. The back of the limo was soundproof, so the driver wouldn't hear her screams.

The man gestured to the girl to come sit beside him. She did as she was expected, her hands wringing in her lap. He grabbed her chin and yanked her face to look at him. His face twisted into an evil grin. "This is going to hurt."

Her eyes grew wide and she tried to pull away from him. He reached forward and yanked a handful of hair out of her head. She cried out and touched her now bleeding scalp. He felt a rush of adrenaline course through his veins. He punched her in the face, hearing her nose crunch under his fist.

She slid off the seat onto the floor and he was on her with all of his weight. She tried pushing him off her, whimpering. "Please, stop. You're hurting me."

"That's what I pay for, you little bitch," he replied, laughing. He took out a pocket knife and slashed her arms as she was pinned under him. He loved seeing their blood.

She quit fighting, knowing it was pointless. He didn't like that, but they usually did. Their eyes would go vacant and he knew by that point, only raping them was left. It wasn't even his favorite part, but he did pay for it, after all. He punched her again a few times, her face becoming disfigured. He wanted to make sure he left his mark on them. That every time they looked in the mirror, they'd remember him.

Once she was good and mutilated, he ripped off her dress, disappointed at the perky breasts under the fabric. He liked them before puberty. He took the knife and cut off her underwear, forcing her legs apart. She lay still, but he could see she was still breathing, and her eyes were watching him. For a second he saw something unfamiliar in them. Primal, almost.

He shrugged it off and pulled his pants down. He wouldn't be gentle. He tried to be as violent entering them as possible, so he could see their pain. He forced himself into her, peering at her face for suffering.

Instead, she looked right at him and smiled. Not the smile of a child. Her mouth curved into a wicked grin. When her voice spoke, it was not the soft, sweet voice from before. It cackled, as her legs clamped around him. "Welcome to hell."

He was pinned and he felt the sensation of teeth biting into his genitals. Searing pain shot through his body as the flesh was torn from his body. He tried to struggle away, screaming for the driver, but the driver couldn't hear him.

Her legs loosened and he felt faint, leaning forward, his face resting on her chest to gather himself. That was a mistake. The perky breasts he'd bemoaned prior, shifted and opened into her chest. The holes planted on his eye sockets and began to draw inward, sucking his eyes from his face. Not quickly, however. Slowly, so he could feel every connection between the eyes and his body snapping.

After his eyes were removed, she pushed him away. He fell against the seat, curling into the fetal position. Blood poured from his body as he quivered in terror. Where his genitals had been, was a gaping hole. His eyes were gone; all he could feel was pain.

The girl tapped on the glass and the limo began to back up. It moved through the streets until it slid up outside a hospital. The door opened and the man was pushed out onto the sidewalk. He tried crawling away, but collapsed after a few feet, too weak to move. The limo driver laid on the horn a few times before pulling off into traffic.

Bobbi Lore watched through the back of the limo as hospital workers came out to see what the ruckus was and found the bleeding and disfigured man. She smiled and adjusted her torn dress over her body.

The limo took her back to where the man had picked her up. She slipped out and stopped by the driver's window. He rolled it down and nodded at her, his yellow eyes meeting hers with a wink. They had completed their task.

The limo pulled off and the pimp came out of the shadows, watching as the limo disappeared into the night. "Is it done?"

Bobbi tipped her head with a delicate smile. "It is done. He'll live to suffer the consequences but will never hurt another child. He is ruined."

The pimp came over and wrapped his arms tenderly around the girl. Under the streetlight, they melded into one being. A beautiful creature with long flowing hair and horns, arms that ended in sharp talons, and a striking, angular face with bright yellow eyes.

The creature moved through the empty streets, pausing to look out for any signs of life. It went on its way, passing a newspaper box. As it moved away from the box, becoming one with the night, the streetlight hit the paper facing out, exposing the headline:

Police Baffled as Another Prominent Figure is Found Alive Mutilated With Their Eyes and Genitals Missing. Victims Claim They Were Attacked By a "Monster." However, Authorities Have No Leads.

Juliet Rose is a multi-award-winning, cross-genre author in contemporary fiction, visionary suspense, sci-fi realism, and supernatural horror. She is adept at blending genres and challenges both herself and the reader to think outside of their comfort zone by introducing new ideas into familiar tropes. She has eleven published fiction books. While she resides in the mountains of Georgia, she's lived all over the United States and Mexico, using these experiences in her writing.

Her website is abovetheraincollective.com and includes all of her social media links and contacts.

IN MY REVENGE, I FOUND SWEET SLEEP
BY BRÝN GROVER

They patted me on my back when
The trophy was presented, then
They lauded me with such fanfare
In all the world I had no care

They said that changes were in store
To help me excel even more
The year ahead was looking bright
As for a trip I packed that night

I went abroad and had success
And I was feeling truly blessed
As with an order in my hand
I had returned to my homeland

But when the next week came around
I found myself on unfirm ground
I should have had such a great week
And yet my knees were feeling weak

My VP and the HR team
Were waiting to upend my dreams
"We're sorry, we must let you go"
"Say what?" I found it quite a blow

Last week I was the best around
I got the trophy and left town
Returning with a new order
From prospects across the border

"A new direction we will go
And it does not include you, though
We thank you for the work you've done."
I heard the words and felt undone

The changes they had promised me
Accompanied by a trophy
With words of praise so uplifting
Were idle with a hollow ring

Ten years of loyalty meant naught
I called my wife. I was distraught
The future had come crashing down
I thought I would in sorrow drown

But when I heard about the smirk
Of an exec who was a jerk
Revenge I decided then would be
Taken so joyfully by me

For orders yet to have been placed
I pushed clients without disgrace
To anyone that I could find
Which to their needs could be aligned

Former competitors and foes
Soon found themselves in the sweet throes
Of business they did not expect
For which their product was not speced

Five million dollars I had moved
From those who treated me so rude
I did not fret. I did not weep
In my revenge I found sweet sleep